MURDER ON HARLEY STREET

CLEOPATRA FOX MYSTERY, BOOK 11

C.J. ARCHER

WWW.CJARCHER.COM

CHAPTER 1

LONDON, OCTOBER 1900

Just when I thought my cousin Floyd had matured, he did something to remind me he was still a feckless youth who'd rather risk his father's wrath than do any actual work. He'd stumbled home at first light on the day he was supposed to begin organizing an important event. The Mayfair Hotel had been hired as the venue for a presentation by a member of the Pharmaceutical Society. Usually presentations were held at the society's offices in Bloomsbury Square, but a last-minute change had become necessary after a burst pipe caused considerable damage. The presentation was scheduled for Saturday, leaving very little time to prepare. Tasked with overseeing the organization by his father—my Uncle Ronald—Floyd ought to be spending as much time as possible making sure it was a success, but instead he was sleeping the day away.

I shouldn't have been surprised. It wasn't long ago that a wayward Floyd had needed rescuing from a ruthless fellow after getting himself into debt. What surprised me more than Floyd's lackadaisical attitude to work was that his assistant, Harmony Cotton, would rather he stay in bed.

"He's more useful when he's asleep," she told me outside my uncle's office on the hotel's fourth floor. I'd just left my suite further along the corridor when she'd emerged after a meeting with my uncle and the hotel's senior staff. I'd waited for them to disperse before signaling to her that I wanted a word.

"How can he be useful while asleep?" I asked.

"Fewer interruptions allow me to get on with it." Harmony's smile may have been a mere wisp of a curve of her lips, but it reassured me that she was indeed satisfied with this arrangement. As one of the hotel maids, Harmony had proved to be an excellent assistant to Floyd when an important guest's wedding had been held at the hotel two months ago. This medical presentation wasn't quite on the same scale, but it was still imperative that it ran smoothly. It was Uncle Ronald's hope that the Mayfair would be the chosen venue for larger conferences if word spread about the success of Mr. Lombardi's event. For Harmony, it was a step closer to a new career that would hopefully see her permanently move away from being a maid.

I indicated my uncle's office door. "Was he upset that Floyd wasn't there for the meeting?"

"I informed Sir Ronald that Mr. Bainbridge was feeling unwell and that I would update him with everything he needed to know when he felt better." She leaned a little closer and lowered her voice. "I'm not sure Sir Ronald believed me, but he didn't seem angry."

"You're too good to Floyd."

Harmony's dark eyes flashed. "Making him eternally grateful to me."

"You run the risk of my uncle finding out that you're covering for Floyd. He could direct some of his anger at you."

"Or he'll be grateful that someone capable is assisting his son and heir."

"I'm not sure I understand."

"Mr. Bainbridge will inherit all this one day, whether he deserves it or not. I intend to make myself indispensable to him by ensuring the events he's tasked with managing are a success. He already realizes how helpful I am, but I plan to make him see how *necessary* I am, so when the time comes for him to step into Sir Ronald's shoes, he'll employ me as his permanent assistant. In the meantime, Sir Ronald will be grateful that someone capable is making his son look good to stakeholders, so he'll not be too concerned that I do more than an assistant should while his son sleeps off the effects of a full social calendar."

Not only did she look like a businesswoman in her sensible navy-blue skirt and matching waistcoat over a crisp white blouse, with her black hair scraped into a tight arrangement, she was sounding like one, too. "Have you become more devious, or am I simply just noticing it now?"

"I prefer to think of it as clever." She jutted her chin at the closed door to Floyd's suite, her smile no longer in evidence. "Should you check to see if he's all right?"

"It's too early. He'll sleep well into the afternoon."

She tucked the clipboard she'd been holding under her arm and removed the watch Floyd had loaned her from her waistcoat pocket. "It's a quarter to eleven. The day is half over for some."

"Perhaps we *should* rouse him. There are things he needs to do. I have a few minutes before collecting Aunt Lilian for her appointment."

Harmony pocketed the watch. "Not 'we', Cleo. *You* check on him alone. I'm merely an employee. He wouldn't want me seeing him in a state of…" She wrinkled her nose in the direction of Floyd's door. "Whatever state he's currently in."

"Floyd wouldn't care."

"Besides, I'm busy."

"As his future permanent assistant, I'm quite sure you'll have to drag him out of bed from time to time to perform his duties."

"Until that time comes, I'll let his favorite cousin deal with him." Her gaze drilled into me. "Unless that cousin plans to move out of the hotel soon."

"I told you I have no such plans, Harmony."

"Plans change."

"Not in two weeks they don't. Well, not in this instance anyway. Harry and I are content the way things are."

Her lips flattened into a firm line, letting me know that she thought I was deluded if I expected Harry to be content to keep our relationship a secret from my family for much longer. Ever since I'd given in to my feelings for him, Harry Armitage and I had decided it was best to wait to make an announcement. As a former employee of the hotel, my family considered him beneath me. Introducing him as the man I wanted a future with would require delicate diplomacy and careful timing. Harmony was convinced that I alone had made the decision to wait, despite me telling her numerous times that Harry wanted it, too.

"As you and Victor are also content with your relationship," I added with more glee in my tone than was polite.

Harmony's face softened at the mention of her beau, one of the hotel's cooks. "Point taken." She shifted the clipboard to her other hand. "Good luck with Lady Bainbridge's appointment. I hope this new doctor proves better than the last one."

"As do I." I glanced at Floyd's door again. "Perhaps your Pharmaceutical Society presenter can advise Floyd on a cure for over-imbibing."

"The best cure for that is to drink less in the first place, but I think the Bella Vita Company do manufacture a restorative tonic."

"Bella Vita!" I grabbed her wrist and lowered the clipboard to read the document. Across the top in neat, bold lettering, Harmony had written Bella Vita Company Presentation.

She frowned at me. "It means The Good Life Company in Italian. It's Mr. Lombardi's company."

I blinked at her. "I think that's the manufacturer of Aunt Lilian's tonic."

She gasped. "The one…?"

I nodded. "The one she no longer uses." Neither of us mentioned the word addiction out loud, but I'm sure she was thinking it.

My aunt had become addicted to the cocaine in the tonic prescribed by one of London's eminent physicians. At first, it gave her a vitality she felt she lacked. She took it before social engagements or when she felt low, but after regular use it became clear to all those who knew her that she was becoming more and more dependent on it to lift her mood. Not only that, it changed her character. She went from a kind-hearted, gentle soul to someone who was easily irritated and sometimes even angry, interspersed with moments of deep melancholy, the very thing the tonic was supposed to cure. Those changes were accompanied by excruciating headaches, restlessness and fatigue.

After months of suffering, Aunt Lilian finally realized she needed to stop. She'd thrown out her bottle of tonic, so I couldn't now check the label to find out who manufactured it.

"We can't allow Mr. Lombardi to have his presentation here," I said. "His tonic is doing more harm than good. He's no better than a quack who peddles so-called remedies on the street corner. I can't believe Boots and other chemists still sell it, let alone eminent doctors recommend it to their patients. Given Aunt Lilian's situation, it would be hypocritical of us to host Mr. Lombardi's event, not to mention unethical."

Harmony chewed her lower lip.

"I know the presentation is important to the hotel," I went on, "but I'm sure Uncle Ronald will cancel the contract once he realizes." We both looked at his office door.

"Are you *sure* the Bella Vita Company is the manufacturer of *that* tonic?" Harmony asked. "The factory is in Italy."

"I'm quite sure, but you're right. I need to be absolutely positive. Uncle Ronald will want proof before he cancels the contract. I'll purchase a bottle while I'm out. I remember the name and what it looked like, as will my uncle." I clasped Harmony's arm and squeezed. "I'm sorry. I know how much hosting this event means to you."

She gave me a reassuring smile. "It's kind of you to think of me, Cleo, but there's no need to worry. I'll have other opportunities to assist Mr. Bainbridge and, like you, I don't want to play any part in helping Mr. Lombardi advertise his medicines to the medical and pharmaceutical professions if he is the producer of that tonic. You're aware he's already staying at the hotel, aren't you?"

I wasn't. It was good to know, however, so I could avoid him.

We parted ways, Harmony heading to the lift while I went to collect my aunt for her appointment. I decided not to check on Floyd. If he was still asleep when I returned, I'd look in on him then.

I was about to knock on the door of my aunt's suite when Flossy emerged from her room.

"Hello, Cleo."

Wearing a soft pink gown that fit snugly across her chest, she was a picture of Rubenesque beauty. Not that I would use that word to her face. Once when a gentleman had innocently described her as such, she hadn't eaten for three days. The fashionably miniscule waistline was simply unattainable for my cousin, unless she starved herself. I wished she saw how naturally beautiful she was, but unfortunately she'd inherited some of her mother's lack of self-confidence.

"Are you going in to see Mother?" she went on. "Perhaps I'll join you, since I have nothing else to do. It's so *boring* at the moment, isn't it?"

"What is?"

"London. Everyone's somewhere else at this time of year."

"It won't be long before they're back again." I knocked on Aunt Lilian's door. "We're going out, as it happens. I'm accompanying her to an appointment with a new doctor."

Flossy pulled a face. "On second thoughts, I'll find something to do." She hurried back to her suite before her mother saw her.

* * *

Aunt Lilian's new doctor didn't have rooms on Harley Street where all the so-called best physicians were located. His practice was located near St. Pancras railway station in a nondescript brick building set in a row of other nondescript brick buildings. He'd been recommended by Dr. Garside, an eminent medical scientist based at St. Mary's Hospital. Dr. Garside assisted the police on occasion, which was how I'd come to meet him when investigating a death by poisoning. As Dr. Garside was an expert at the leading edge of a rapidly changing profession, Harry suggested we ask him for the name of a doctor who could treat Aunt Lilian's addiction. With many doctors prescribing cocaine, opium, and other highly addictive substances for treating all manner of ailments, Dr. Garside sometimes came under fire from colleagues unwilling to admit they were wrong, but that was precisely why Harry and I sought his advice. Dr. Garside didn't have consulting rooms himself, but he'd given us the name of a friend who did.

Aunt Lilian emerged from the consulting room with an air of hope. When she instructed Cobbit, the hotel's coachman, to stop at a chemist on the way home, I waited until we were seated inside the carriage to ask why.

Aunt Lilian told me the doctor had not only given her a written plan of medication to take, but he'd spoken with her at length, unearthing the root cause of her addiction—her lack of self-worth. I suspected it was the unburdening of her mind rather than the medicinal plan that lifted her spirits most. She handed me the written plan. "The doctor wants me to take a powder, but in decreasing amounts over time. It will help with the headaches and other symptoms. He suggested someone else keeps it hidden from me and is the one to measure out the doses."

I supposed that was to stop her replacing her addiction to one medicine with an addiction to another. I looked over the plan as we drove. It stipulated precise measurements of the powder be mixed with a cup of water, the doses to decrease a little each week until the content of the cup was mostly water. The idea was to slowly wean Aunt Lilian off her cocaine dependency.

"It's beginning to rain," I said, peering out of the window as we pulled up in front of a Boots chemist. "You stay in here and keep dry."

"Thank you, dearest." She reached forward and clasped

my hand. I could feel her bones through the soft kid leather of her glove. "You are good coming with me today, Cleopatra. Your Uncle Ronald offered, but I didn't want him there. Some things should not be seen or heard by one's husband."

Her relationship with Uncle Ronald was different to the one I wanted with Harry. I wanted to share everything with him—the good and the bad. Not that he'd formally proposed, but there was an understanding between us.

The fact that I was even thinking such thoughts after years of convincing myself I would never marry left me feeling lightheaded as I entered the pharmacy. It wasn't a terrible feeling. Quite the opposite. I looked forward to seeing Harry again, to wrap my arms around him and feel his arms around me, too. Although we wanted to see each other every day, it wasn't always possible. He was very busy with his investigations, and I couldn't get away in the evenings without raising the suspicions of my family.

I purchased a packet of the powder prescribed by Aunt Lilian's new doctor and a bottle of Nerve Elixir, the tonic she used to take. The small print on the bottom of the Nerve Elixir label did indeed sport the Bella Vita Company's name. I buried it in my handbag so she wouldn't see it.

Once back at the hotel, Frank the doorman held an umbrella over my aunt's head as she traversed the short distance between the carriage and hotel door. I waited for him to return and offer me the same protection, but he simply stood by the open door. I waited some more. With a sigh, he released the door and joined me, umbrella raised high.

I stepped down from the carriage. "I like that you consider me your equal and a friend, Frank, but it would be nice to be afforded the same privileges you give the Bainbridge family when it's raining."

The grumpy middle-aged doorman was all smiles and "how do you do" for the guests and my family, but I usually received little more than a grunt in greeting. I knew it wasn't unfriendly—he treated the other staff the same way—and I wasn't lying when I said I liked that he was comfortable enough with me to be himself.

"You're always correcting folk who call you a Bainbridge, reminding them you're a Fox," he pointed out as he held the umbrella over the both of us as we walked.

"Yes, but—"

"And it's not far, the rain is light, and you have an enormous hat to protect your hair and face."

I touched the brim of my straw hat. "Yes, but the flowers and ribbons are silk."

He opened the hotel door. "Seems to me you're becoming more Bainbridge and less Fox the longer you live here."

"What does that mean?"

He cleared his throat. "Sir Ronald wants a word with you." He nodded at my uncle, standing in the foyer under the blazing light of the crystal chandelier where he was trying to catch my attention. A guest with a spectacular thick, black moustache with upward pointing ends stood beside him.

I joined them, smiling my best niece-of-the-owner smile. "Good morning, Uncle."

"Cleopatra, may I introduce a guest at the hotel, Mr. Lombardi. Or should I say *Signor* Lombardi?" Uncle Ronald's chuckle made his jowls tremble.

My smile froze.

In a cultured Italian accent, the guest said, "Mister Lombardi, please. When in England, do as the English do. Is that not what they say, Sir Ronald?"

The variation to the common idiom had both men's moustaches twitching with mirth.

"Well then, *Mr.* Lombardi, may I present my niece, Miss Fox."

Mr. Lombardi took my limp hand and kissed the back of it. "A pleasure to meet you, Miss Fox."

What did one say to the man who manufactured a medicine that made their aunt ill? And in front of my uninformed uncle, no less? He would expect me to be charmingly polite. I could manage the politeness but not the charm. "Good morning, Mr. Lombardi. How do you find the Mayfair Hotel so far?"

"It is a fine establishment. My room has a balcony with a very nice view over the park. What is it called?"

"Green Park."

"If all parks were named for their color then all of England's would be called Green Park." He laughed lightly.

It was difficult to gauge his age. Both his moustache and hair were thick and black without a hint of gray, but the wrinkles fanning the outer edges of his eyes and across his forehead would suggest he was at least fifty. I suspected he used hair dye.

"Mr. Lombardi was just telling me how he has thirty-five pharmacists and another twenty-three doctors coming to his presentation next week," Uncle Ronald said proudly. "Some of those are from outside London and will be staying here in the hotel. Isn't that marvelous, Cleopatra?"

It was indeed, particularly with the hotel being rather quiet in October. The best thing to say at that point would be to praise the number of attendees, or ask Mr. Lombardi if he regularly showcased his products to that many, and perhaps whether he was looking forward to the event. But I found I couldn't pretend enthusiasm. I simply murmured agreement.

Uncle Ronald frowned at me, but if Mr. Lombardi noticed my reticence, he gave no indication. He checked the time on his watch and made his excuses.

Once he was out of earshot, Uncle Ronald asked if everything was all right.

"We need to talk," I said.

"Is it your aunt? I was with Mr. Lombardi when she entered the hotel and couldn't ask how the appointment with the new doctor went, but she didn't seem unhappy." He gazed in the direction of the lift where John the operator bade two departing occupants a good day.

"The appointment went well. I'm sure she'll tell you all about it when you have a moment." I pulled out the bottle of tonic from my handbag, checked the vicinity to make sure no one was watching, and showed him the label.

"He prescribed the same stuff that made her ill?" he whispered loudly.

"No. He prescribed a powder. I purchased this to show you something. Look at the manufacturer name."

Uncle Ronald snatched the bottle off me and squinted at the label. His face drained of color. "Lombardi makes this?"

I nodded.

"That bloody scoundrel. I ought to chase after him and tell him what I think of his blasted tonic." He didn't move, however.

"Or you could cancel the presentation."

"I could…"

I waited for more, but he stopped there. "Uncle?"

"Damn and blast. We need the presentation to be held here."

"We *need* for Aunt Lilian to get well."

"Hosting the presentation won't make her ill again. She's on the mend and will be back to her old self in no time." I wasn't sure if he was truly optimistic about the outlook for her health or if he was trying to convince himself. His outlook may be heartening, but it wasn't the point.

"Uncle, you can't let him present here. It would be condoning the manufacture of this…" I took the bottle of tonic back and dropped it into my bag. "…this quackery."

"It's not as simple as that, Cleopatra. There are other considerations."

"Such as?"

"Mr. Lombardi's presentation is the only important event on the horizon. We need more."

"Isn't October typically quiet anyway?"

"October is, but the rest of the year is looking lean, too." He tugged on his shirt cuffs as he peered around. "I don't want to trouble you with the details, but suffice it to say, I expected the ballroom we created from the old restaurant to be more in demand after the Hessing-Liddicoat wedding."

"I am sorry it's not, but even so—"

"Even so, I won't make a rash decision about something so important. Hobart!" he called out. "Do you wish to speak to me?"

The hotel manager had been hovering nearby. He now

approached and greeted us both warmly. "Actually, I wanted to speak to Miss Fox."

Uncle Ronald looked relieved. "Good, good. I'll leave you to it. I have to see Lady Bainbridge." He went to walk off, only to stop. "Have either of you spoken to Harry Armitage about my proposal?"

Mr. Hobart glanced at me. "Um…"

"He won't be interested, Uncle," I said.

"You don't know if you don't ask." Before I could respond, he strode in the direction of the lift.

Mr. Hobart blew out a breath. "He asked you to ask Harry to return to his former position here, too?"

"Not quite the same position, but yes he did. I keep forgetting to mention it to Harry."

"I did ask him, and you're right. He wasn't interested. I just don't know how to tell Sir Ronald in a way that will cause the least offence."

"I'm quite sure that whatever you say will be less offensive than what I say. You're diplomatic, whereas I can be too blunt, particularly when speaking to my uncle."

He watched as John welcomed Uncle Ronald into the lift. "Sometimes bluntness is best. Sir Ronald appreciates forthrightness."

"We'll think of a way to manage him," I said. "Has Harry telephoned asking for me? Is that why you needed to speak to me?" Sometimes Harry would place a call to his uncle's office directly from his own office, although he kept such calls to a minimum. They were rarely necessary anyway, since Harry and I saw each other quite a lot lately and were able to say what we needed to say in person.

Mr. Hobart looked worried. "He asked me to ask you to meet him at the medical rooms of Lady Bainbridge's former doctor as soon as possible, if you have the time."

"I do, but why does he want to meet me there?"

"Apparently he needs your expertise as both an investigator and as someone who knows that particular doctor. He hired Harry today, and Harry wants your opinion on the doctor's trustworthiness."

As far as I knew, Mr. Hobart didn't know Aunt Lilian was addicted to the cocaine in the tonic that doctor prescribed, but he did know that her health had not improved while she was his patient. "I'll go now. What has he hired Harry to investigate?"

"He wants Harry to prove him innocent of the murder of a patient."

<h1 style="text-align:center">CHAPTER 2</h1>

I was rather glad the victim's body had been removed from the crime scene by the time I arrived. Despite solving several murder cases, I'd not seen many of the bodies, and apparently the effects of electrocution were more gruesome than most people expected. Discovering the patient died by electrocution in a doctor's consulting room was somewhat of a surprise at first, until Harry explained that she'd been receiving electric shocks from the Electro Therapy Machine. The device was supposed to send mild currents through her system, but something had gone wrong in that morning's session, and a much stronger current had been given.

We stood in the room with Detective Sergeant Forrester, a man I'd worked alongside on previous occasions. He was relatively young and good at his job, but, most importantly, he had an open mind. Like us, he was keen to uncover the truth. He'd recently taken to calling me Cleo and insisted I call him Monty, something that had been noted by several friends, including Harry. While it wasn't unusual for men and women to call one another by their first names, it sometimes signaled they were *more* than friends. I suspected in D.S. Forrester's case, that was his hope.

Apparently he'd planned to leave the scene some time ago, but stayed when Harry said he'd telephoned me. In the meantime, Dr. Iverson had been taken to Scotland Yard for questioning, while the two other staff working at the consulting suite—his nurse and receptionist—had been sent home. D.S. Forrester had already questioned them, collected enough evidence to satisfy himself that Dr. Iverson needed further interrogation, and was merely extending Harry the professional courtesy of letting him look around before locking up the crime scene. As a friend and former colleague of Harry's father, a retired detective inspector, D.S. Forrester was willing to make such a concession.

I studied the contents of the wooden box positioned beside a daybed. The industrial-looking device with its wires, brass cylinders and knobs seemed out of place in the otherwise calming room with its tall potted palm in the corner, daybed covered with luxurious maroon velvet and soft leather armchairs.

"Don't touch it," Harry said. "While it should be safe now, I'd prefer you not to test it."

"What does it cure?" I asked, straightening.

I'd addressed my question to Harry, but it was D.S. Forrester who answered. "It improves circulation of the blood and the function of the organs."

"Apparently," Harry added.

"You don't believe it works?" I asked him.

"I telephoned Dr. Garside after learning the victim had died while using this contraption, and he doesn't think it's effective. Although some medical professionals swear electro-therapeutic shocks can help cure all manner of conditions, there's little evidence to support their claims. Dr. Garside says he wouldn't personally recommend their use."

D.S. Forrester cleared his throat. "Aren't you on Dr. Iverson's side, Armitage?"

"I was hired to prove him innocent, not to prove the efficacy of his treatments."

D.S. Forrester removed his notebook from his jacket pocket and began to flip pages. "You're wasting your time.

He had means, motive and opportunity. He's probably guilty."

"Then our investigation will prove it, and I'll not receive a penny from my client."

At the mention of 'our' investigation, D.S. Forrester looked up from his notebook. His gaze flicked between Harry and me and his lips thinned before he returned to reading his notes.

Harry continued. "The fact that Iverson hired me would suggest he's innocent."

"Or it could be a ruse to make himself *appear* that way." D.S. Forrester sounded a little terse.

While Harry agreed that was a possibility, I did not. "If Dr. Iverson hired a private detective purely as a ruse, he wouldn't have chosen Harry. He's been in the newspaper quite a lot these last few months thanks to solving several cases, some of them rather high profile."

D.S. Forrester pointed his notebook at me. "Thanks to *you*, you mean, Cleo. We know *you* solved them."

"I couldn't have done it without Harry. We're a team."

D.S. Forrester once again glanced at each of us in turn before frowning at his notes.

Harry handed me a brochure from the device manufacturer, his lips tilting with his wry smirk. If he was offended that D.S. Forrester gave him no credit for helping solve the cases, he didn't show it. Indeed, he was more interested in flirting with me in front of the detective sergeant. As he passed the brochure, his thumb caressed my fingers before letting go.

Even though D.S. Forrester appeared to be concentrating on his notes, I suspected he'd seen the exchange.

I lifted my gaze to Harry's and smiled. He smiled back before dropping his hand to his side. It was good to see him, despite the circumstances, and I hoped my lingering gaze told him so.

When D.S. Forrester cleared his throat, I broke the connection and read the brochure from the manufacturer of the

Electro Therapy Machine. The device was purported to cure backache, headache, rheumatism, dyspepsia, kidney troubles, heart irregularities, sleeplessness, piles, weakness, nervous disorders, hernias and ladies' ailments. The brochure was a piece of art, with winged cherubs holding scrolls upon which were written the chief claims of 'Cures Debility' and 'Cures Hysteria'. A smiling woman and a strongman with bulging muscles stood below the cherubs, alongside a large building radiating bolts of electricity from its rooftop. According to the print underneath, it was the office for the manufacturer, the Medical Electrical Company, with an address on Oxford Street.

"That's quite a varied array of ailments," I said. "If it worked, it would be a wonder cure."

"A lot of people claim it does work," Harry said. "Turn it over and you can read the testimonials of some."

According to the quotes on the reverse of the brochure, several well-known actresses, sportsmen, and a number of medical professionals based in England, Europe and America thought the device a miracle of modern medicine. Even Dr. Iverson was noted as having called it 'an exhilarating health-giving current to the whole system.'

"I presume you've ruled out a fault with the machine?" I asked D.S. Forrester.

"The device had been tampered with, according to the engineer from the manufacturer who inspected it this morn-ing." He scratched his sideburns with the corner of the small notebook. "I don't really understand the science, but appar-ently one or more of the wires were disconnected. He has put them back the way it should be to make it safe."

Harry pointed to the offending wire. "I think it's a little more complicated than that, but essentially this connects to a transformer, here. When the handle is turned, a safe low voltage current is emitted along these other wires, into the zinc discs which are placed against the patient's skin. When that wire *isn't* connected, instead of a small electrical shock, the patient receives enough volts to kill her. Isabel Kempsey's death wouldn't have been painless, I'm afraid."

"How awful," I murmured. "It's a terribly dangerous machine."

"It is, but the killer had to know what they were doing. I have some knowledge of how electricity works, but I'm not sure if my explanation is correct. I'm not an electrician."

He may not be, but he had a keen scientific mind. His interests were in architecture and the engineering of buildings and structures, but his clever mind was capable of understanding many scientific theories. I wasn't surprised he had already grasped how the machine worked. Having Harry involved in the case would be a great help, but D.S. Forrester didn't look inclined to ask him for assistance. Indeed, he seemed satisfied that he already had the right man in custody. That wasn't like him. I'd always found him to be willing to accept possibilities other than the obvious. He must know something that we didn't.

Harry pointed to the cupboard where the machine was usually housed. "There are extra components, including a corset with these discs sewn into it, as well as a wide belt, and what appears to be trousers. They can all be connected to the machine and the patient will receive mild electric shocks while wearing them as they recline on the bed."

D.S. Forrester pulled out the accessories from the cupboard and held them up for me to see. As he held up the trousers, he pulled a face. "A fellow would need to be desperate to wear this." He suddenly flushed and quickly returned the items to the cupboard. "Isabel Kempsey wasn't wearing any of these, however. Only those discs in the box you see there were connected to her face, chest, and arms."

"When was the device last used safely?" I asked him.

"Friday. The patient walked out perfectly well, according to Dr. Iverson, the nurse and receptionist. Mrs. Kempsey was the first patient to use it today. Dr. Iverson didn't notice the wire had been disconnected from the transformer until too late. The device is stored in that cupboard when not in use. He is supposed to lock the cupboard, but thinks it possible he forgot on Friday."

"You sound like you don't believe him," I said.

"Hence why I want to interrogate him further at the Yard. He's the only one with a key to that cupboard."

"If he planned to murder Mrs. Kempsey, why do it in his own clinic? He could have poisoned her with a tonic or powder." I indicated a display cabinet full of medicines in amber, green and blue glass bottles. "He could claim someone added poison to the bottle. It's more convincing. So, if we discount him, who else would have been able to get into this room without drawing attention to themselves?"

"You're suggesting one of his staff used their key to enter the premises over the weekend and tampered with the device?" The sergeant flipped back through his pages of notes. "Mrs. Iverson must be added, too. She could have stolen her husband's key while he slept beside her then returned it before he awoke."

While D.S. Forrester responded to all my questions with patience, Harry had begun to search the outer office. Clearly my questions weren't new. He and the sergeant must have already covered this ground.

D.S. Forrester watched Harry open the top drawer of the desk. "Armitage wanted to involve you, Cleo, because of your personal knowledge of Dr. Iverson. What can you tell us about him?"

"Not a great deal. I've never met him."

D.S. Forrester paused. "I see."

"My aunt was a patient of Dr. Iverson's until recently. She decided to see a different physician after Dr. Iverson repeatedly prescribed a tonic to her, even though it was making her more ill. He wasn't interested in trying a new treatment, nor did he believe the claims of leading scientists who theorize that a particular substance in that tonic can be addictive and harmful. So you see, my opinion of Dr. Iverson as a medical professional isn't a favorable one." I waved at the Electro Therapy Machine. "I wouldn't be surprised if he was taken in by the manufacturer's claims, just as he has been taken in by the manufacturer of the tonic."

D.S. Forrester closed his notebook with a snap. "Thank you for your insights." He glanced at Harry, rifling through the contents of the desk drawers, then stepped closer to me. "The exchange between the two of you just now... Am I to believe that you and Armitage are...more than friends?"

"You miss nothing, detective sergeant."

As if he sensed we were discussing him, Harry suddenly looked up. His gaze softened as he cast me a fleeting smile before returning to the task of searching the desk drawers.

D.S. Forrester cleared his throat. "Found anything, Armitage?"

"Nothing of note." Harry picked up a framed photograph from the corner of the desk. "Mrs. Iverson, I presume." He turned it around to show us the couple standing side by side in the picture, neither smiling. Dr. Iverson was a middle-aged man, but his wife looked considerably younger. She was quite striking with strong features, and rather tall for a woman, unless Dr. Iverson was very short.

"Does she know her husband has been arrested on the suspicion of murdering one of his patients?" I asked.

"Not arrested," D.S. Forrester said. "Merely taken in for further questioning. And yes, she has been informed. She lives close by. She was here all day on Friday, acting as the front desk receptionist. Apparently the usual girl was sent home first thing when she arrived to work sick."

"We'll question Mrs. Iverson ourselves," Harry said. "And the nurse and regular receptionist. Could I trouble you for their addresses, Forrester?"

D.S. Forrester hesitated then reopened his notebook. He picked up a pencil from the desk and wrote. He tore off the page and handed it to me. "Please keep me informed of anything that may be relevant, Miss Fox."

Miss Fox again, not Cleo? It would seem we were returning to formalities. It was probably more appropriate, given my relationship with Harry, and for the best. Following his lead, I said, "Thank you, Sergeant. You're a good man. I knew you'd do the right thing and cooperate to ensure the right person is arrested."

D.S. Forrester gave me a flat-lipped smile and nodded. He seemed a little sad, but I meant every word. He was a good man, and he would one day find a good woman who was right for him.

Harry didn't seem to have noticed the second meaning in our exchange. He attempted to open the window, only to give up when it wouldn't budge. "Locked," he announced.

"With the key in Dr. Iverson's possession," D.S. Forrester added. "Hence why he is my main suspect. Are you finished here? I need to get back to the Yard and question him."

Harry indicated I should walk ahead into the waiting room, where a constable stood near the door clutching a large leather wallet. Like the consulting suite, the waiting room was simply but expensively furnished. The chairs positioned against the wall were antiques that had been reupholstered with the same maroon velvet as the daybed. The desk and occasional tables were also fine-looking pieces that wouldn't have looked out of place in a Regency-era drawing room. A separate filing cabinet behind the desk was more functional and modern.

Seeing it sparked another question. "May I see Mrs. Kempsey's file?"

D.S. Forrester held out his hand to the constable who passed him the leather wallet, then pulled out some documents. "She was suffering from a nervous condition, but was otherwise healthy. She came twice a week for a session on the Electro Therapy Machine."

Aunt Lilian had been originally diagnosed with a nervous condition by Dr. Iverson, before being treated with the Nerve Elixir tonic, so I didn't have much confidence in his diagnoses. Others certainly did, however. He had a well-appointed practice on Harley Street, the location of all the prestigious London physicians.

I looked over the documents, noting Isabel Kempsey's address and the name of her next of kin, before handing it back to D.S. Forrester who gave it to the constable.

Harry and I left the medical practice, bypassing another constable standing at the base of the steps. Something was bothering me about the length of time it took for death to occur, but before I could discuss it with Harry, he said something that proved he wasn't thinking about the murder at all.

"So it's back to D.S. Forrester now, not Monty."

I regarded him from beneath my hat brim, but I didn't need to be quite so sly about it. His gaze was fixed firmly on the pavement ahead. "I knew you were pretending not to notice."

"I'm quite a good detective, even though you are the one who apparently solved all of the cases alone."

I tilted my head up to regard him fully. "Are you jealous of Forrester's personal regard for me or his professional one?"

"Neither." His lips twitched with a mischievous smile. "But I am contemplating whether to kiss you here in full view of the constable so he can report it to his superior."

"Don't you dare. But when we're somewhere private, I'll kiss you so thoroughly that you'll be left in no doubt that I'm very happy I chose you over him."

He removed his hat and flapped it at his face. "You make me blush, Cleo."

I laughed softly. "Seriously though, Harry, it doesn't bother you?"

"Not at all. I got the girl."

"I meant about him giving me all the credit for solving the cases."

"You have solved them."

"With your help."

He placed his hat back on his head. "Don't worry. I'm quite sure Forrester knows. He only made that comment because his masculine pride is a little bruised after you didn't choose him. It was his way of scoring a point against me."

"Why do men think everything is a competition?"

"I suppose it's not a healthy trait."

"I'm glad to hear you say that."

"Even so, I won."

I rolled my eyes.

Harry veered off course and looked both ways to cross the street.

"Mrs. Iverson's house is this way," I said before he stepped off the curb.

"I know."

"Then where are you going?"

"Somewhere private so you can kiss me thoroughly." He took my hand and led me across the street, flipping a coin to the lad who cleared away the horse muck in our path as we passed him.

I laughed as I held onto my hat. "You're incorrigible."

"It's been two days since I kissed you, Cleo. I need to do this if I want to focus my whole mind on the case, otherwise I'll be too distracted."

We entered a quiet lane then, after a glance back toward the lane entrance to check that we were alone, he removed my hat pin, took off my hat, and kissed me. I never ceased to be amazed at the effect his kisses had on me. It was as if a sort of impenetrable bubble enveloped us and we became the only two people in the world. I sank against Harry's chest, wrapped my arms around his neck, and savored the moment of utter bliss.

When we finally drew apart, he returned my hat to my head and slotted the hat pin back into place. He adjusted its angle then settled his warm gaze on me. "I've missed you, Cleo."

"It's only been two days."

"Too long."

I stood on my toes and pecked him lightly on the mouth before taking his hand and leading him back out of the lane. "Unfortunately, we can't stay here all day. We have work to do."

"Cruel employer."

"*You're* the employer this time. I'm your assistant."

"Ha!"

I released his hand as we returned to the busier street. The sweeping lad leaned on his broom, watching us with a grin. He knew what we'd been up to. "Are you implying that I'm incapable of following instructions?" I asked Harry.

"Not at all. I'm implying that you're no one's assistant.

You'll be the one with all the good theories and I'll be scrambling to keep up with your quick mind."

"You are sweet for saying it, but we both know what I said to D.S. Forrester is true. You and I are a team."

"We are," he said, his voice matching the tenderness in his gaze. "And a good one."

"Yet only one half of this team is humble."

He laughed and I couldn't help grinning, too.

We headed in the direction of Dr. and Mrs. Iverson's address, discussing the particulars of the case along the way. By the time we reached the handsome four-level redbrick townhouse, we'd decided that Dr. Iverson was almost certainly innocent. He'd be a fool to tamper with his own device, in his own clinic, and not change it back again to the way it was before the police arrived. He certainly had the opportunity to do so, and it would have given D.S. Forrester reason to believe the machine was faulty. Suspicion would have fallen on the manufacturer, not the doctor.

Being quite sure the doctor who hired Harry was innocent, we felt confident that we were looking for someone who wanted Isabel Kempsey dead *and* Dr. Iverson blamed for her murder. The most obvious culprit was a jealous wife, but I was reluctant to accuse Mrs. Iverson without evidence that her husband was having an affair with the victim.

Harry had no such qualms, but ever the gentleman, he managed to broach the subject delicately. "I'm afraid I have to ask you some sensitive questions, for your husband's sake. Firstly, was he a particularly attentive doctor?"

Margaret Iverson folded one bare hand over the other in her lap and leveled her gaze with his. She was just as she appeared in the photograph on her husband's desk. She was extraordinarily tall, but slender to the point of angular. She had strikingly chiseled cheekbones and jaw, and chestnut brown hair without a hint of gray. She was aged about forty, making her considerably younger than her husband. Framed photographs of a son at varying stages of his life, and no other children, would suggest they were a family of three. In one photograph, he was a young man standing in front of

King's College Chapel at Cambridge University, a building I knew well as my father had taught mathematics on campus and I'd grown up nearby. Mrs. Iverson must have been quite young when her son was born.

"It's all right, Mr. Armitage. You can be direct with me. I appreciate candor, particularly now. I believe candor will get my husband out of this situation and help you find the killer of poor Mrs. Kempsey as quickly as possible." Her tone was direct but not unfriendly. She seemed keen to get on with it and resolve this situation. "You want to know if my husband and Mrs. Kempsey were having an affair, is that correct?"

"It is," Harry said.

"If they were, I was unaware of it, and I believe I would have noticed. I'm quite observant."

"Are you able to make that judgment, considering you wouldn't have seen them together very often?"

"I've seen her in the waiting room from time to time, when I've also been there. She hasn't shown any sign of guilt, or that they are—were—lovers. No little glances or flushed cheeks, that sort of thing." She suddenly turned to me, catching me unawares. "You know what I mean, Miss Fox."

My face heated. Did she detect there was something between Harry and me? Had I given it away? Had he? "I, uh, yes. I believe I do know what you mean. You were working there on Friday, weren't you, Mrs. Iverson?"

She nodded. "My husband telephoned me first thing, after he sent the regular girl home. I used to be a receptionist at his first practice, years ago. That's how we met. I know what to do and have helped him occasionally. Miss Wainsmith has been with him almost a year and is an adequate receptionist, but my husband sent her home on Friday when she arrived sick."

"She was there today."

"Of all days, yes." Mrs. Iverson sighed. "She's a good girl, but apparently she became quite hysterical when it was clear what had happened."

"D.S. Forrester told you that?"

"Sister Dearden did, my husband's nursing assistant. She

stopped by after the detective sent her home. A constable had already informed me about the death and my husband's predicament, but she was able to give me the particulars. She knew I'd want to know, you see, so came here directly."

"Has Sister Dearden worked for your husband long?"

"About five years." Mrs. Iverson twisted the gold band on her ring finger. "It's good that you've taken on my husband's case, Mr. Armitage. I know how it looks, and that's why D.S. Forrester believes my husband is guilty, but I can assure you he is not. He's not the murdering type. If he was, he'd hardly do it in his own consulting rooms, would he? He's no fool. Someone must have staged it to make it look as though he's guilty."

"Do you know of anyone who'd want to see your husband hanged for murder?" Harry asked.

She seemed ready for the question, neither shocked by it nor hesitant in answering. "Last week a man caused a scene at my husband's rooms, accusing him of medical malpractice. His late wife was a former patient, you see. He was upset and looking for someone to blame. Her doctor is an obvious choice."

"How did she die?" Harry asked.

"She had a nervous condition that caused her to stop eating. She wasted away." Mrs. Iverson gave a little shrug of her shoulders. "Clearly that's not my husband's fault. He can't make someone eat when they don't want to. The patient's husband couldn't accept the truth, though."

"The truth?" I asked.

"His wife had a weak mind that allowed dark thoughts to creep in. It's those dark thoughts that upset her to the point of seeking medical help. But a doctor and medicine can only do so much. In such cases, the patient must *want* to get better. It seems this particular patient did *not* want to get better, and her husband can't accept that."

I blinked at her, not quite believing that someone could be so unsympathetic. I'd expected a doctor's wife to be caring and compassionate, but Mrs. Iverson was unfeeling, to the point of being mechanical. "Perhaps she had good reason for her dark thoughts," I said.

"We all have good reasons for our dark thoughts, Miss Fox. However, some of us just get on with it." Getting on with it seemed to be Mrs. Iverson's mantra. "I wasn't there the day that man came in. I heard about the incident secondhand, from both my husband and Sister Dearden. Apparently, Sister Dearden was the one who got him to leave."

"How?" Harry asked.

"She talked to him. I don't know what she said, but he saw reason and left without the police needing to be called. We thought that was the end of it, but perhaps it wasn't. Perhaps he plotted this revenge on my husband."

"By murdering an innocent woman?" Harry asked.

"Perhaps Mrs. Kempsey wasn't all that innocent, but that is something for you to find out, Mr. Armitage." Mrs. Iverson turned to me, her sharp features softening a little. "And you too, Miss Fox. I can already tell you are clever and forthright, so I feel sure you'll get to the bottom of this and prove my husband is innocent."

Her compliment threw me off, and I took a moment to respond. "Harry and I make a good team." I'd been so thrown off that I called Harry by his first name. I wasn't usually so unprofessional in front of a client.

Mrs. Iverson's shrewd gaze flicked to him then back to me.

"Do you know the name of the angry man?" Harry asked.

She shook her head. "I don't, but Sister Dearden and Miss Wainsmith will."

"We have an address for Sister Dearden, but not Miss Wainsmith. Do you know where we can find her?"

"They live at the same boarding house. That's how Miss Wainsmith came to work for my husband. She'd just moved into a room there when she first came to London last year, and my husband was looking for a new receptionist after the last one got married. Sister Dearden told her about the vacancy and suggested she apply after she learned Miss Wainsmith could type. She has a friendly manner but isn't particularly bright. Sister Dearden and my husband don't seem to mind, though."

We thanked her for her assistance, and she showed us to the front door. Once it was closed behind us and we were out of earshot, I asked Harry for his thoughts.

"She was somewhat direct, but I don't mind that," he said. "She seems to have unsettled you though. Do you think she lied?"

"It's not that. It was her manner. I can't really explain it, but she was almost *too* direct."

"Her answers were prepared, but I put that down to her expecting us or the police to ask them, so she'd already thought of her answers."

We walked on, but my mind wasn't as made up as Harry's. The unsettling feeling wouldn't go away.

CHAPTER 3

We found Sister Tuppence Dearden and Miss Emma Wainsmith together in the front parlor at their boarding house. Miss Wainsmith had clearly been crying and Sister Dearden seemed to be attempting to comfort her when we entered. The older woman had her arm around the younger's shoulders and was speaking gently to her.

The nurse was by no means *old*, it was just that the receptionist was quite a bit younger. She couldn't have been more than twenty-five, whereas Sister Dearden was mid-thirties. She looked up as the landlady led us through to the parlor, but Miss Wainsmith turned her face away and dabbed at her eyes with a handkerchief.

Harry introduced us and the reason for our visit. "May we ask you some questions about the incident?"

"Please, do," Sister Dearden said, indicating the spare chairs. "Anything to help prove Dr. Iverson is innocent."

"You believe he didn't do it?"

"Of course he didn't. He wants to save lives, not..." Sister Dearden patted a hand against her chest. "He isn't a perfect man, but he's not a murderer. And poor Mrs. Kempsey deserves justice."

Dressed in a simple outfit of navy blue skirt and matching jacket, her dark hair was parted down the middle with a thick plait wound into a bun at the nape of her neck. Although she didn't wear a uniform, it was easy to imagine her dressed in a crisp white apron with a white cap perched on her head. Likes Mrs. Iverson, she had a no-nonsense air about her, but I didn't feel as unsettled with her as I had with the doctor's wife. Perhaps it was the fact she showed more sympathy in the two minutes of our acquaintance than Mrs. Iverson had shown the entire interview.

"I've read about your agency, Mr. Armitage," Sister Dearden went on. "You've solved a number of murders recently. I am very glad Dr. Iverson hired you."

Miss Wainsmith blinked damp lashes at Harry. "Oh, you're *that* detective. You must be very clever."

Harry indicated me. "Miss Fox is the clever one. I merely take the credit."

Both women smiled politely at me, then turned back to Harry. I suspected they didn't believe him and assumed he was simply being chivalrous. The receptionist in particular barely even glanced at me. Her attention was focused on Harry, the tears on display when we arrived having dried up, leaving behind a smear of lash-darkening substance under her eyes. If I'd not seen that smear, I'd have guessed she darkened her lashes anyway. No strawberry blonde I knew had jet-black lashes. I also suspected she wore rouge on her cheeks. Their color was too pink against the rest of her pale face. Her outfit was more fashionable than Sister Dearden's, with the butter-yellow dress belted at her waist to draw attention to her thin frame. The lace belt, collar and cuffs, however, were a little yellow and somewhat frayed. I suspected she'd taken them from an older outfit and sewn them onto this one. Usually when young women did that, it was to give the appearance she'd purchased new clothes.

I suspected neither woman was well-off, since they lived in a boarding house, but unlike Sister Dearden, Miss Wainsmith wanted to appear to be more comfortably off than she was.

"It's our understanding that Dr. Iverson is the only one with the key to the cupboard where the Electro Therapy

Machine is kept," Harry said. Both women nodded. "Does he always lock it?"

"He'd be a fool not to," Sister Dearden said. "And he is no fool."

"What about a key to the premises? Do either of you have one?"

"I do," Sister Dearden said. "If Dr. Iverson has a house call, I'll open up the clinic of a morning. Although only the doctor takes appointments, sometimes patients show up without one and he wants me there to answer any questions they may have."

"I don't have a key," Miss Wainsmith added.

"Does Mrs. Iverson?"

"No," Sister Dearden said.

"But she would have access to her husband's," Miss Wainsmith pointed out rather enthusiastically, until she realized the implication of her comment. "Not that she would have stolen it and sabotaged the machine. Please don't think I am accusing her, Mr. Armitage."

"They have a good marriage?" he asked.

The younger woman looked at the nurse.

Sister Dearden gave a shrug. "I've not seen anything in their behavior to imply otherwise. On the occasions she has helped at reception, Mrs. Iverson was as professional as her husband."

Miss Wainsmith stared down at the handkerchief she was twisting around her slender fingers.

Sister Dearden suddenly gasped. Frowning, she turned fully to the receptionist. "Do you recall last Thursday, when I couldn't find my key?"

It was Miss Wainsmith's turn to gasp. "I do. You found it before you left for the day, but that was several hours after you noticed it had gone missing. Oh my! Could someone have taken it, made a copy, and returned it later?"

Sister Dearden got up and began to pace the small parlor with short, brisk strides. "One of the patients was there twice on Thursday. Firstly, for her appointment in the morning, then she returned at the end of the day. Do you recall, Miss Wainsmith?"

"I do." Miss Wainsmith nodded eagerly. "This particular patient was new. She paid in full after her appointment and didn't make another, yet she returned just before we closed. I distinctly remember her. She was pretty, confident and younger than our typical patient."

"Her name was Mrs. Linton," Sister Dearden added. "She wanted the doctor to treat her with the Electro Therapy Machine, even though it was her first appointment. Usually, first appointments are an introduction. Dr. Iverson talks to the patient, diagnoses their condition, then discusses treatments. Sometimes he'll prescribe medicine, but a session on the machine requires a full appointment, so the patient needs to return. Mrs. Linton insisted she needed it then and there."

"And Dr. Iverson obliged?" I asked. "Without first deciding if that was the treatment she required?"

Sister Dearden chewed her lower lip as she returned to her seat. "I'll be honest with you. I don't think the machine is a very effective treatment. It emits a mild current that gives the skin a vibrancy for a little while afterward, but once it wears off, the patient's health has not improved."

Miss Wainsmith drew in a sharp breath. "It's a fraud?"

Sister Dearden looked pained. "I don't know, but I think so. I've tried it myself and while somewhat exciting at first, it didn't really do much. Whether Dr. Iverson believes it's effective, I cannot say. I assume he must, since he continues to encourage sessions with it as a treatment."

Miss Wainsmith leaned forward and fixed Harry with an unblinking stare. "It must work. Dr. Iverson wouldn't continue to prescribe such a treatment if it wasn't effective. He's an *excellent* doctor, Mr. Armitage. He *must* be to have rooms on Harley Street."

Harry removed a pencil from his pocket and wrote down Mrs. Linton's name in his notebook. "What reason did she give for returning later that day?"

"She'd lost one of her gloves," Miss Wainsmith said. "She remembered removing them in the waiting room and thought it must have fallen out of her bag when she paid. A thin excuse, if you ask me."

"You don't happen to know where she lives."

"Her patient file will have that information," Sister Dearden said. "If you'd like to return to check, you may borrow my key to let yourselves in. I don't think I'll be needing it until Dr. Iverson is released."

"Thank you," Harry said.

"It's in my uniform pocket."

"Before you retrieve it, I have some more questions. Apparently, a man came to the premises last week and caused a scene, accusing Dr. Iverson of medical malpractice. Do you remember that incident?"

Before he'd even finished, it was clear they both did. Sister Dearden nodded, her expression grim. The incident clearly had a more troubling effect on the young receptionist. She pressed the handkerchief to her mouth as tears filled her eyes. Sister Dearden, seated beside her, put her arm around the younger woman's shoulders.

"It was awful," Miss Wainsmith said. "He barged in like a madman and began shouting, demanding to speak to the doctor. He called him a murderer for treating his wife with an addictive tonic. He said the cure was worse than the ailment. I was terrified. Fortunately, there was only one patient in the waiting room, and one other in with Dr. Iverson. The doctor came out of the consulting room and spoke to the man, but that didn't calm him down. If it wasn't for Sister Dearden, we would have had to call the constables."

"What did you say to him?" I asked the nurse.

Sister Dearden shrugged. "I don't really recall. I think I told him he needed to leave because he was upsetting the ladies. I may have mentioned telephoning the police. Or perhaps he just ran out of steam after getting it all off his chest. Anyway, he left."

"Not before he threatened Dr. Iverson, shouting that he'd pay for what he'd done." Miss Wainsmith waved her handkerchief at Harry's notebook. "You should write down his name—Mr. Pierce. It was also Thursday, the same day Sister Dearden's key went missing."

Harry dutifully wrote. "Do you know of anyone who would want to kill Mrs. Kempsey and have Dr. Iverson arrested?"

Both women shook their heads, although Miss Wainsmith hesitated.

"Sister Dearden, would you mind fetching that key now?" I asked.

The nurse rose and left the parlor.

Once she was gone, I moved to sit in the spot she'd vacated on the sofa. "Miss Wainsmith, I think you have something you wish to tell us?"

She glanced at the doorway through which Sister Dearden had just gone.

"Something about the marriage of Dr. and Mrs. Iverson?" I prompted.

The receptionist twisted her handkerchief more vigorously. "I can't say…" Her voice was barely above a whisper and her face flamed. She wouldn't meet my gaze, or Harry's.

I gave him a look.

He understood its meaning and got up. "I need to stretch my legs," he said, leaving the parlor.

I tried again. "Miss Wainsmith, if you know something then you must tell me, even if you don't think it matters. Even if you think it implicates someone you like."

She pressed the handkerchief to her nose and seemed to reach a conclusion. "You're right. My loyalty is to Dr. Iverson, no one else. Not that I think Mrs. Iverson is guilty, you understand. Anyway, it'll be good to get it off my chest. I haven't told a soul, and it's been eating away at me. It's rather shocking you see. I can't even look at you while I recount it." She turned away from me and spoke to the blue lampshade on the side table. "About two or three weeks ago, at the end of the day, Sister Dearden and I walked home together. But when I got here, I remembered I'd left a letter from my mother that I'd been reading in my desk drawer at work. I wanted to finish it that night, so I told Sister Dearden that I was going back to retrieve it. She loaned me her key and I used it to re-enter the clinic. I assumed Dr. Iverson had gone home, but then I heard a noise coming from his consulting room. I thought I'd poke my head in to tell him why I'd returned but when I opened the door and looked in, I saw…" She covered her mouth with the handkerchief. After a moment, she removed it. "I saw the doctor on top of someone on the daybed. They were both naked."

I bit my lip to stop myself making a sound of surprise. Reminding Miss Wainsmith that I was there might stop her divulging more out of embarrassment.

"I'll never forget the look on his face. He was horrified. As was I. I quickly left, but not before I saw the woman's face. It was Isabel Kempsey."

This time I couldn't stop myself uttering a small sound. Miss Wainsmith had seen the doctor in a very compromising situation with the victim! He hadn't informed Harry, which might or might not mean anything. What I really wanted to know was whether Mrs. Iverson had lied to us, and did indeed know about the affair. If she did, she'd just become the main suspect. Not only would murdering Mrs. Kempsey get rid of her husband's lover, he'd be hanged for the murder.

"Do you think anyone else knows?" I asked.

"I'm not sure. I haven't told a soul. Not even Sister Dearden. Dr. Iverson never acknowledged the incident. Neither he nor I mentioned it the following day. We went about our business as if nothing was amiss."

Harry's voice was loud and clear as he thanked Sister Dearden for the key in the corridor. They both appeared in the doorway. Sister Dearden arched her brows at Miss Wainsmith, who blushed again and looked away. Sister Dearden offered to walk us to the door.

I wasn't quite finished, however, but my question was for her. "You say the Electro Therapy Machine doesn't work, but what do you think of Dr. Iverson's other treatments? The tonic that Mr. Pierce's wife took, for instance. What's it called?" I watched Harry out of the corner of my eye. If he knew I was fishing, he didn't try to stop me.

Sister Dearden seemed to suspect, however, going by her hesitation as she thought through her answer. "I don't have anything to say about that," she finally said. "The thing is, Dr. Iverson is a good man. He's generous, easy to get along with, and treats me like an equal when most doctors would look down their noses at a nurse. I shouldn't have said what I said about the Electro Therapy Machine not being particularly effective, and I won't repeat it, so please don't ask me to. As far as tonics and pills are concerned, if an eminent doctor says they work, then who am I to say they don't?"

I opened my mouth to speak, but Harry got in first. "We appreciate your predicament, Sister Dearden. Thank you. If you think of anything else, please contact me." He handed her a business card.

"Your name isn't on here, Miss Fox. Mr. Armitage introduced you as his associate earlier, not assistant."

"This is Mr. Armitage's case," I said. "This time I *am* his assistant."

"We're a team," Harry countered. "I can't solve my cases without her."

"How nice to hear a man give a woman the credit she's due," Sister Dearden said with a smile for him. "That's how it is with Dr. Iverson and me. I'm fortunate that he asks my professional opinion from time to time."

Once Harry and I were out of earshot, I asked him if he thought the nurse was being *too* effusive in her praise for the doctor.

"You mean, is she his lover?" he asked.

"I meant is she infatuated with him, but perhaps you're right and she's his lover, too."

"Too? Is that what Miss Wainsmith wanted to tell you in private? That *she* is his lover? She was even more effusive in her praise than the nurse... If she is his lover, the man has gone down further in my estimation. He's taking advantage of the girl. Not only is she a lot younger than him, she's his employee. It's wrong."

"*She's* not his lover, but I think your estimation of the

doctor will remain low when you hear that his lover was in fact Isabel Kempsey."

Harry stopped and gawped at me. He made a noise, part scoff, part humorless laugh, part grunt. "I need a stern word with my client."

I looped my arm through his and massaged the tense muscles through his sleeve. He soon relaxed, and we ambled rather than walked, our direction aimless. Neither of us wanted to part, but the afternoon was growing late, and we both knew I didn't have time to join him in questioning more suspects. Even though my aunt and uncle afforded me considerable freedom to come and go from the hotel as I pleased, they didn't like me to be out after dark. Besides, a family dinner was planned for that evening, and I'd need to change and have my hair done.

Harry guessed what I was thinking and suggested we question the suspects together tomorrow. "I'll return to Iverson's clinic after I escort you back to the hotel and retrieve the addresses we need from the files."

"You don't have to wait until tomorrow," I said. "It's your case. You should call on the suspects now if you can."

"And miss a golden opportunity to spend more time with you? Not a chance."

I tightened my grip on his arm. "Thank you."

"I also want to visit the manufacturer of the Electro Therapy Machine and check that my understanding of it is correct, and whether its malfunction could have been a fault after all. There's still a lot we don't know about the device. We should also talk to the victim's husband, particularly in light of what Miss Wainsmith admitted."

"It's going to be a long day," I said. "I'll have an early night and meet you at your office at nine."

"Do you have evening plans?"

"Just a dinner in the hotel restaurant. As far as I know, we aren't dining with any of the guests, but that may have changed. Uncle Ronald makes a habit of inviting people to sit at our table at the last minute." I wrinkled my nose. "I hope he doesn't invite Mr. Lombardi."

"Who is Mr. Lombardi and why don't you want to sit with him?" He stopped and rounded on me, eyes narrowed to slits. "Your uncle isn't trying to marry you off to him, is he?"

"No. Mr. Lombardi is not a suitor. He's the owner of the company that manufactures the tonic Aunt Lilian used."

His brows rose. "And he's staying at the hotel?"

"Not just staying there. He has hired the ballroom to make a presentation to dozens of attendees from the pharmaceutical and medical professions. We realized too late that his company makes that tonic, and now it's all arranged, and Uncle Ronald doesn't want to cancel. It's too important to the hotel, he says, but isn't his wife's health more important? If she finds out that Mr. Lombardi makes that tonic and her husband knew and still supported the business, how will that make her feel? She's delicate at the moment. She needs to know he's prepared to put her well-being above the hotel's reputation and profit. By letting the presentation go ahead, he's sending the message that the hotel is more important to him than she is."

Harry took both my hands in his. "I think you need to spell it out to Sir Ronald. He won't knowingly upset Lady Bainbridge for the sake of the hotel, but he's not the most perceptive when it comes to women."

He was right. Not all men were as empathetic as Harry. His understanding of women probably had a lot to do with being brought up by his birth mother while living in an all-girls school where she taught. He'd had no father figure, and had been surrounded by women in his formative years.

Before we turned onto Piccadilly, he kissed my gloved hand warmly before releasing it. When I reached Frank at the Mayfair Hotel's door, I turned and gave Harry a little wave. He waved back then joined the many other pedestrians hurrying along the pavement.

In the foyer, I smiled a greeting to Goliath, the extremely tall porter, as he passed me wheeling a trolley laden with luggage. To my surprise, he smiled back. He'd been rather low in spirits lately, ever since his sweetheart decided to end their relationship after she'd been dismissed from her position at the hotel. Although his friends all told him she didn't care about him enough to fight for their relationship, he'd still felt as though her dismissal was all his fault. I was glad to see him happy again.

"Mr. Hobart has been looking for you for quite a while, Miss Fox," he said.

"I've been assisting Mr. Armitage with a murder investigation."

I hadn't noticed Frank come up behind me until he spoke. "Can't Armitage work alone?"

Goliath winked at Frank. "Where's the fun in that?"

The lines on Frank's face settled into their usual curmudgeonly pattern. "He shouldn't have asked you. If Sir Ronald hears about it—"

"It won't matter," I said.

"Tell us about the murder," Goliath said, keeping his voice low as two guests passed.

"Not here." I smiled at another guest I recognized. "And not now. Mr. Hobart is signaling me."

I joined the hotel manager who'd emerged from the corridor where the senior staff offices were located. It was almost time for him to leave for the day, but he didn't yet hold the leather satchel he carried with him to and from work.

"How did it go with Harry?" he asked.

"Splendidly." Realizing how that sounded in light of the reason why I'd met with Harry, I tempered my enthusiasm. "That is to say, it was interesting. We have a great deal to get on with tomorrow."

"Together?"

"Yes." I tried to keep my features schooled, but a small smile and a blush managed to escape.

"Marvelous. I am pleased. I'm sure you'll have it solved within the week, Miss Fox. You two have an excellent partnership. Before you go up, I ought to inform you that your family want to speak to you."

"All of them?"

"I believe so. They're waiting for you to return to have a

family meeting in your aunt and uncle's suite. I said I'd send you there directly if I saw you before I left."

I glanced over my shoulder toward the lift. "It sounds ominous."

"I'm sure it's nothing to worry about. They certainly didn't hear it from me that you were meeting with Harry or that you're investigating a murder."

My uncle had forbidden me to associate with Harry, but I'd managed to get him to change his mind and allow me to see Harry when we investigate together, knowing anything more would be too much for my uncle to bear. The time would come when I'd have to inform him about our relationship, but not yet. I needed to soften his attitude to Harry first.

How I would do that was still a mystery.

I thanked Mr. Hobart and took the stairs up to the fourth floor, where I planned to go directly to my aunt and uncle's suite. I was accosted by my two cousins in the corridor before I reached it, however.

"Have you both been waiting for me?" I asked.

Flossy shushed me with a finger to her lips. "We've all been summoned to their suite. I think Floyd is in trouble."

"Me?" Floyd's bellow earned another shushing from Flossy.

"It must be you," she shot back. "It's always you. It's never me."

"That's because you're as dull as a loaf of bread."

"Are you calling me fat?"

"No! But you are stupid."

She thumped his arm. Honestly, sometimes they behaved as though they were children, not nineteen and just turned twenty-four.

"If it was about Floyd, we wouldn't all be summoned," I pointed out. "It's probably something to do with Mr. Lombardi. Have neither of you been told?"

"That he's hosting a presentation here?" Floyd asked. "Yes, I know. I'm organizing it."

"Harmony is organizing it," Flossy said petulantly. "You're merely providing the Bainbridge name."

"I do more than that, Floss, but you wouldn't understand, so I'm not going to bother explaining it."

She planted a hand on one hip and gave an indignant *humph.*

Before they descended into a verbal fight, I rapped on the door. "Let's see what this is all about."

Uncle Ronald answered my knock and invited us into their suite. The most spacious suite in the entire hotel, it was tastefully furnished by my aunt with a mixture of modern comforts, and antiques that Uncle Ronald had inherited along with the building itself. Aunt Lilian's keen sense of style was evident in the placement of the furniture, the muted color scheme, and the cluster of family photographs on one of the occasional tables. I noticed a new one had been added of Flossy, Floyd and me lounging in the sunshine on a picnic blanket in the garden at Hambledon Hall.

Aunt Lilian indicated we should all sit on the sofa while she sat in an armchair opposite. Uncle Ronald took up a position behind her, his hand resting on her shoulder. They were presenting a united front for what was to come, which was pleasing to see after Aunt Lilian had deliberately distanced herself from her husband in recent times. It was also pleasing to see that she was taking charge of the meeting. It meant she was feeling more confident within herself. The visit to her new doctor was already working wonders.

We exchanged the obligatory pleasantries before Aunt Lilian got to the point. "You all know about the event for Mr. Lombardi's company that will be held in our ballroom. You know how important it is to the hotel. But you may not know that Mr. Lombardi's company is the one that makes the tonic I used to take."

Flossy and Floyd glanced at each other, then at me. "You knew," Floyd said.

I nodded. "I learned it this morning, as did Uncle Ronald."

"And he told me," Aunt Lilian said. "Except I already knew, of course. I recognized the company name when I first heard it."

"Then why not say something before the contract was signed?" I asked.

"Because I want our hotel to host his presentation. Like your uncle, I believe corporate events could prove lucrative."

He patted her shoulder.

"But by hosting Mr. Lombardi's event, it makes it appear that we approve of his medicines," I said. "How can we approve of the tonic after knowing how it affected you, Aunt?"

Her eyes briefly fluttered closed, as if it hurt to keep them open. She already looked quite exhausted, with the dark circles under her eyes against pale skin. I regretted my vehement tone, but she spoke before I could apologize. "Mr. Lombardi's company produces other medicines. We can't make a sweeping judgment based on one product. Especially not when it would be to the hotel's detriment."

I appealed to my cousins for support, but neither looked inclined to disagree with their parents. "I think it's wrong," I said. "We're putting profits ahead of our moral duty."

"It's not our duty to prove his tonic is ineffective," Aunt Lilian said.

"It's more than ineffective. It's dangerous."

Her fingers twined together in her lap. "It's the duty of the medical profession to police such things. *Our* duty is to our guests, and Mr. Lombardi is a guest. Please treat him with the respect you would treat others."

"But—"

"Your aunt has made her decision, Cleopatra," Uncle Ronald said. Although his words were stern, his tone held a hint of apology. I suspected he felt more conflicted about continuing to host the event than she did.

Aunt Lilian winced and pressed her fingers to her temple. "I have a headache and won't be joining you for dinner tonight, but if Mr. Lombardi is dining alone, then I've asked Ronald to invite him to join you. If not tonight, then another night. You will all be polite to him. No one is to mention the Nerve Elixir and my...condition in his presence. Is that clear?"

Flossy and Floyd both murmured their assent.

"Is that clear, Cleopatra?"

"Quite." I rose. "If you'll excuse me, I must dress for dinner."

I filed out of the suite along with my cousins, but didn't stay to talk to them. I marched off to my room where one of the housemaids was laying out a dress for me to change into. I'd momentarily forgotten that Harmony wouldn't be assisting me, since she was working on the event. Her ladies' maid duties had been temporarily handed to Jane.

My nerves were still on edge when I entered the restaurant. I didn't head for the family table directly but stopped to speak to Mr. Chapman. "Does Mr. Lombardi have a reservation for tonight?"

The steward raised one perfectly plucked eyebrow. "No, Miss Fox. Apparently, he is dining elsewhere."

I released a held breath. "Good."

"You're not the first member of the family to ask that question." He looked in the direction of Uncle Ronald and Floyd, both seated at our usual table, chatting amiably to some guests at the adjacent table. "Nor the first member to seem relieved with my answer. Is there a problem?"

"That's none of your concern," I snipped off. He could be quite the nosy busybody. I'd caught him listening at doors on more than one occasion.

Instead of apologizing for his nosiness, he simply leaned a little closer, giving me a strong whiff of the cologne he used. It was an expensive brand. "Do I need to alert you when Mr. Lombardi does have a reservation with us?"

"Of course not." I went to walk off but stopped. "On second thoughts, perhaps that's a good idea. Thank you, Mr. Chapman."

I was gratified that he was being so agreeable after he and I had clashed on occasion. That was until I noticed the slight change in his handsome features. They'd taken on a slyness that I was more familiar with.

"I'm happy to do you this *favor*, Miss Fox."

Now I understood. He was being agreeable so that I

would grant him a favor in turn. I was about to retract my response to his offer, but decided to let it stand. That favor would probably come in the form of me keeping his secret to myself—Mr. Chapman's proclivities leaned toward men, not women—which was something I was happy to grant anyway.

Flossy arrived and took my hand. She scanned the faces of the other diners in the restaurant. "Is he here?"

"Not tonight," I said as Mr. Chapman politely melted away.

"Good. We can enjoy our meal."

I doubted I could enjoy my food until the week was over and Mr. Lombardi had left the hotel. My appetite vanished at the thought of being agreeable to the man who profited from something that made vulnerable people even more ill.

CHAPTER 4

$\mathcal{H}$arry was on the telephone when I arrived at his office the following morning. The recently installed device was a boon to his business, saving him a great deal of time, but it was also a testament to his agency's success since installing it must have been expensive. Although I suspected he could afford new furniture now, I was glad he hadn't replaced the secondhand desk, or the old leather armchair worn smooth from years of use. They gave the office—and therefore his business—an air of comfort and steadiness, both desirable traits for a detective agency.

He hung up the receiver as I placed two coffee cups on the desk. I'd stopped in at the Roma Café downstairs where Luigi, the owner, informed me that Harry had guessed I'd do just that and prepaid for the coffees. I slotted my umbrella into the holder by the door and hung up my coat on the stand then took a seat at the desk opposite him.

He sipped his coffee before telling me he'd just had a conversation with D.S. Forrester. "He's refusing to allow me to see Dr. Iverson."

"Why?"

"He didn't say, but he seemed cross."

I lowered my cup without taking a sip. "Do you think he's punishing us because I chose you over him?"

"I don't think he's that petty."

I hadn't thought so either, but why else would he be blocking Harry's investigation? "So you haven't had a chance to ask the doctor why he didn't tell us about his affair with the victim?"

"Or whether anyone else had access to the cupboard where the Electro Therapy Machine was kept."

"Ah," I said, realizing what he meant. "If it was locked, just like the front door, the killer would have needed *both* keys. But we've only been asking about the key to the clinic, not the one that locked the cupboard door."

"Precisely."

"The killer may have picked both locks." It was a consideration we'd overlooked earlier. "I can't believe we didn't think of that immediately."

"To be fair, we were distracted."

"By what?"

"I was distracted by you, and you by me."

"You don't distract me *that* much, Harry."

He smiled into his coffee cup.

I cleared my throat and took a sip of my coffee, too, while avoiding looking directly at him.

He lowered his cup to the desk. "I had another look at both doors when I went back yesterday. There were no signs of forced entry, and no scratches around either lock, but that doesn't rule out the use of lockpicking tools altogether." He passed me his notebook, opened to a page showing a list written in his neat hand. "What do you think of the plan of attack for today?"

"I think it's a good idea to start with the manufacturer. The more we know about the device, the better armed we'll be when we question the suspects."

We finished our coffees and Harry pocketed the notebook. As he assisted me into my coat, his fingers lightly brushed the back of my neck. Then he kissed the bare skin there. I turned and tipped my head back to receive a kiss on my lips.

When we drew apart, our fingers remained twined together. As we were both wearing gloves, it wasn't as intimate as it could be, but the touch still felt as thrillingly improper as the kiss. If my family knew what Harry and I were doing in the privacy of his office, they'd be shocked.

I quickly withdrew my hand and retrieved my umbrella while he collected the empty cups.

Harry seemed to guess the direction of my thoughts. "What excuse did you give your family for being out all day?"

"I haven't. I didn't see any of them before leaving the hotel. I'll have to think of something by the time I return, though. There's an exhibition at the Tate Gallery. I could say I was there."

"All day?" He opened the door for me. "I think you should say you're helping me with this case. Sir Ronald hasn't forbidden you to see me if we're investigating. And it is the truth."

"But he loathes me investigating murders. He thinks a lady detective should limit herself to finding missing puppies."

"Perhaps it's time he knew just how many murders you've solved. You did his friend an enormous favor last time. I think he can overlook your penchant for murder cases now as thanks."

I wasn't so sure. My favor for Lord Kershaw had been repaid by Uncle Ronald when he allowed me to continue to see Harry at all.

Harry locked the office door and followed me down the stairs. "Is the Tate open on Sundays?"

"Are you going to take me to the exhibition? That would be lovely. I do want to see it."

"I was thinking you could use it as an excuse when you join us for lunch. My parents asked me to invite you."

I glanced at him over my shoulder as we descended the staircase to street level. "All right, unless your mother plans to interrogate me." Harry's adoptive mother was very protective of her only son. Although she seemed to have forgiven me for getting him fired from his job as assistant manager at the hotel, I often wondered if she had, deep down.

"I doubt she will. She wants to mark the occasion with joy."

"What occasion?"

He flashed his dimples. "You've forgotten."

I gasped, then followed it with a groan. "It's your birthday. Sorry, Harry. I did forget." I placed a hand to his chest and stood on my toes to kiss him. "I'll make it up to you by buying you a special gift."

He circled his arm around me and gently pulled me against his body. "More of this is gift enough."

"But you can't unwrap it in front of your mother."

I kissed him thoroughly, causing him to drop the coffee cup that was balanced on top of the other. Neither of us hurried to pick it up.

* * *

THE HEADQUARTERS of the Medical Electrical Company on Oxford Street was brightly lit, as if warding off the darkness of midnight, not an overcast morning. The owner of the company and inventor of the Electro Therapy Machine, Mr. Reid, refused to see us at first. We overheard him ordering his assistant to throw us off the premises. Going by the way he shouted the order, he wasn't in a good mood.

The assistant emerged from his employer's office with a sheepish expression on his face. "I apologize, but Mr. Reid is busy."

The door opened again and a bearded gentleman with bushy black eyebrows appeared. "On second thought, they can come in." The eyes beneath the brows skewered us with a sharp glare. "They could be useful."

"Thank you for seeing us," Harry said as we sat at the desk. "I'm not sure your assistant adequately explained why we're here."

The office was as large as my suite in the hotel. Indeed, it was part office, part inventor's workshop. Although the desk where we sat was limited to paperwork, a second one and a long bench were occupied by all manner of interesting devices, tools and machine parts. Another wall was covered in floor-to-ceiling bookshelves crammed with books. Harry's gaze kept moving to the devices, but I couldn't stop staring at the picture of a life-sized skeleton made up of several X-ray images pinned to the wall.

"He said you're private detectives hired by Dr. Iverson to prove my machine is faulty," Mr. Reid said, those ponderous eyebrows still severely drawn together.

Harry shook his head. "That's not correct. It's true that we've been hired to prove him innocent, but that doesn't necessarily follow that your machine is at fault. It may have been sabotaged."

Mr. Reid pointed a stubby finger in the air. "Yes! That's what I think happened. Good man. We are in agreement." He picked up a newspaper from his desk and showed us the front page. The attention-grabbing headline declared WOMAN DIES USING MEDICAL DEVICE. "Will you go to this newspaper and tell them? I've demanded a retraction, but the editor refused. Until the police prove she didn't die on an Electro Therapy Machine, he stands by the article."

"I read that this morning," Harry said. "It doesn't blame your machine for the murder."

"But it's mentioned! It's murder by association."

"Not really."

Mr. Reid sniffed. "Murder of my reputation. Sales of the device will slow after this." He shook the newspaper at us.

Harry took the paper and set it down to one side on the desk. "Mrs. Kempsey did die on one of your machines. That is a fact. What we think happened, however, is that someone tampered with it to lay blame on Dr. Iverson."

Mr. Reid seemed satisfied that we were still on his side. He crossed the room to the bench where a similar wooden box to the one in Dr. Iverson's consulting suite sat. "I was called to the doctor's clinic by a Detective Sergeant Forrester yesterday morning. It was I who informed him the machine had been tampered with. According to this paper, Dr. Iverson is the main suspect. Would you both care to join me and I'll prove it can't harm anyone, let alone kill, unless it's been sabotaged?"

We joined him at the bench and watched as he removed the zinc discs.

"I believe I know how it works," Harry said. "May I run my knowledge by you and you can tell me if I'm correct?"

"By all means."

Harry explained that the transformer should ensure a safe low voltage of electricity was passed along the wires into the zinc discs that are placed on the body, but instead, a high voltage was transmitted because a wire had been disconnected.

Mr. Reid tapped one of the wires. "You are essentially correct. However, this other wire must also be disconnected. It acts as a secondary safety mechanism in case the first wire is accidentally dislodged." He held up two discs. "Would you care to try it on your hand, Miss Fox? It's quite safe."

I removed my gloves. "Certainly."

Harry leaned over the box and gave the device inside a thorough inspection. "Perhaps I should go first."

Mr. Reid placed one of the discs on the back of my hand. "If she is electrocuted, you may prosecute me and take all my money, Mr. Armitage. Does that set your mind at ease?"

"Hardly," Harry ground out.

Before Harry could protest further, Mr. Reid cranked the handle on the side of the box. A small jolt at the site of the disc tingled my skin. It continued for some time, even though Mr. Reid no longer cranked the handle.

"Is that it?" I asked.

Mr. Reid removed the disc. "That was merely a simple demonstration. When all discs are placed on a particular area of the body and the device is connected to an electrical switch, or the handle is cranked several times, the patient enjoys an invigorating sensation that awakens the blood, muscle, and bones. Many women find it rejuvenating, restoring youthful vitality that has been lost."

"Only women," I said wryly.

"And weak men."

I bit back my sarcastic retort and focused on the death instead. "We're trying to discover how Mrs. Kempsey could have died during her appointment on this device with only Dr. Iverson present. Have you ever seen someone fatally electrocuted before?"

"No, although I have read about it in science journals. It's used as a humane mode of execution in America." He closed the lid on the box. "I think I know what you're going to ask, Miss Fox. How could Dr. Iverson not know his patient was being electrocuted? She should have shouted, or made a noise, and he would have had time to turn it off, saving her life."

"Yet she died instantly, right before his eyes," Harry added.

"Interesting," Mr. Reid murmured, tapping his chin in thought.

Harry and I exchanged grim glances. Mr. Reid's idea of interesting was rather macabre.

"What you're describing is instant death, with no opportunity to even turn the machine off," he said. "To my mind, that means she died in one of two ways."

He had Harry's and my full attention now. "Go on," I said, impatient.

"Either Dr. Iverson is lying, and her death *wasn't* instantaneous. He ignored her pleas for help and watched her die. Or she had an underlying condition that caused her heart to fail when her body received the dangerous level of volts, killing her instantly. The first scenario means he's a murderer, which I don't believe. Dr. Iverson is a good man, and surely there are easier ways for a doctor to kill a patient. The second scenario means the saboteur knew about the heart condition *and* knew a high voltage would be instantly fatal."

There was also a third scenario. "It's possible the saboteur *didn't* know about her heart condition but *assumed* the machine would kill her instantly. They didn't know electrocution can take longer than a mere second or two."

Mr. Reid agreed. "If you rule out Dr. Iverson being the murderer—and I believe you can—then the machine must have been sabotaged by someone else with access. It's the only conclusion. Not even a weak heart would give out while attached to the Electro Therapy Machine if it was working correctly." He patted the box's lid. "The currents it transmits are so minimal they barely register on a galvanometer. That's a special instrument we use to measure electricity," he told me.

"If the currents are that low, how can it be effective in curing anything?" Harry asked.

Mr. Reid bristled. "Are you calling me a fraud, Mr. Armitage?"

"I'm merely asking a question about the medical science."

Mr. Reid snorted. "I don't expect you to understand. You're not an electrician or doctor. I have many testimonials stating the excellent health benefits of the device. Just this month the *Pope* wrote to me to tell me it helped his rheumatism." He pushed past Harry and strode to the door. "If you're looking for someone with a reason to sabotage my device and my good name along with it, look at my former employee, now rival. Duncan Hamlin of The Hamlin Electrical Company is peddling a device he claims is better than mine, but is in fact essentially the same. I taught him everything. I treated him like a son, even allowing him significant time off when he was going through some difficulties. How does he repay me? He steals my idea and leaves. He's a greedy thief who'll stop at nothing to besmirch my name and that of my most celebrated client, Dr. Iverson."

"Even murder?" I asked.

Mr. Reid opened the door. "I'm afraid Duncan Hamlin has no morals. I was quite taken in by him at first, but his true nature came out in the end. He threatened me when I dismissed him. You'll find him in a grubby little workshop in Rosebery Avenue, Clerkenwell." He sniffed. "He can't afford premises in this part of the city."

Harry thanked him and we left. As we walked along Oxford Street, he removed his notepad and pencil from his pocket. I peered down at the page as he wrote another question to ask Dr. Iverson—did Isabel Kempsey have a weak heart?

"I've thought of another question for the doctor," I said.

"Did any of his staff know how the Electro Therapy Machine worked, and do they have the knowledge to sabotage it?"

Harry wrote the question down then flipped the notebook closed and pocketed it. "The rival manufacturer certainly has the knowledge, but his motive isn't very strong. Even if Duncan Hamlin wanted to ruin his former employer's reputation, I can't believe he'd stoop to murdering an innocent woman and blaming it on an innocent man."

I agreed. We may not have met Mr. Hamlin yet, but it was a stretch to think someone would go to such dreadful lengths for profit. Unless... "We discussed three scenarios in Mr. Reid's office, but I've just thought of a fourth. What if the saboteur didn't know Isabel Kempsey had a heart condition? Indeed, what if he didn't know who Dr. Iverson's first patient was yesterday morning, or didn't think it mattered? Maybe he presumed sabotaging the device would badly shock the next patient to use it, not cause her death because he didn't know that patient had a heart condition."

"A tragic miscalculation? It's a good theory, Cleo. It fits if the saboteur is the disgruntled Hamlin. He'd want to make the device look bad to Iverson. Come on. We need to speak to him. That bus will take us to Clerkenwell."

He ran to catch it and asked the driver to wait for me. I hurried as quickly as I could and was assisted on board by Harry. The driver didn't wait until we were seated before urging the horses forward, and Harry had to steady me as he paid the conductor for our tickets. There was no room inside, so we headed up the stairs to the open-air seats on top.

Once settled, Harry asked me if I'd managed to avoid Mr. Lombardi the previous evening.

"Fortunately, he was dining elsewhere," I said. "If he was in the hotel restaurant and dining alone, Aunt Lilian told us to invite him to sit with us. It was practically an order. Uncle Ronald went along with it, but I think that was more because he didn't want to upset her. I could tell he didn't like the idea."

"Yet he's fine with Lombardi hiring the hotel's ballroom for his event?"

"They both are. They say company events will be a good future revenue stream for the hotel, and we need this one to be a success to attract more."

"If it's your aunt's decision, then you can't go against her wishes. As long as she's not being coerced into it by Sir Ronald, that is."

"She's not, I'm quite sure of it." I sighed. "You're right. It is her decision. Very well. I will dine with Mr. Lombardi if necessary, and not call him a quack to his face."

"Very good of you to add that last part, Cleo."

I leaned against his side. "It will cost me a great deal to be gracious, but I'll do it for my aunt's sake."

When we reached Rosebery Avenue, Harry assisted me onto the pavement then assisted a woman with a large leather handbag up onto the omnibus. The Hamlin Electrical Company workshop wasn't far. According to the sign painted on the red bricks, the company manufactured quality electrical medical machinery. A white lace curtain in a window above moved with the gentle breeze. I wondered if it was the private residence of Mr. Hamlin or whether he rented the rooms to someone else.

The front part of the ground floor was occupied by a small office. Mr. Reid had called the premises grubby, but the space was quite the opposite. Like Mr. Reid's office, all of the electric lights were on, and with the newly painted white walls, it felt modern, clinical and fresh.

A man had been about to walk through a door behind the counter. He let the door swing closed upon seeing us, but not before I saw the untidy workshop of an inventor beyond. He blinked at Harry through round spectacles. "Good morning. How may I help you?"

Harry gave him a business card, which wiped the smile off the man's face. "I'm Harry Armitage and this is my associate, Miss Fox. Are you Mr. Hamlin?"

"I am Duncan Hamlin." He placed the card down on the counter with a deliberate, precise motion. "Private investigators? How curious."

"We've been hired to investigate the death of a woman at

a doctor's clinic yesterday. She died while undergoing a session on the Electro Therapy Machine."

"I read about it in the newspaper. Quite awful. Aren't the police investigating that case?"

"We've been hired by the doctor whose clinic was the scene of the murder."

"So it *is* a murder. Even more curious." He regarded us levelly through his spectacles. He was a young man, no more than thirty, with a very thin frame and sallow skin. He looked like he needed a good feed and some sunshine. "How can I help?"

"You used to work for the company that manufactured the Electro Therapy Machine," Harry said. "You know how it works."

Mr. Hamlin frowned. "Are you accusing me of tampering with it?"

"It had to have been tampered with to transmit a lethal voltage."

"Perhaps it was faulty," he said as he absently slid Harry's business card around on the counter. "If you compare it to another, you should be able to tell. Or bring it to me. I can take a look and give an honest opinion."

Harry pressed his fingertips down on the card, halting the movement. Mr. Hamlin finally looked up again. He swallowed.

"You don't believe it was faulty." Harry released the card. "The police will have an independent electrician check it, but I think we both know they'll find it couldn't have killed anyone unless it had been deliberately tampered with."

Mr. Hamlin swallowed again. "Perhaps you are right. It's been some time since I looked at one, I can't remember how it worked."

"I'm sure it would quickly come back to you. In fact, as someone with an excellent understanding of electricity, as well as knowledge of that particular machine, plus a motive—"

"Motive! For murder! Are you mad?"

"A motive for sabotage. It seems likely the victim had a

heart condition, something you couldn't have known. You merely wanted to shock her badly—or any unfortunate patient who happened to be first to use it yesterday."

The rather awkward inventor became a different person as he vehemently denied sabotaging the device. He even thumped his fist on the counter. "You've already been to see Reid, haven't you? He put into your minds that I sabotaged his machine, because I'm a disgruntled former employee."

"Who stole his ideas," Harry finished.

"I did not! I've developed a superior machine through my own ingenuity. That man is a liar and fraud. You can't believe a word he says. If it wasn't for me, he wouldn't even have the Electro Therapy Machine. That was *my* invention. He bought it from me, then hired me as his chief engineer. I continued to refine it, making it more portable, while all he did was pay doctors with famous patients to say it worked wonders. Any monkey can do that." He pointed to his chest. "Without me, he would be nothing. When I finish refining my newest invention, he'll be nothing once again. Mine will become the more popular product on the market, because it will actually work."

His pale face had become quite red by the time he finished. I was worried he was overdoing it, so decided a calmer, less accusatory tone was required. "Perhaps someone can vouch for your whereabouts. Your wife, perhaps?" I indicated the framed photograph on the wall of a doe-eyed young woman seated beside Mr. Hamlin.

He looked down at the card again. "My wife died last year. As to my whereabouts, I worked late in the workshop." He indicated the door leading to the back room. "I went to bed about two or three. I live upstairs, alone."

"What about other employees?" Harry asked.

"I have no employees. It's just me. A small factory in Shoreditch assembles my device to order." He picked up Harry's card and tucked it into his pocket. "Hardly a serious rival for Reid, am I?" He gave us a pointed look. "Is there anything else?"

"Just one more question," Harry said. "Why did you leave Mr. Reid's employ? You mentioned you were disgruntled."

He glanced at the photograph. "I was grieving my wife, but Reid wouldn't allow me more time to…compose myself. I decided I'd had enough of working with him. My wife always said I should never have sold my idea to Reid, and I suppose it took her death for me to realize she was right." He lowered his head, causing his glasses to slip down his nose.

"Thank you for your time," Harry said. "Please telephone if you think of anything further."

"Actually…" Mr. Hamlin cleared his throat. "I think I ought to tell you, my wife was a patient of Dr. Iverson's before she died."

Harry and I glanced at each other.

"I know how it looks," Mr. Hamlin said. "But I want to assure you, I don't blame him for her death. Not altogether."

"What did she die from?" Harry asked.

"Cancer of the breast."

"We are truly sorry for your loss, Mr. Hamlin," I said.

"Thank you. I know what you're thinking now, but I assure you I didn't tamper with the machine to ruin Dr. Iverson. As I said, I don't blame him. Nothing could have saved her." He looked down at the counter as his eyes filled with tears.

"I do have another question for you. Did you know the victim, Isabel Kempsey?"

His head jerked up. "No! I've never met her, heard of her, or know anyone named Kempsey."

I felt his gaze bore into my back as we left.

"What do you think?" Harry asked as we walked away.

"I think Hamlin is still angry with Reid."

"So much so that he was prepared to harm a woman he has never met to get revenge on his former employer? He may not have known about her heart condition and that the machine would kill her instantly, but he must know that electrocution—even for a mere few seconds—causes terrible injuries."

"Mr. Hamlin didn't *seem* cruel enough to do it," I admitted, "but I've been wrong about people before."

* * *

WE DECIDED to call on Mr. Pierce, since we were closer to his house than any of the other suspects. He was the fellow who'd accused Dr. Iverson of malpractice after he'd prescribed what we suspected was Nerve Elixir to his now deceased wife. He'd made quite a scene in the waiting room, shouting and carrying on until Sister Dearden calmed him down.

Mr. Pierce lived in a respectable neighborhood, if not an affluent one. We thought he might be at work, but fortunately he was home. He met us at the door and did not invite us inside.

Harry handed him a card and explained that he'd been hired by Dr. Iverson. He'd hardly finished getting the words out when Mr. Pierce went to shut the door. Harry muscled it back and forced his way inside.

"I wouldn't try that again," he said. "It makes you look guilty."

Mr. Pierce rubbed his stubbled jaw and mumbled something under his breath. I caught a whiff of alcohol and cigarette smoke, but I wasn't sure if it was coming from him or the depths of the house. "I know you want to blame someone for what happened to that woman, but it wasn't me. Yes, I want Iverson to suffer, but I wouldn't kill a woman I'd never met."

"Where were you over the weekend?" Harry asked.

"Here, drinking myself into a stupor."

"Can anyone vouch for you?"

"My dead wife's ghost." Mr. Pierce pressed his thumb and finger into bloodshot eyes. "Apologies. No. No one can vouch for me. I was alone."

"No servants?" I asked.

"Do I look like I can afford live-in servants? I used to have a charwoman come, but I dismissed her. I'm not wealthy. It was a stretch to afford that damned doctor's fees." He put up a hand. "Sorry for my language, Miss, but talking about him aggravates me."

"I understand." I hesitated then decided to use a weapon that could be effective in this instance. "I have a close relative who was prescribed the Nerve Elixir by Dr. Iverson. She became addicted to the cocaine in it and is now suffering the ill effects of that addiction. Is that what your wife was taking?"

Mr. Pierce suddenly grasped my hand. Harry took a step toward him, but I shook my head and he stayed back.

"Yes! Then you *do* understand." Mr. Pierce squeezed my hand. "You know how terrible it is to watch your loved one waste away while continuing to pay more and more money to that *charlatan*. I couldn't help my wife. She believed Iverson was right, that the tonic would cure her. But it did the opposite. Not only did it slowly kill her, but before her death, her character changed entirely, and I blame that *blasted* tonic. She used to be good and gentle, but she became angry, cruel. The last few months were unbearable. What did you say your name was?"

"Miss Fox."

He squeezed my hand again, rather too firmly, and I winced. He started to say something but stopped himself, then released me. He raked his fingers through his hair, which didn't improve its already disheveled state.

"It's gloomy in here," Harry noted, looking around the dark hallway.

"I keep the curtains closed. There's no point opening them when you just have to close them again at the end of the day."

"Why not put the light on in here?" Harry indicated the single lightbulb dangling from the ceiling.

"There's something wrong with it." Mr. Pierce shrugged. "No idea what."

I mentally struck Mr. Pierce off our list. Clearly he had no electrical knowledge.

Harry thanked Mr. Pierce for his time and invited me to leave ahead of him.

"Miss Fox, wait." Mr. Pierce angled himself between Harry and me, blocking Harry out of the conversation. Mr. Pierce leaned close. I held my breath against the stink of alcohol and smoke that clung to him. "Miss Fox, you may be interested to know that there is a way to punish the man behind the tonic."

"I think Dr. Iverson is already suffering."

"Not Iverson. The manufacturer of the Nerve Elixir, an Italian by the name of Lombardi. He's here in London to present to pharmacists and doctors at a fancy hotel on Saturday."

I held my breath again, but not because of the stench this time.

"I'm going to cause a scene at his event, something that will draw the interest of all the newspapers. They'll be forced to listen to me, and then the whole world will find out Lombardi's tonic is as dangerous as poison."

Suddenly feeling ill, I pressed a hand to my stomach. "What sort of scene?"

"I don't know yet. But I can assure you, it will be something spectacularly disastrous for Lombardi."

For Lombardi, and by association, the Mayfair Hotel.

CHAPTER 5

"We need to alert the police," I said to Harry as we walked away from Mr. Pierce's house. "Thank goodness he didn't know the hotel belongs to my family or he wouldn't have confided in me."

"I think you should tell Sir Ronald and let him decide whether to notify the police or not."

"But Mr. Pierce plans on creating a disturbance of some sort. The police can stop him before it happens."

"They can't arrest him until a crime has been committed. All they can do is caution him and I'm not sure that will work. Pierce is a drunkard and determined, a combination that usually finds a way in my experience."

"They can post constables at the entrance to watch for him on the day of the event."

Harry's pace slowed. "That's the problem. Sir Ronald won't want a police presence on the day. It's too visible and will worry the guests. But if you tell him, then he can alert the staff. Frank and the other doormen are very good at keeping undesirables out, but if Pierce manages to get past them it's unlikely he'll also get past Goliath. The front-of-house staff are experienced at keeping calm and being discreet. Or perhaps Sir Ronald will decide to notify the police. Either way, it's his decision to make."

He had a point. It should be my uncle's decision. However, telling him about Mr. Pierce's threat meant I had to tell him how I'd gained the information. Should I lie and pretend the case was something milder, and not a murder investigation?

Harry watched me struggling to think of the best way to broach the topic. "I can be the one to tell him if you want. That way you don't have to lie. I'll say I stumbled across the information while investigating the murder at Dr. Iverson's clinic. It's all true anyway."

It was an excellent idea. Not only did it keep me out of it altogether, but my uncle would be grateful to Harry for the information. The more grateful Uncle Ronald was to Harry, the better for us when it came time to inform him about our relationship.

"It's a neat solution," I said.

"I'll tell him later today. So where to next? The address we have for the victim's husband is closer than the address for the suspicious patient who may or may not have taken Sister Dearden's key."

"Then we'll call on him first."

Hopefully Mr. Kempsey could shed light on possible motives and give us a reason as to why his wife had been murdered. We were still no closer to knowing if she was supposed to die, or whether she was an innocent victim in a plot to ruin Dr. Iverson.

* * *

MY EXPERIENCES in dealing with the loved ones of the deceased had taught me that grief manifested in various ways. During this investigation so far, two men had shown quite different reactions to the deaths of their wives. Mr. Pierce had taken to drink and Mr. Hamlin had thrown himself into his work.

Mr. Kempsey seemed more irritated than angry, as if his wife's death was an inconvenience that was taking him away from more important things. He refused to let us into the house at first, until Harry told him it wouldn't look good if he didn't speak to us. As Mr. Kempsey led us through to a library, I caught a glimpse of mourners in the front reception room. Several men and women spoke quietly among themselves, many with handkerchiefs in hand. One, a middle-aged woman, craned her neck to watch us.

"Well then?" Mr. Kempsey prompted once we were in the library. "Let's get this over with quickly. I have a funeral to organize." He was a thickset man with a ruddy complexion and strands of gray hair that he'd combed over his head in an attempt to hide the bald patch. I saw no hint of sadness in his eyes.

Harry's first question got straight to the point, as requested. "Do you know why anyone would want to murder your wife?"

"Of course not. My wife was popular. Everyone liked her. What happened must have been a dreadful accident. A faulty machine, something like that." Mr. Kempsey rocked back on his heels, hands clasped behind him, and regarded Harry levelly. Too levelly. He didn't blink.

"Did she have a heart condition?" Harry asked.

Finally Mr. Kempsey blinked. "What do you mean?"

"Was she seeing Dr. Iverson for her heart?"

The hands behind Mr. Kempsey's back slapped together. "She saw him for her nerves. She was otherwise in good health, as far as I'm aware. The doctor will know more, I'm sure."

"She didn't confide in you?" I asked.

"That's what the doctor was for, Miss Fox." He glanced at the clock on the mantelpiece. "While I appreciate you're trying to clear Iverson's name, I'm sure the police will release him soon. There is no reason for him to have harmed my wife. None at all." He indicated the door. "Now, if you don't mind."

He saw us out of the library, but was waylaid by the housekeeper, waiting to speak to him. They re-entered the library while the butler saw us out of the house. We'd just set foot on the pavement when the front door reopened. The woman who'd taken an interest in us upon our arrival slipped through the gap and raced down the steps. She clasped a black-beaded drawstring bag in both hands.

"A moment, if you please. I overheard you introduce yourselves to my brother-in-law as private detectives investigating the death of my sister."

"I'm Harry Armitage and this is Cleopatra Fox. We're very sorry for your loss, Mrs…"

"Miss Rowbottom. Isabel is—was—my baby sister." Tears welled in eyes rimmed red from crying. "I can't believe she's gone. She was so full of life, so vibrant. Everyone adored her." She sighed. "That may have been her downfall."

"What do you mean?" Harry asked.

"She was very popular, and she welcomed that popularity. I think it got her murdered."

My gaze moved beyond her to the house. "You mean popular with men?"

Miss Rowbottom blushed. "She was having a liaison with Dr. Iverson, but there may have been at least one other." She removed a packet of letters from the bag, tied together with a pink ribbon. "I found these yesterday in her belongings." She glanced over her shoulder at the door then pressed them into Harry's hand. "Take them to the police if you think it's necessary."

"Your brother-in-law knows about them?" he asked.

She nodded. "I showed them to him after I found them. He wanted them destroyed, but I saved them. They prove that Mrs. Iverson had a motive for killing my sister, so I didn't want to get rid of them."

"They prove Mr. Kempsey also had a motive."

"No! That's not true! I *told* you, he didn't know about them until I showed them to him yesterday. Their very existence is proof that he's innocent. If he had found them, he would have destroyed them."

Just because he didn't know the letters existed didn't

mean he was also unaware of the relationship, but I didn't point that out to her. Instead, I said, "He may not have known about the letters or affair before her death, but he knows about them now. Yet he didn't mention them to us."

"Well, of course he didn't. What man likes to admit to being cuckolded? He's very proud, and if this case goes to court, it will become a torrid, salacious business. He wants the affair to remain private. Which is why he doesn't want the police to see these, but I think it's necessary. Please don't let them get into the wrong hands."

Harry slipped the letters into his jacket pocket. "Thank you, Miss Rowbottom. I must warn you, if these letters are key to finding the murderer, I cannot guarantee they or the affair will remain a private matter."

"I understand, but do your best." She looked over her shoulder at the house again. "If it does get out, then we'll deal with whatever comes together. I won't abandon my brother-in-law. Now, I must go. He needs me to act as hostess."

"One more question," Harry said. "What does Mr. Kempsey do?"

"He works for the Post Office. He was heavily involved in the transfer of the trunk lines held by the National Telephone Company to the Post Office a few years ago. He worked his way up from nothing, so he's always been careful with his reputation. As I said, he's a very proud man. He won't like admitting that Isabel had an affair right under his nose and he knew nothing about it."

I watched her hurry back up the stairs and wondered if Mr. Kempsey had been as oblivious to Isabel's affair as her sister seemed to think.

"She seems keen," Harry said.

"To assist her newly single brother-in-law or to besmirch her sister's name?"

He patted the pocket containing the letters. "Both."

"Do you think someone who works on the telephone system for the Post Office will have electricity knowledge?"

"It's highly likely."

We walked the short distance to Regent's Park and sat on a bench near the large griffin vase floral display to read the letters. There were only four from Dr. Iverson to Isabel Kempsey, but they were quite long. They expressed his admiration for her laughter, her bright personality, and her 'plump, womanly hips'. I had to bite my lip to stop myself giggling at that line. Although the language was a little overblown, each letter got quite repetitive. Each of the four letters began 'To my darling Izzy' and were signed 'Your loving Will I' for William Iverson.

The fifth letter was different, however. For one thing, it was dated last Wednesday, five days prior to Mrs. Kempsey's death. The others were undated. It also had no name at the bottom or top, and it was written in capital letters.

"To disguise the handwriting," Harry suggested.

I pointed to the capital letter W on one of the letters from Will and compared it to the W on the anonymous missive. "These are different. The anonymous one is more rounded, the one from Dr. Iverson is quite sharp. They're written by different people."

"'I dare to write this knowing I may be rebuffed,'" Harry read from the brief letter. "'Yet I must write it. I admire you and would like to know you and be known by you, if you dare. If you are curious to see who sent this, meet me outside 59 Regent Street at nine next Tuesday evening.'"

"That's tonight. What's at 59 Regent Street?"

Harry shrugged. "Just shops, I think. We can check now. It's on the way to the address we have for Mrs. Linton." He folded the letter in half and placed it on top of the others before retying the ribbon around them. "So Isabel Kempsey had a second admirer, one who is more succinct than the doctor."

"Her husband and sister did say she was popular," I said, taking his arm to stroll along the tree-lined path. "He must be considered a suspect now, in light of the affair with Dr. Iverson, and perhaps this second one."

"As should Mrs. Iverson. She could have killed her husband's lover at his clinic to punish him. Even if he doesn't ultimately get arrested, the murder will damage his reputation."

"Damaging her husband's reputation will damage her own as well, not to mention cause financial hardship, which would also affect her. She'd be a fool to risk it."

"Perhaps she acted out of rage, rather than with a cool head."

"I'm not convinced," I said. "Mrs. Iverson struck me as very practically minded."

"Even practical minds can be overruled by strong emotions."

The gruesome discussion was at odds with the beautiful setting of Regent's Park. The cooler weather kept most people away, so it was peaceful, yet stunningly beautiful with its display of autumn leaves in varying shades of gold. I would have liked to stroll with Harry a while longer, especially since it was far enough from the hotel that I wasn't worried about being caught by anyone we knew. We had a great deal to still accomplish, however, and idle walks would have to wait for another time.

We maintained a swift pace all the way to Regent Street and took shelter under the awning of the jewelry shop at number fifty-nine as it began to rain. We peered through the window, past the glittering display of gemstones and gold to a couple inspecting a ring under the bright light of a lamp at the counter. The jeweler stood ready with more to show if that one proved not to their taste.

"Shall we go inside and speak to the jeweler?" I looked at Harry to discover that he was no longer peering through the window. He surveyed the street.

I followed suit. We were at the Piccadilly Circus end of Regent Street where most of the shops catered to the well-heeled residents of Mayfair, but it was also near the theater district and more eclectic area of Soho. Harry's office wasn't far, and the Mayfair Hotel was a short walk in the opposite direction. On one side of the jeweler's was a leather goods seller, and a toy shop occupied the other premises. Across the way were the four columns marking the entrance to the Café

Royal, and next to that was a bootmaker and a dressmaker's clothing boutique. Was the venue for the meeting place significant or random?

"Why tonight?" Harry mused.

I watched as two gentlemen left the Café Royal and simultaneously put up their umbrellas. "What do you mean?"

"The letter was dated last Wednesday, so why not meet earlier than tonight? Why wait?"

"Perhaps the letter writer was busy."

Harry turned back to the jewelry shop and once again peered through the window.

"It will be closed at nine PM," I pointed out. "It'll be night, but not too dark with all these streetlamps on, so privacy isn't guaranteed."

"Especially since they're electric. Regent Street was converted from gas years ago. It was easier to have clandestine meetings in those days. The light was softer."

"Did you have many clandestine meetings in those days?"

His lips curved with his wicked smile. "Not on Regent Street."

"Dare I ask more?"

"If you do, I'll answer you honestly. I have no secrets from you, Cleo."

I knew Harry was more experienced than me when it came to relationships. I'd even met one of his former lovers during a previous investigation. But I decided not to delve any further into his past. It would change nothing between us.

As much as I wanted to loop my arm through his as we walked, I kept my hands by my sides. We were much too close to the hotel to risk it.

* * *

HARRY HAD OBTAINED the address of Mrs. Mary Linton from her file at Dr. Iverson's clinic. She lived quite a distance from Harley Street, in a short street lined with two-story row houses. The street was so short that it quickly became obvious the address was wrong. It had been listed as number twenty, but there were only twelve houses. We walked up and down twice before giving up.

"Perhaps it was noted down incorrectly," I said. "Miss Wainsmith may have misheard."

"Or Mrs. Linton gave a false address."

A woman and little girl emerged from number twelve. The woman clutched the girl's hand tightly as Harry smiled at them. He removed his hat and politely asked if she knew anyone named Mary Linton.

The woman frowned, glanced at me, then looked at Harry again. "If this is a joke, I don't understand it."

"It's not a joke," Harry assured her. "We're private investigators looking for Mary Linton. She gave her address as number twenty, but we can see it doesn't exist."

The woman apparently did understand the joke this time. "Seems to me someone's pulling your leg, sir." She pointed to the adjoining road where another street met it on the opposite side. "That there is Mary Street. Follow it and you reach Linton Street."

Harry thanked her and we did just that—followed Mary Street until we arrived at the intersection with Linton Street. The coincidence was too great to ignore. The patient who'd claimed to return to the clinic to look for her glove had given a false address located near to two real streets of the same names as her own. Her own equally false name, that is.

"Miss Wainsmith called the patient young, pretty and confident," I reminded Harry. "Not their typical patient, she said."

Harry looked around at the buildings near the intersection. "Sister Dearden said Mrs. Linton wanted to use the Electro Therapy Machine in that session, even though it was her first appointment, and the doctor hadn't yet diagnosed her." He sighed up at the sign for Linton Street. "We've been led on a wild goose chase."

"Not necessarily."

Like him, I studied the buildings. On two corners were houses, each one at the end of a row of identical houses. They were bigger than those located at the address Mrs. Linton had given us, although not as large as those found in Mayfair. The occupants coming and going were well dressed, and there were basement service rooms accessible from the pavement. Arlington Square Gardens occupied a third corner of the intersection, and a pub stood on the fourth.

I pointed to the houses. "I think she used Mary and Linton as her name because she sees these street signs every day. Perhaps she often walks through this intersection, or perhaps she lives in one of these buildings, either as a resident or servant."

Harry didn't agree, however. "If I were choosing a false name and address to disguise my identity, I wouldn't choose them based on real places near where I lived."

"Not everyone is as smart as you, Harry. Most people would say whatever came to mind."

"In that case, we need to find out what the woman who calls herself Mrs. Linton looks like. Then we'll return here and watch the vicinity. But first, shall we eat a late lunch?"

* * *

AFTER LUNCH HARRY used a silence cabinet in a local pharmacy to telephone D.S. Forrester and update him on our progress. The troubled look on Harry's face when he emerged from the booth worried me.

"They released Dr. Iverson," he said as we exited the pharmacy.

"That's good news! So why are you frowning? Do you think the doctor will cancel the contract he has with you now?"

"He may, but it's not that. Forrester wasn't interested in hearing about our progress. He was curt on the telephone, cutting me off mid-sentence."

"That's not like him," I agreed. "Should we go to Scotland Yard and insist he listen?"

Harry placed his hand at my lower back as we walked. It

was comfortably reassuring. "Not yet. Not until we've solved the murder. He won't be able to ignore us then."

I leaned into him a little, and he shortened his strides to match mine. "Where to now, lead investigator Armitage?"

"We call on the doctor. He has a lot of questions to answer."

CHAPTER 6

For a man who'd just been released from a Scotland Yard holding cell, Dr. Iverson didn't look particularly pleased to be home. Indeed, I suspected he and Mrs. Iverson had been having a tense discussion moments before our arrival, going by the strained faces.

Although signs of exhaustion circled his eyes, Dr. Iverson was still a very handsome man. The flecks of gray through his thick brown hair suited him, and the lines across his forehead did nothing to detract from the strong planes of his face. The way he looked at me when Harry introduced me made me feel as though I was important. Where most men tended to treat me like Harry's assistant, even when I wasn't described as such, Dr. Iverson gave me his full attention.

As did his wife. She rose from the sofa and offered me her seat. "May I say, I am pleased to see you still working with Mr. Armitage, Miss Fox. It's refreshing to see women take on traditional male roles."

"You'd be surprised at how many female private detectives there are in London," I said as I sat. "Despite popular belief to the contrary, we make up a good proportion."

"But are they involved in important cases? Or are they merely hired to trap wayward husbands?"

The mention of wayward husbands threw a blanket over

us, smothering the friendly greeting so that the air once again thickened. "You are quite right," I said, keeping my tone light in an effort to diffuse the tension. "I've been fortunate to work on some very interesting investigations. Others may not be so lucky."

"I would very much like to hear about them some time."

Dr. Iverson cleared his throat. "I want to assure you, Armitage, I intend to continue with your services. The police may have released me, but my name is not yet in the clear."

"Thank you," Harry said. "I believe I've made progress."

"Oh?"

The housekeeper entered carrying a tray of tea things. Mrs. Iverson dismissed her and poured the tea into cups, which she handed out.

Harry waited until the housekeeper closed the door behind her before speaking again. "I'm afraid we have to ask some delicate questions, but we would very much like you to stay, Mrs. Iverson."

"I understand. I must be considered a suspect in the murder of Isabel Kempsey, since she was having an affair with my husband."

Dr. Iverson's face flushed. "I only told my wife this morning, so she is *not* a suspect."

"They only have your word for that, and since you omitted to tell Mr. Armitage about the affair in the first place, he quite rightly must doubt everything you say now."

Dr. Iverson mumbled an apology to Harry.

"It would have been helpful if I knew," Harry said.

"My husband hoped it wouldn't come out," Mrs. Iverson said. "But these things always do in the end, don't they, Miss Fox?"

I was caught off guard, but managed to cover my surprise at being addressed by nodding. "How long had it been going on?"

"Since June," Dr. Iverson said. "It has been over for a few weeks."

"They ended it when Mr. Kempsey found out." Mrs. Iverson turned to her husband. "It's important to be honest with Miss Fox and Mr. Armitage. They are here to help you, and they cannot do that unless you speak truthfully."

"You are right, my dear. You always are." He regarded Harry. "As my wife said, the affair ended because Kempsey found out. I'm not sure how. I think he guessed and confronted Isabel. We thought it best to stop our liaisons at that point. We didn't want to ruin her marriage. She didn't love her husband, but she didn't want to leave him, and I had no intention of leaving my wife."

So, Mr. Kempsey *had* known before her death, despite what his sister-in-law, Miss Rowbottom, claimed. That placed him very much near the top of our suspect list.

I watched Mrs. Iverson, but she showed neither surprise nor annoyance at her husband's admission. They'd said he'd only just informed her, so I expected more shock and hurt on her part. Although I was quite sure our arrival had interrupted a tense discussion, that tension seemed to have already dissolved, at least as far as the affair was concerned. Had they been discussing it at all, or something else?

"If the affair was over, why did Isabel Kempsey continue to see you professionally?" Harry asked.

"I'm an excellent doctor." Dr. Iverson said it with conviction, not a hint of doubt in his voice. He truly believed it. Clearly, he didn't know why my aunt was no longer his patient. Since he hadn't asked about her, I presumed he didn't know we were related.

Even though I was listening to Dr. Iverson, I watched his wife's reaction. As one of our main suspects, she might give something away with a look or movement. But she simply calmly sipped her tea.

"Some of your letters to Isabel Kempsey were found in her things," Harry went on.

Dr. Iverson's face blanched.

Mrs. Iverson set down her teacup in the saucer with a clatter. She shot her husband a steely glare. "I *told* you. Never write anything down unless you don't care who sees it."

Dr. Iverson rubbed a trembling hand over his jaw. Perhaps this was what they were discussing when we arrived. Mrs.

Iverson wasn't angry with her husband about the affair; she was angry because evidence of it existed.

She turned to Harry. "Can you acquire the letters? We'll double your fee."

"I'll see what I can do," he said, noncommittal.

I studiously avoided glancing at his jacket pocket where the packet of letters was safely hidden. "One of the letters was different to the others and appears to be written by someone else," I said. "Do you know anything about it, Doctor? Could it have been from another of Mrs. Kempsey's lovers?"

"There were no others," he spluttered in his eagerness to deny my remark.

His wife rolled her eyes and sipped her tea.

"Perhaps Mrs. Kempsey had another lover *after* you," I went on. "The letter was dated five days before she died and asked to meet her tonight on Regent Street."

He frowned. "I've seen that letter, although I can't recall which day exactly. Last week, I do know that much. It wasn't Isabel's, so I don't know how it came to be in her possession."

"Who was it addressed to?" Harry asked.

"No one. It came to the clinic. It was given to me along with some other mail. I threw it away since it made no sense to me. Isabel must have taken it out of the wastebasket and kept it, although I can't think why. Perhaps she thought I was seeing someone else and was jealous, even though our relationship had ended." He seemed quite surprised by the revelation.

"She was at the clinic the day you received it?" Harry asked.

"That day, and twice more last week. Her nerves required a great deal of treatment."

Mrs. Iverson smiled tightly. "Many of the pretty patients have frayed nerves that require several appointments per week. More tea, Miss Fox?"

Once again, I was caught out by her sudden attention. Was she using me to score a point in the battle of wills with her husband? If so, I couldn't quite work out what she was trying to achieve. Was she trying to draw the doctor's attention to me? Encourage him to flirt with me and thereby catch him in the act and accuse him of being flirtatious with other women? If so, it was clumsily done.

Harry seemed quite oblivious to the strange exchange. He was still focused on the fifth letter, the one that was different to the others. "Why do you get the mail, Doctor? Isn't it Miss Wainsmith's job to go through it before passing on only what is relevant?"

Mrs. Iverson tutted. "That silly girl probably didn't know what to do with it and simply handed it over along with the other correspondence."

Dr. Iverson merely shrugged. "That must be it."

"Speaking of Miss Wainsmith," Harry went on. "Did she know about your affair with Isabel Kempsey? Did Sister Dearden?" He looked quite sincere, giving no sign that Miss Wainsmith had been the one to inform us.

Again, Dr. Iverson shrugged. "If they did, they didn't mention it to me."

"Mrs. Iverson?" Harry prompted. "Do you think either of them knew?"

"I don't know, Mr. Armitage. You'd have to ask them."

Harry moved on. "Doctor, can you say for certain that the cupboard where the Electro Therapy Machine is kept in your consulting suite was locked?"

"I can't, no. I informed the police that I think I left it unlocked. Sometimes I am in a hurry and don't get around to it."

His wife tutted again and rolled her eyes for good measure.

Dr. Iverson stiffened. "The murderer still had to get into the building. The front door was locked, I'm very sure. He or she must have stolen the key."

That led Harry to mention the woman calling herself Mary Linton, who'd returned to the clinic at the end of the day last Thursday in search of her glove, although it may have in fact been to return Sister Dearden's key which had gone missing earlier that day. He explained how the address she'd given didn't exist, and we believed she'd derived her false name from the two streets, Mary and Linton. "It's possible she lives nearby and saw those streets regularly." He removed his notebook from his inside jacket pocket and flipped to a blank page. "Can you remember what she looked like?"

Dr. Iverson settled back into the chair as he thought. "She wanted to use the machine, which I don't ordinarily do during first appointments, but she insisted."

"They want to know what she looked like," his wife prompted.

"She was young. Younger than most of my patients. Quite attractive, too."

"And confident?" I asked, recalling how Miss Wainsmith had described her.

"I thought so at first. But then when she lay down on the daybed to receive her treatment, her wig moved. Usually women wear wigs when they lose confidence in their appearance—when their hair falls out or it goes gray, that sort of thing. But the glimpse of her real hair that I saw was a glorious shade of red, and seemed quite thick, although I admit I only saw a little of it at her forehead."

My experience of people wearing wigs was a little different to his. Usually they did it as part of a disguise. It was looking more and more likely that the woman calling herself Mary Linton had a reason for seeing Dr. Iverson that day that had nothing to do with her nerves.

Harry was busily writing in his notebook. Without looking up, he asked, "Aside from the red hair, was there anything else notable about her?"

"She was pretty."

"You already said that," Mrs. Iverson pointed out. "In what *way* was she pretty?"

Dr. Iverson shrugged. "In the usual way. Clear skin, large eyes, generous mouth and a slim figure."

"I'm sure that description will help Miss Fox and Mr. Armitage find her." It was difficult to tell whether Mrs. Iverson was being sarcastic or not.

Her husband once again cleared his throat. "Are there any

other questions, Armitage? It's just that I didn't get much sleep last night. I'm rather tired and have a raging headache."

"A pity we don't keep any of that tonic you like to prescribe in the house," Mrs. Iverson said. "Shall I send the housekeeper out for a bottle?"

"Don't bother," he muttered.

I was tempted to press him about the tonic but Harry quickly changed the subject. "Do either Miss Wainsmith or Sister Dearden have any understanding of electricity?"

For the first time, Dr. and Mrs. Iverson were both shocked by a question. "Are you accusing one of them of tampering with the machine?" he asked.

"We have to consider all possibilities." Harry poised his pencil above the notebook page, waiting.

Dr. Iverson shook his head. "If they do, I'm not aware of it."

"Nor I," Mrs. Iverson added. "Furthermore, we trust them both implicitly. Don't we, dear?"

Dr. Iverson gave an emphatic nod. "They are excellent employees."

It seemed on that score, they were united.

Harry flipped the notebook closed. "One last thing. Did Isabel Kempsey ever complain about her heart?"

"As a matter of fact, she did," Dr. Iverson said. "She once mentioned an erratic beat. I listened to it, but detected nothing unusual." He leaned forward, his entire focus on Harry. "Are you saying she had a bad heart, and that killed her?"

"The high electrical current in the Electro Therapy Machine killed her, but her instantaneous death would imply her heart was already weakened. Otherwise she'd have taken longer to die. Long enough for you to switch off the machine and perhaps save her life."

Dr. Iverson rubbed his hand across his mouth. It still trembled. "It was an awful thing to witness. But yes, it was instant albeit not pain free."

Mrs. Iverson pressed a hand to her throat. "Poor woman."

After a respectful moment of silence, Dr. Iverson asked

Harry if he'd proved the machine had been tampered with. "D.S. Forrester wouldn't tell me for certain, but he persistently asked me about my understanding of electricity, so I presume it had been."

"It was," Harry confirmed.

Dr. Iverson held up his hands. "Then I am certainly not the one who tampered with it. I know how to switch the lights on and off, not how they work."

"Nor do I," Mrs. Iverson added. "Just in case either of you were thinking I'm the murderer."

Harry and I rose to leave, just as two newcomers were shown in by the housekeeper. Sister Dearden and Miss Wainsmith both exclaimed with joy upon seeing Dr. Iverson released.

Sister Dearden gave him a hearty embrace as his wife watched on, her gaze narrowed. "We received your message and came immediately. We are *so* relieved."

"So relieved," Miss Wainsmith echoed, as she also embraced her employer. "We've been terribly anxious, haven't we, Sister Dearden?"

"Very worried indeed. How have you held up, Mrs. Iverson? You look a little peaky, if you don't mind me saying."

Mrs. Iverson gave her a curt nod. "I'm quite well, thank you, Sister. We've just been hearing a report from Miss Fox and Mr. Armitage. They're making thorough progress in the investigation. Indeed, I believe they may have one or two questions for you both."

Harry removed a key from his pocket. "Thank you for loaning this to me, Sister. Mrs. Iverson is correct. I have one question." He glanced at the doctor. "It's not an easy thing to ask in a group. Perhaps we can go somewhere more private?"

"That won't be necessary," Mrs. Iverson said. "There's no point being discreet now. Mr. Armitage wants to know if you were aware of my husband and Mrs. Kempsey having an affair. Don't feel as though you need to hide anything for my sake. I am aware of it all."

Miss Wainsmith's face flushed scarlet as she avoided

everyone's gaze. "I was aware, as you know," she murmured, so softly that I doubted anyone other than me heard her.

Sister Dearden didn't look surprised. She merely gave Mrs. Iverson a grim smile. "Are you all right?" she asked gently.

Mrs. Iverson folded her arms and inclined her head in a nod. Her husband patted her shoulder in what seemed to be a test to see if she would flinch or pull away. She did not, and he rested his hand there, a look of relief on his face.

"Miss Wainsmith, may I ask one more question?" Harry asked.

Miss Wainsmith looked like a startled rabbit as she nodded.

"Do you recall seeing a letter arrive at the clinic last week? It was written in all capital letters and had no recipient or sender on the letter itself. We're not sure if it arrived in an envelope. Do you remember it?"

She blew out a long, relieved breath. "It doesn't ring any bells."

"Does the postman hand the post directly to you?"

"The first delivery of the day is already there when I arrive. Either Sister Dearden or Dr. Iverson collects it and places it on my desk for me to sort through. For the other mail deliveries throughout the day, I'm there. What was the letter about?"

"It was found in Mrs. Kempsey's possession after her death, but Dr. Iverson says he saw it at the clinic days before her death. Are you sure you never saw it?"

"No. Never. Sister?"

Sister Dearden shook her head. "I haven't either. How did it come to be in Mrs. Kempsey's possession if Dr. Iverson saw it at the clinic?"

Everyone turned to look at him. Throughout the exchange, he seemed to be pretending he was elsewhere and hadn't overheard a single word. Now that he was being directly addressed, he shrugged, proving he had been listening. "She must have taken it out of my wastebasket. We may never know now. Perhaps it's not even relevant to the investigation."

"Perhaps not," Harry agreed with a reassuring smile.

As we took our leave, Dr. Iverson once again complained of being tired due to lack of sleep. The ladies got the hint and they, too, gave their leave.

As the Iversons walked us to the front door, Miss Wainsmith mentioned cooking a hearty broth for the doctor's health. "Our landlady has an excellent recipe that she claims does wonders for a strong constitution. I'll bring some tomorrow."

"We'll be at work tomorrow," Sister Dearden reminded her.

"Not so soon, surely." Miss Wainsmith appealed to her employer.

Dr. Iverson gazed longingly at the exit and sighed. "I think I need another day to recover."

"Miss Wainsmith and I will go in to rearrange appointments and set everything to rights." Sister Dearden held up the key Harry had just returned to her then took Mrs. Iverson's hand and regarded her warmly. "Do come and see us if you need anything."

"Yes, do," Miss Wainsmith echoed, blinking large eyes at the doctor. Large, pretty eyes, in a pretty face, with clear skin and a slim figure. Just the doctor's type.

We walked out with the two women, then went our separate ways. Thanks to the long omnibus journeys between our destinations across London, it was growing late. Harry suggested we return to the hotel.

"I'll speak to Sir Ronald and warn him about Mr. Pierce's threat, then I'll return to Islington and watch the area at the intersection of Linton and Mary Streets." When I didn't respond, his little finger touched mine. "A penny for your thoughts."

"Did you think the exchange between Dr. and Mrs. Iverson strange?" I asked.

"Do you mean the fact that she wasn't particularly upset about her husband's infidelity? Perhaps Isabel Kempsey wasn't the first and there was a long line of lovers before her. Mrs. Iverson's caustic comments implied she knows what he's like."

"I agree, but it was more than that. Mrs. Iverson drew attention to me from time to time. It was a little unnerving. Why would she do that? Was it a ploy to trick her husband into flirting with me? But he wouldn't; not in front of you."

"They don't know we're together."

That was true, although I suspected the more intuitive people we met guessed. "It was odd," I said again.

"All I saw was a woman who greatly admired you for your career, Cleo."

"If you think that's all it was, I won't read any more into it."

The finger that touched mine now hooked around it. "She isn't the only one who admires you for your skill as a detective."

"Thank you, Harry. That is very sweet."

"I do admire you for other reasons, too," he quickly added. "Not just because you've helped my business."

I laughed at the panic in his voice as he tried to clarify his response.

"There are many, many reasons I admire you," he went on. "Your kindness, bravery, insight into the human character…"

"You'd better stop there. It's starting to rain, and an omnibus is coming." We could have walked back to the hotel, but at least we'd keep dry on our journey and it would get us there faster.

Once seated in the cabin, we discussed in low voices what we'd learned from the interrogation of the Iversons. When a woman sat beside Harry, we stopped talking altogether and traveled the rest of the way in silence. As the omnibus drove down Regent Street, however, Harry and I turned to one another as we passed number fifty-nine. We both had the same idea, but didn't discuss it until we alighted outside the hotel.

"I'll wait at the rendezvous point tonight at nine and see if someone comes," Harry said.

"*We* will wait there together," I countered. Before he could protest, I pointed out that nine wasn't too late. Respectable people were out and about, coming and going from the theater or parties.

"That's the problem," he said. "We shouldn't be seen together."

"I'll wear a cloak and keep the hood up at all times." I spied Frank watching us as he opened the door for two guests to enter. "Collect me from across the road here at eight-thirty. That will give us plenty of time in case the letter writer is early."

We greeted Frank amiably and received a grudging, "Good afternoon," in response. It was a positively friendly greeting for Harry, considering Frank had sided with my uncle when Harry was dismissed from the assistant manager position. Frank tended to side with my uncle on most things. He was a loyal employee, a quality I admired, even though it was sometimes misguided.

Although October was a quiet month for the hotel, the foyer was quite busy. Late afternoons tended to be one of the busiest times of the day, with ladies coming and going from the main sitting room for the Mayfair's famous afternoon teas. Mr. Hobart and Peter, the assistant manager, were chatting to different parties, while the front desk clerk was on the telephone. The lift door opened and Floyd emerged. He struck a direct course toward Harry and me, but before he arrived, two elderly ladies who recognized Harry from when he was assistant manager drew him away.

Although Floyd regarded Harry with a flinty glare, it was me he wanted to see. "Have you seen Harmony? I need to speak to her."

"I've just come in. Is something wrong?"

"You mean aside from you being here with Armitage?"

"He needs to talk to Uncle Ronald, as it happens."

Floyd's eyebrows rose. "He's not coming back to work for us, is he?"

"Lord, no. As part of his investigation, he stumbled across something that affects the hotel. A man may be intending to sabotage Mr. Lombardi's event."

Floyd's gaze sharpened. "Is this an investigation that you are conducting with him?"

"Is that the first question you wish to ask? I thought you'd be more concerned about the potential sabotage."

He tugged on his cuffs. "I am. Although I'm conflicted. I would rejoice to see Lombardi fail, and not just because of his tonic. Harmony and I had a long meeting with him today. He treated her poorly."

"Oh dear. Because of the color of her skin?"

"It could be that, or it could be because she's female and in a subordinate position to him. He was a little too tactile to be considered a gentleman." He put up his hands and wiggled his fingers. "After she slapped his hand away when he went to touch her, I had to tell him not to do it again or he'd be looking for a new venue for his presentation."

"Well done, Floyd. Is Harmony all right?"

"She's more all right than I am, or seems to be. I'm worried Lombardi will complain to Father who'll take out his irritation on his favorite whipping boy." He poked himself in the chest.

"He won't do that. He'll be on your side, once he knows the details."

"I don't trust Lombardi to give him the correct details, but you are probably right. Knowing what we know about the Nerve Elixir, Father is unlikely to think favorably of Lombardi." He smiled at a regular guest who passed by. Once the gentleman was out of earshot, the smile vanished. "So you haven't seen Harmony? Lombardi has changed one of his requests for the event and I need to inform her."

"Have you checked the staff parlor? She often enjoys a cup of tea in the afternoons with the others."

He pulled a face. "It's not my place to enter their domain during their time off. You shouldn't go in either."

"They don't see me the same way as they see you. I'm a Fox, not a Bainbridge."

"Ha!"

I ignored his reaction and changed the subject. "Is Flossy with your mother? How is she?"

"Mother is resting in her room. Flossy is having afternoon tea with friends." He nodded in the direction of the sitting room.

"How lovely. I am pleased to see your parents giving her more freedom." Usually if Flossy wanted to go out socially, she had to be chaperoned. With her mother often ill, and me out investigating, her social engagements had been limited. Lately, however, she'd been allowed to meet her friends for afternoon tea as long as they stayed within the hotel.

When Harry finished chatting to the two ladies, Floyd made sure to catch him before anyone else waylaid him. He said he wanted to know more about the potential threat to Mr. Lombardi's event, but I suspected he also wanted to warn him to stay away from me. That was a discussion Harry could handle without me.

I left them and headed to the staff parlor, where Harmony was indeed enjoying a cup of tea and game of cribbage with Goliath and Victor. She invited me to join them, but I declined.

"I can't stay long. I ought to go and look in on my aunt. Harmony, Floyd wants to talk to you."

She rose to leave, but I asked her to stay a moment longer.

"He told me about Mr. Lombardi's advances," I went on.

Victor had been shuffling the deck of cards, but his quick hands suddenly stilled. "Advances?"

Harmony flipped her hand, dismissing our concern. "It was nothing. I've experienced far worse from other guests."

"You have?" I asked, dismayed.

Again, she dismissed my concern with a gesture. "Housemaids are used to it. We learn how to deflect unwanted interest in a way that doesn't cause offence."

"While I'm glad you're not upset, it isn't all right for men to treat you like that, whether they're important guests or not. I'm glad Floyd was a witness. He and my uncle need to be aware of these things so they can do something about it. You should inform Mrs. Short when it happens while on maid duty."

"Nothing will change."

"Then inform me," Victor growled. "I'll see that it doesn't happen again."

I eyed his knife belt on the table where he'd laid it beside the cribbage scoring board so that he could sit more comfortably. Like all the cooks, he brought his own tools of the trade to work. Dressed in crisp, clean chef whites, he must be employed on the dinner shift, due to start shortly. While I didn't think Victor would actually cut anyone who made an inappropriate advance toward his girl, I worried that he'd use a blade to threaten them. That was a dismissible offence, not to mention an arrestable one.

Harmony changed the subject. "How is the investigation coming along?"

"Slowly but surely," I said. "We have a number of suspects, including a woman who acted suspiciously at the clinic on the day one of the keys went missing. We're not sure how she is connected to the victim, but she gave a false name and address."

"I read about the murder," Goliath said as he stretched out his long legs and crossed them at the ankles. "Apparently the doctor was arrested. Am I right in saying he is Lady Bainbridge's doctor?"

"Goliath," Harmony snapped. "That's none of our business."

Goliath shrank a little from her harsh tone. "Sorry," he mumbled.

"It's all right," I said. "Dr. Iverson was her doctor, but she is seeing someone else now. The doctor wasn't arrested, merely taken in for questioning. He was released this morning. Harry and I have already interviewed him."

"Do you think he murdered his patient?"

Before I could respond, Victor made a scoffing sound. "In his own consulting rooms? He'd be an idiot to kill someone there."

"That's the theory Harry and I are working on, too," I

said. "It's most likely someone else tampered with the machine with the plan of besmirching the doctor's reputation."

Goliath pointed a finger at me. "Or that's what he wants you to believe because it's a bluff." He frowned. "Or is it a double bluff?"

Victor clapped a hand on the big porter's shoulder as he stood. "Don't think too hard, something might explode."

"You sound like Frank."

As if he'd been summoned, Frank entered the parlor. He stopped short upon hearing his name. "If this is about Mrs. Crighton's pet dog, I'd like to point out that it's just a small dog and the hotel doesn't have a written policy against guests bringing their animals."

We all stared at him.

"No?" he squeaked. "Forget I spoke."

Goliath wasn't prepared to do so, however. "It's not against any policy, but that's probably because Sir Ronald never thought of it before. How could you just let her waltz in with it? What if it does its business in the room? Think of the poor maids who'd have to clean it up."

"She takes it out three times a day for it to do its business in the park. Anyway, who am I to stop a guest from doing something a little naughty?"

"It is your job," Victor pointed out. "She paid you, didn't she?"

Frank sniffed. "Mrs. Crighton slips me a few coins to look the other way when she smuggles it into the hotel inside her bag."

Goliath sat forward and lowered his voice. "Next time she has it with her, give me a sign. I can keep quiet for a fee, too."

Harmony signaled for me to leave the parlor with her.

"One moment," I said. "Before I go, I have a question to ask the men. If I were to buy you a gift, what would you like?"

Goliath smiled shyly. "That's kind of you, Miss Fox, but you don't have to."

"It's not for you. I simply need ideas. I thought polling a few men might help."

"A watch," Frank said. "Mine's broken."

"New knives," Victor added, collecting his knife belt.

Goliath tugged on his lower lip in thought. "Two tickets to the theater, one for me and the other so I can win back my girl. She likes theater shows, particularly something with jaunty tunes."

"Perhaps you should think about the recipient and what *he* would like," Harmony said.

"Is it for your uncle?" Victor asked. "Cousin?"

"It's not their birthdays," Frank said, frowning.

Before they remembered the date of Harry's birthday, I grabbed Harmony's hand and together we left the staff parlor. As we re-entered the foyer, she asked if I thought the afternoon tea would go on for much longer. "I need to speak to Mr. Chapman about Mr. Lombardi's dinner arrangements this evening. He has asked me to inform Mr. Chapman there'll be one less at his table."

"Why are you liaising for Lombardi? His dinner plans for this evening are not part of his Saturday presentation."

"It is, in a way. The dinner is for Mr. Lombardi's most valued clients, who will also come to the presentation. A sort of pre-event gathering to discuss business."

At least his prior engagement meant my family was saved from having to invite him to join us at our table. Given I needed to meet Harry at an early hour, I was relieved. I would order my meal through the speaking tube in my room and dine there. Hopefully no one wanted to join me.

* * *

AT EIGHT-THIRTY, dressed all in black, I flipped up the hood of my cloak as I left the stairwell on the ground floor. The daytime staff had gone home and there weren't many guests in the foyer. Most would be in their rooms or at dinner or the theater. I was quite sure that with my head down, no part of my face was visible, so I was surprised when my name was called. No, not *called*. Barked out, as if I were a prisoner fleeing from jail.

"Cleo! Halt! Where are you going at this hour?"

CHAPTER 7

"Floyd, what a lovely surprise," I said, smiling. "You look handsome." A strong whiff of cologne preceded him as he drew closer. "Are you dining out?"

"Don't avoid the question, Cleo. Are you sneaking out of the hotel for an investigation or for a man?"

"I am not sneaking."

He tugged the hood back from my head and arched his brows.

There was no use lying to Floyd. He was too perceptive. He also had some secrets to hide—secrets I was privy to—so I knew I could convince him to keep quiet about my nocturnal activities in exchange for keeping quiet about his. "An investigation, of course. I would never meet a man in the night."

He pointed his top hat, which he held in his hand, at the exit. "So I won't see Armitage waiting for you outside?"

"It's his investigation, so he is out there. He was hired by Dr. Iverson to find out who murdered a patient in his consulting suite. Harry asked for my help, since I am familiar with the doctor and his somewhat dubious methods."

"You shouldn't have told him about Mother. That's a private family matter."

"He won't splash it about."

"Besides, I fail to see how you can be of any help to him.

It's not as though you can offer any insights about the doctor that he can't glean from other sources." He pointed the hat at me. "This is a ruse so he can get closer to you, Cleo."

Should I deny it? Give in and admit that Harry and I were together?"

Before I could answer, he added, "Don't fall for it. You must be strong and look past the charming manner, the handsome face, and see him for what he really is."

I bit down on my tongue before I rattled off all of Harry's good qualities.

"He's off-limits, Cleo, that's what he is. Understand? If you must have a dalliance, choose someone else. Someone who isn't a former employee of the hotel who has feelings for you."

"Such a vast pool to choose from," I bit back. "Thank you for approving of me having dalliances, Floyd. That's very progressive of you."

The muscles in his cheeks bunched as he ground his back teeth together. "That's not what I'm saying."

"Speaking of dalliances, I have noticed that you didn't answer my question about where you were going tonight. Is that because you're meeting a woman? Perhaps auditioning for a new mistress?" My cousin had kept a mistress until a few months ago. As far as I was aware, he'd not found himself a new one in the meantime.

"How did you know?" he asked, his tone somewhere between incredulous and impressed.

"You're wearing an expensive cologne and your favorite waistcoat with the gold thread that you think impresses women. Also, you've done the front of your hair in an elaborate sweep, which will be ruined once you put your hat on, hence you're holding it. Added to which, you didn't answer me immediately when I asked, which meant you hadn't yet thought of a story to explain where you were going. For future reference, when a woman asks, just say you're going to your club. It's not as though we can check."

He gave in with a sigh. "Is the cologne too much? I accidentally spilled it as I was applying a dab."

I sniffed in his general direction. "It's not too potent."

"By the way, one does not *audition* for mistresses. I'm not filling a role in a play."

"Aren't you?"

He scowled. "You're exhausting, Cleo."

"Then give in and let's walk out together. You can say hello to Harry." I flipped up my hood then took his arm.

He didn't move. "I'm not condoning you seeing him in the middle of the night."

"It isn't the middle of the night; it's only eight-thirty. And you *will* condone it, otherwise I'll be forced to blackmail you and I would rather I didn't have to." He still didn't move, although he no longer glared at me. That was a good sign that he was wavering. A little more encouragement ought to have him giving in completely. "Floyd, please don't do this. You know Harry will be the perfect gentleman. You also know this is for an investigation, nothing else."

He grunted. "I'm not happy about it."

"I'm not asking you to be."

Floyd delivered me to Harry, standing one streetlamp away from the front entrance of the hotel. "Armitage," he said flatly.

"Bainbridge," Harry replied, equally monotone.

"I trust you'll be careful."

"Cleo is safe with me, both physically and reputationally."

"Unless someone sees you together."

"My hood covers my face," I pointed out. "Go, Floyd. Don't make your candidate wait."

Floyd finally put his hat on. "Good evening to you both." He returned to the hotel entrance where he climbed into a waiting hansom.

Harry offered me his arm. "Does your cousin know he's wearing too much cologne?"

"I decided not to tell him. Some women like it that strong."

"Has he been keeping out of trouble lately?"

"I believe so. Nothing has reached my ears, and he does seem content. He still goes out regularly and stays out all night, which irks my uncle because it means he's too tired the next day to be of any use. But at least he's not gambling anymore. Speaking of my uncle, did you tell him about Mr. Pierce?"

"I did."

I waited for more, but he offered nothing.

"How was Uncle Ronald with you?"

"Professional, polite. Did you expect him to throw me out on sight?"

"I expected him to offer you your old job back. Perhaps it wasn't the right time."

Harry chuckled. "Perhaps not."

As we turned the corner onto Regent Street, we both stopped. A short man with a thin moustache stood outside number fifty-nine. I didn't recognize him, but when he saw us watching him, he hurried away in the opposite direction.

"That was suspicious," I said.

We walked past number fifty-nine and stopped a few doors down outside a draper's shop. There were no lights on inside the shop, and the nearest streetlamp was broken, so we felt somewhat invisible in the shadows with our dark clothing. Although we weren't far from the theater district, it was rather quiet on our side of the street. On the other, piano music, voices and laughter spilled out of the Café Royal every time the door opened. It was a lively venue.

"Have you ever been inside?" I asked Harry.

"A few times, but not for a while. It's popular with the artistic set. As the former assistant manager of a hotel and now private detective I never felt like I fit in there."

It was hard to imagine Harry not fitting in anywhere. He got along with everyone and was generally well-liked.

Although I couldn't see the dial of my watch in the dark, I was quite sure nine PM came and went. No one stopped at the jewelry shop at number fifty-nine or even slowed their pace as they passed it. The longer we waited, the cooler the night air became. It nipped at my nose and cheeks and, despite wearing gloves, I had to tuck my hands under my arms for warmth.

Harry began to undo his coat buttons. "Put this around your shoulders."

"Then you'll get cold." I snuggled into him and rested my head against his chest. I sighed into his warmth. "That's better."

He went quite still for a moment, then gave in and circled his arms around me and rested his chin on the top of my head. "I told your cousin I'd be careful with your reputation, and we're quite close to the hotel here."

I hugged him tightly, enjoying the purr of his deep voice in my ear. "No one can see my face."

"Even so, I think it's best if I take you home. The person who wrote that letter isn't coming."

"I agree. But not until I've done one thing."

He drew away and looked down at me. "Should I be worried?"

"Very."

I ushered him back into the recessed doorway where it was even darker than the pavement, and kissed him. He offered no resistance.

* * *

After breakfasting with Harmony in my suite the following morning, I met Uncle Ronald waiting at the fourth floor lift. My heart fluttered wildly in panic before I realized Floyd wouldn't have informed his father that I met Harry the previous night. For one thing, Floyd would still be in bed, and for another, he couldn't afford for me to follow through on my threat to reveal his secrets. Besides, I was quite sure he didn't think I was serious about Harry. Because I'd been vocal about not wanting to get married, Floyd believed Harry would never be more than a mere dalliance. The day would come when I would disabuse him of that notion. Until then, I was happy for him to continue to be wrong.

"Good morning, Cleo." There was no cheer in Uncle Ronald's tone, but neither was there anger or censure.

"Good morning, Uncle. Do you have a busy day ahead?"

"Yes, as always. There's a staff meeting today at five-thirty in the ballroom. I want you there to talk about the man threatening Lombardi's presentation."

"Certainly."

The lift door opened and John the operator greeted us amiably.

As we rode the lift down, I asked my uncle if the preparations for Mr. Lombardi's presentation were going smoothly, even though Harmony had already told me they were. I wanted his opinion.

"They are," he said gruffly. "I'm eager for this entire thing to be over with."

"I imagine so." I didn't want to say more in front of John. The staff weren't aware of my aunt's addiction to Mr. Lombardi's tonic. "Events like these are hard work."

"It's not that. It's Lombardi himself. He's a demanding guest."

"Oh?"

"He complained to Chapman after dinner last night that the food served in the restaurant is ordinary, the wine second-rate, and atmosphere too stuffy."

"Poor Mrs. Poole." The hotel's *chef de cuisine* took her menu seriously. She'd received high praise since she took over the kitchen, so Mr. Lombardi's criticism was unexpected.

"I'm not going to tell her, since I disagree with everything he said. Mrs. Poole is a magnificent chef. Everyone in London says so." Uncle Ronald made a scoffing sound that had his jowls wobbling like one of Mrs. Poole's jellies. "Lombardi just likes being obnoxious. Even Floyd complained about the way he was treating Miss Cotton, and you know Floyd, he's rather untroubled by most things."

I was glad Floyd had mentioned it. I wanted to ask my uncle if he was going to have a word with Mr. Lombardi about his behavior, but the lift door opened and there was no more privacy.

Uncle Ronald and I parted in the foyer, but I held my breath until the hotel door closed behind me. Although he'd given his consent for me to investigate alongside Harry—

albeit reluctantly—I still expected him to forbid it, or to demand I take a chaperone with me when I leave. He did not, so it seemed I'd won that particular battle.

Harry had some work to conduct for another case, so I waited for him in the Roma Café below his office. I sat at the table in the window and read the newspaper, noting the time and venue of Isabel Kempsey's funeral listed in the obituaries. I was surprised to see it being conducted already, considering there was a murder investigation going on.

"Another coffee, Miss Fox?" Luigi asked as he collected my used cup. Although he was of Italian descent, his accent was as Cockney as any Londoner's.

"No, thank you. Do you have any other newspapers? I've finished this one."

"Not in English."

"You get Italian newspapers here?"

He indicated the two elderly men sitting on their stools at the counter. Every time I came into the café, they were there. I was beginning to think they'd glued themselves to the seats. "They like to read the news from back home, even if it is out of date by the time the papers arrive."

"We have an Italian man staying at the hotel at the moment. I should send Mr. Lombardi here for some authentic food since he doesn't like our restaurant's offerings."

"Lombardi? From the Bella Vita Company?"

"The same. Do you know him?"

"I know *of* him. I read he was in London." He said something in Italian to the two regulars. The only word I picked up was Lombardi.

One reached for a nearby newspaper, flipped the pages until he found the article he wanted, then held it out for Luigi.

Luigi read the relevant part to me, translating into English. "The Bella Vita Company's Nerve Elixir has come under fire from pharmacology researchers at the University of Bologna for its addictive qualities.'" He showed me the text, but I could only understand a few words. "They're calling for a ban on its sale, as well as the sale of other medicines that contain cocaine, saying they cause addiction, which can lead to other health problems and eventually death."

"Do you think they'll ban it?"

Luigi repeated my question in Italian for the two men. They both shrugged and started speaking over each other. Even if they spoke in English, I doubted I'd be able to follow both at the same time, but Luigi seemed to have no trouble.

"They say it's unlikely to happen soon," Luigi said.

"That's similar to what's happening here in England. Despite some experts condemning cocaine, most doctors are still prescribing medicines that contain it. Some patients become addicted and their health actually gets worse."

One of the men held out a second Italian newspaper and said a few words to Luigi. Luigi then interpreted for me. "This article says the Bella Vita Company has borrowed heavily and must increase sales internationally or face ruin."

"But sales of its tonic are excellent, aren't they?"

"The article says the Nerve Elixir sells very well, but the company has developed a number of other medicines that have failed in a heavily saturated market abroad. The Bella Vita Company built too many factories in the wake of its success with the Nerve Elixir, but most will have to close soon unless sales improve." He lowered the paper. "A great deal must be riding on the presentation he's doing at your hotel."

"Indeed," I murmured.

Harry entered the café and apologized for his tardiness. "I hope you haven't been bored, Cleo."

"Not at all. In fact, it's been very enlightening. Oh, and the funeral starts soon. Shall we go?"

"All right. I'd like to see how upset Mr. Kempsey is."

"And Miss Rowbottom," I added.

I paid for my coffee at the counter and thanked the two old men in Italian. One after the other caught my hand then kissed me on each cheek before concentrating on their coffees again.

Harry held the door open for me. "Did I miss something?"

I told him about Mr. Lombardi's company troubles while

we walked, and he agreed I needed to mention it to my uncle so he could get full payment for the event up front.

"And if Mr. Lombardi refuses?" I asked.

"Then Sir Ronald will have grounds to cancel the whole thing."

"That will damage the hotel's reputation."

"Unfortunately it will, but it's that or risk being out of pocket."

* * *

THE DRIZZLING rain seemed appropriately gloomy for a burial. Harry and I watched from a distance as mourners huddled under umbrellas in the cemetery. Once the formalities finished, they dispersed quickly along the gravel path. It wasn't the weather for lingering.

We had decided not to disturb Isabel Kempsey's husband or sister on this difficult day and be content with picking up any clues we could by simply observing. While we couldn't make out facial expressions from a distance, we did notice Miss Rowbottom dogging her brother-in-law's steps. Whenever he moved, so did she.

When he made directly for us, so did she.

I thought our own umbrellas and the mausoleum hid us well, but apparently not. By the time we realized we'd been spotted, it was too late to leave with dignity.

Mr. Kempsey was understandably cross, but not as much as I expected. "You could have chosen a better time and place if you needed to speak to me again, Armitage."

"We're terribly sorry for the intrusion," Harry said. "We'll call on you tomorrow."

"Get on with it now. No point putting it off."

Before Harry could begin, Miss Rowbottom asked if she could say something. "The police told us the doctor has been released. If that's so, then why are you persisting with your inquiries, Mr. Armitage? Your client is free now."

"His name isn't completely cleared," Harry said.

"I see." She pressed the handkerchief edged with black

lace to her chest. It was damp from crying, and her eyes were red and swollen. "So…he may have killed my sister?"

"Nonsense," Mr. Kempsey spluttered. "I told you, it was an accident. The infernal machine must have been faulty."

Miss Rowbottom sidled closer, causing her umbrella to clash with his. She grasped hold of his arm. "I'm sure you're right." She blinked up at him. "You always are."

Mr. Kempsey stamped the end of his walking stick into the soft earth. "Go on then, Armitage. What do you want to know?"

Harry hesitated. Even for someone as smooth as Harry, the topic wasn't an easy one. "I'm afraid I have to ask you a difficult question."

Mr. Kempsey smacked the end of his walking stick against his shoe, dislodging a chunk of mud. "Can't be helped."

Part of me admired his no-nonsense fortitude, and his eagerness to get to the truth. But it did make me wonder if he'd cared for his wife at all. There was no sign that he'd shed any tears for her. Was that merely his nature? Or did it confirm what we already suspected—that their marriage wasn't a happy one, hence she'd had an affair.

"Dr. Iverson told us that his affair with your wife came to an end before her death because you became aware of it, sir. Yet we were led to believe you only found out afterward, when you discovered the letters."

"Don't say anything, Ian! It's a trap!" Miss Rowbottom's loud outburst proved that first impressions could often be misleading. She may appear to be a timid spinster, but there was a fiercely protective side to her. She glared at Harry. "My brother-in-law is grieving. Please leave this instant!"

Mr. Kempsey stared wide-eyed at Miss Rowbottom. Perhaps he'd never seen this side of her either. "If I don't answer, they'll think me guilty. I've done nothing wrong." He tried to move away, but she tightened her grip on his arm. "It's true," he told Harry. "My sister-in-law brought the affair to my attention some weeks ago. I was angry. Isabel and I had a row about it, at which point she promised to end the liaison.

I had no reason to doubt her and we spoke no more about it. I did *not* kill my wife."

"Thank you, Mr. Kempsey," Harry said. "Again, we apologize for the intrusion."

I wasn't prepared to leave yet, however. Not without more answers. "How did you find out about the affair, Miss Rowbottom?"

Miss Rowbottom lifted her chin, defiant. "Isabel told me."

Being an only sibling, I could never truly understand the relationship between sisters, but I doubted I could ever betray my two cousins, and I'd not even known them an entire year. For Miss Rowbottom to break that trust and tell her brother-in-law about the affair meant she must have disliked Isabel, perhaps even hated her.

Or she wanted what Isabel had for herself.

Miss Rowbottom jutted her chin even further forward. "I can see what you're thinking, Miss Fox, and I'd like to point out that my sister was boastful about her affair with the doctor. She enjoyed rubbing my nose in the fact that she was able to get a wonderful husband *and* a lover, and I had no one. I couldn't let her get away with it."

Mr. Kempsey extricated himself from her grip, all the while blinking at his sister-in-law as if he'd never seen this side of her before.

Miss Rowbottom reached for him, but he moved away. Her eyes filled with tears as she appealed to him. "Isabel showed no guilt or remorse, because she knew she could get away with it. So I did the only thing in my power to make her pay for her crime."

We waited, holding our breaths, hoping for a confession.

When she realized the implication of her words, she quickly shook her head. "I didn't kill her! I simply meant I told Ian what she'd done, to bring it all out into the open."

Mr. Kempsey flexed the fingers that clutched the head of his walking stick. "You did the right thing."

Miss Rowbottom sucked in a shuddery breath of relief.

"An affair is not a crime," Harry pointed out.

"It should be, when the injured party is a decent man and

good provider." Again, she reached for Mr. Kempsey. This time he didn't step away.

"If you'll excuse us," he intoned.

They walked off, arm in arm like a married couple.

"I wonder what the future holds for them," I said. "It's illegal for him to marry his sister-in-law, but perhaps she'll keep house for him."

"Is that a euphemism?"

I simply smiled.

He offered me his arm and we departed on the path leading to the cemetery gates. I couldn't help glancing over my shoulder at our suspects, mingling with the few remaining mourners near the gravesite.

"Miss Rowbottom may have denied killing Isabel, but I'm not ruling her out," I said. "There was no sisterly love between them. In fact, I'd say Miss Rowbottom loathed Isabel. She certainly envied her life."

"I'm not ruling Kempsey out either," Harry added. "He may not show much emotion, but that doesn't mean he isn't furious underneath the cool facade."

"Where to now?" I asked.

"Back to Mary and Linton Streets. I want to show you something."

* * *

AFTER WARNING my uncle of Mr. Pierce's threat the previous afternoon, Harry had left the Mayfair Hotel and returned to Islington to watch the intersection of the two streets that had given Mary Linton the inspiration for her fake name. He'd kept watch until darkness fell, for a woman matching the description given by Dr. Iverson and his staff. He'd not seen her, but a sign on an office door had caught his attention.

It was that office we now watched. Positioned several doors down from the pub, we'd not passed it the day before, having approached the area from a different direction. But I agreed with Harry. It may be where Mrs. Mary Linton worked.

According to the sign on the door, it was the office of R. Bolton, Private Detective Agency.

Private detectives sometimes had to disguise themselves while investigating and the one thing we knew about Mary Linton was that she'd put on a wig to cover her distinctive red hair. She was trying to be unobtrusive, to blend in, perhaps so no one would notice her when she stole Sister's Dearden's key then returned to the clinic at the end of the day to put it back, using the excuse that she'd left her glove behind. Few ladies left the house without gloves, and if she did, she'd notice immediately, not hours later. All of those points added up to suspicious behavior, and happening mere days before Isabel Kempsey's murder made the woman even more suspicious.

But how was a private detective involved in the murder of a woman at a medical clinic?

It wasn't until a slim redhead left the office carrying a bag that the pieces began to fit into place. "It's her. Come on, Harry, let's confront her before she disappears."

He fell into step beside me as we crossed the street. "How do you know that's the woman calling herself Mary Linton?"

"Do you see her bag?" The leather handbag wasn't as large as a doctor's medical case, but it was quite big. Few women carried one that large on their everyday outings. It was too unwieldy. It was the sort of bag a woman who worked in an office carried with her, a little like Mr. Hobart's satchel that he used to carry paperwork to and from the hotel.

"What about it?" Harry asked.

"A woman who caught the omnibus outside Duncan Hamlin's workshop carried the same bag. She had her wig on then, I think, but it's definitely the same bag." We were only a few steps behind the woman now. "Excuse me," I called out. "May we have a word?"

She glanced over her shoulder, gasped, and ran off.

CHAPTER 8

arry could have easily caught the woman, but he
allowed me to chase her and force her to stop.
She tried to pull free, but I tightened my grip.

"Enough!" I snapped. "You won't get away."

She settled a penetrating glare on me that I found rather unnerving. "Unhand me or I'll scream." With her firm jaw and hard eyes, she looked prepared to follow through on her threat.

Before I gave in and released her, Harry made a good point. "Don't try running away unless you want us to believe you murdered Isabel Kempsey."

I relaxed my grip and she jerked free, but did not run off. She shifted her glare to Harry and scanned his face and form, which she hadn't done with me. A subtle softening of her jaw signaled a lowering of her guard, proving once again that a handsome man could disarm some women without even trying.

She wasn't ready to lower her guard all the way, however. "I didn't murder her." Just as Dr. Iverson had described, the woman calling herself Mary Linton was quite pretty with clear skin and a slim figure. He'd also said how determined she was to use the Electro Therapy Machine at her first appointment, and now that I'd met her, I understood how she could railroad a person into giving in. There was a determination about her, a trait I admired, although not always in a suspect. It was a trait she'd need as a private detective.

"May we go into your office to discuss this further?" Harry asked.

The woman glanced past us to the building from which she'd just emerged. The hesitation was at odds with the set jaw and direct glare. "We'll talk out here."

"Are you R. Bolton?"

"He's my father. I'm his assistant, Miss Madeline Bolton." She adjusted her grip on the handle of her bag. Strands of brown hair were caught in the clasp. "Who are you and what do you want?"

"We're also private detectives. This is Miss Fox and I'm Harry Armitage."

"Armitage! I've heard of you. You've solved some important murder cases since opening your agency. My father and I are great admirers of your work." Her flawless cheeks turned pink as a shy smile touched her lips, which apparently Dr. Iverson found to be generous. "You're a marvelous detective, Mr. Armitage. So clever."

"Miss Fox solved the murders with only a little input from me."

He may as well not have spoken. She didn't even acknowledge me. "May I ask you something? How do you manage to find such interesting investigations? We seem to get lumped with lost cats and cheating spouses."

"There is a lot of that, but the murders seem to find us, not the other way around." Harry cleared his throat. "Is Duncan Hamlin your client?"

"No."

"We saw you near his workshop."

She once again glanced at the door of the P.I. firm. "I should speak with my father."

I blocked her path as she tried to move past me and plucked the hair out of the clasp of her bag. I dangled it from my fingers. "You carry a brown wig in there to hide your natural red hair, but I suspect if we asked Dr. Iverson if he recognized you now, he would say you were the new patient who'd insisted on using the Electro Therapy Machine at her first appointment. If we asked his nurse and receptionist if they recognized you, I think they would also say you were that patient, and that you returned later the same day looking for your glove. I may not know you, Miss Bolton, but I am quite sure you don't have a nervous condition that required a session on the machine."

Still, she hesitated. She was a very stubborn woman.

"Duncan Hamlin is your client, isn't he? We saw you outside his workshop," I went on. "Did he hire your father to steal a key to Dr. Iverson's rooms?"

Her lips parted with her silent gasp.

"You weren't as subtle as you thought you were," I said.

"Miss Bolton," Harry said firmly, "if Duncan Hamlin is the murderer, then you are an accessory."

She gave in, but I sensed reluctance. "He hired my father to discover precisely where Dr. Iverson kept his machine, and to find a way into his rooms after hours. My father gave the assignment to me, since the clinic specializes in female conditions. I insisted on using the machine so I could see where and how it was stored. After my appointment, I saw the key on the reception desk and took it. I had a copy made then returned the original. I passed on the copy to Mr. Hamlin that very same day."

"Why would he want access to the machine if not to tamper with it?" Harry asked.

"He simply wanted to break it to inconvenience the doctor and make the manufacturer seem incompetent. He was going to return every week or so and break it again and again, so that eventually the doctor would stop using the Electro Therapy Machine and instead purchase *his* revitalizer device. Mr. Hamlin used to work for the Medical Electrical Company, you see, but he went out on his own and has a superior product that he plans to market soon. He's convinced that once the medical profession discovers his version, they'll be impressed. Dr. Iverson is well connected within the medical community and has been vocal in his support for the Electro Therapy Machine."

"Did you know Mr. Hamlin left the Medical Electrical Company under a cloud?" I asked. "He and the owner, Mr. Reid, had a falling out with Mr. Reid blaming him for stealing his ideas. Mr. Hamlin felt unappreciated by his former employer."

Miss Bolton glanced at Harry. "Is that true?"

He nodded.

"I'm sure Mr. Hamlin never intended to harm anyone," she went on.

"And yet a woman is dead," I said.

"He's a nice, unassuming man."

"In our experience, nice people are capable of murder," Harry said.

She shifted her weight from foot to foot. "I will admit that it's not beyond the realms of possibility that he might want to destroy his former employer, but to do so by murdering an innocent woman...that's monstrous."

"Are you quite sure he didn't know Isabel Kempsey?" I asked. It wasn't just a question for Miss Bolton. It was for Harry and me, too.

"I'm sure."

We had no further questions and thanked her.

"Wait," she said. "Please don't let my father know I spoke to you. After he read about the murder in the papers, he became worried about our involvement, but I assured him my disguise was perfect and that my real identity wouldn't be uncovered. I'm somewhat embarrassed that you found me so quickly, and he'd be furious. He already thinks women shouldn't be detectives, but I convinced him to hire me." A shadow passed over her pretty face. "My brother used to work for our father, but he died and...and now Father just has me."

Harry gave her a sympathetic nod. "Perhaps don't use identifiable places in your false name next time, nor choose an address in a street near your office."

She chewed her lower lip before releasing it. "Thank you

for the advice. I'm still quite new at this, but I'm a very quick learner, and very willing to do everything required of me in an investigation. Mr. Armitage, this may be bold of me, but no woman got anywhere by being demure. If you need another assistant then please do consider me. I don't want to work for my father for long."

"Miss Fox isn't my assistant; she's my partner. I'll keep you in mind if we have more work than we can handle." He touched the brim of his hat in a polite farewell, then made a rather obvious point of offering me his arm.

I didn't think it a very professional thing to do in front of a rival private detective, but given Miss Bolton may have been admiring Harry for more than his investigative skill, I took his arm anyway.

"Do you think she spoke the truth?" I asked him, once we were some distance away.

"I don't see why she would lie. She wouldn't want to risk being an accessory to murder if Duncan Hamlin turns out to be guilty."

Indeed.

I glanced over my shoulder, but Miss Bolton had moved on. She wasn't continuing in the direction she'd been heading in when we caught up to her, however. She was re-entering her father's office.

* * *

THE DOOR to Duncan Hamlin's office and workshop was locked. He may have gone out, or he may have been warned by Miss Bolton that we might call on him. When I shared my thoughts with Harry, he agreed she may have telephoned him.

He stepped away from the door, tipped his head back, and peered up at the open window on the first floor. "Let's try around the back. There's probably a door leading directly into the workshop from the lane or a courtyard."

"And if it's locked, too?"

"We wait."

A short lane led us to the back of the row of shops, including Mr. Hamlin's. The gate's lock was broken, but if Mr. Hamlin was inside, he would have heard our arrival thanks to the squeaking hinge. The courtyard was paved with the same red bricks as the building. The door to the outhouse stood ajar, but the door to the workshop was closed. Harry tried it only to discover it, too, was locked. No one answered his knock.

I huffed out a frustrated breath.

Harry merely smiled at me. "Do you want to pick the lock or shall I?"

"I thought you said we'd wait."

"We will. Inside." He removed his lockpicking tools from his pocket and got to work on the lock.

At that moment, the door opened from the other side. Upon seeing us, Duncan Hamlin emitted a yelp and tried to shut the door. Harry put his shoulder to it and forced it open.

I entered behind him. "Have something to hide, Mr. Hamlin?"

The inventor backed up until he hit a long desk covered with sketched plans of mechanical devices. Without taking his gaze off Harry, he slipped around the desk to the other side. "I, er, of course not. I simply have too many things to do and I know talking to you both will take up my time." From the way he eyed Harry carefully, I suspected he thought he needed protecting from him.

Given his concern, it may have been a good plan for Harry to interrogate Mr. Hamlin and use some of that worry to intimidate him. Harry seemed to have a different idea, however, and encouraged me with a nod. Meanwhile, he browsed the workshop, inspecting tools, spare parts, and the drawings. Mr. Hamlin's watchful gaze tracked him.

I cleared my throat to get his attention. "Why didn't you tell us you hired a private investigator to find where Dr. Iverson kept his Electro Therapy Machine, so you could break in and sabotage it?"

Mr. Hamlin showed no surprise at my question. Miss Bolton must have telephoned him after we left her, although

I couldn't see a telephone in the workshop and there hadn't been one in the front office. "I know how it looks, but I assure you I didn't go through with it. I never sabotaged the device. I've never even entered the premises, with or without a key." He sat heavily on a stool near the door. "I'm a coward."

"Or sensible."

He opened a drawer and plucked out a key. "You should take this and give it back. I don't want it."

I placed the key in my bag. "Has it been in that drawer the entire time?"

"Yes."

"Does anyone else have access to this workshop?"

"Just me nowadays."

Harry bent to study a framed photograph on the workbench. "You may not have gone through with it, Mr. Hamlin, but you planned to tamper with the machine in order to kill."

Mr. Hamlin leapt off the stool. "No! I never wanted to turn the machine into a weapon. I was going to damage it in such a way that it simply failed to work at all. I wanted the doctor to think it was faulty. I certainly wasn't going to increase the voltage the patient receives." He pressed his palms together, pleading. "You must believe me, Mr. Armitage.

Harry seemed not to be listening. He was intent on the photograph. "Why did you hire the R. Bolton Detective Agency?"

Mr. Hamlin blinked. "You already know the answer. To find out where the machine was kept and find a way to get into the premises after hours."

"But why that agency specifically? He's not local to you."

Mr. Hamlin studied the floor at his feet, which caused his spectacles to slip down his nose.

"Why did you hire Mr. R. Bolton?" Harry asked again. "Did you use that agency because you wanted to hire Miss Madeline Bolton?"

I wasn't sure why Harry persisted with that line of questioning, but I knew he must have a reason. Indeed, from the guilty look on Mr. Hamlin's face, I suspected he not only knew the reason but was also about to give in. A little more stern prompting from Harry had him finally surrendering.

"There is no Madeline Bolton. The R in the agency name stands for Rose. She's Rose Bolton, and the agency is hers. I hired her because I knew a woman would more easily get an appointment with Dr. Iverson."

I understood Miss Bolton's reason for pretending her father owned the agency. It gave it a legitimacy that a young woman would struggle to gain on her own. I'd probably have done the same thing, if I were in her position.

Harry turned the photograph around. It was of the same woman from the photograph in the office we'd seen during our first visit, except this time it wasn't in black and white. The photographer had meticulously painted it to add color. The woman's hair was the same shade of red as Rose Bolton's.

"Is this your late wife?" Harry asked.

Mr. Hamlin snatched the photograph off him and pressed it against his chest. "It is."

"She bears a resemblance to Miss Bolton. Are they sisters?"

"They are. I have no reason to hide that fact."

"Miss Bolton clearly thinks *she* has a reason to hide it," Harry said. "Not only did she lie about her name and the agency's ownership, she failed to mention that you are her brother-in-law."

Mr. Hamlin returned the frame to the corner of the workbench, adjusting the angle twice before being happy with the position. "I never asked Rose to lie to you. She must have her reasons."

Murder would be a valid reason. Did she blame Dr. Iverson for the death of her sister? Perhaps she believed he should have cured her of her cancer.

Harry moved so that he blocked Mr. Hamlin's exit to the office door while I remained near the back door. "Whose idea was it to sabotage the machine? Yours or Rose's?"

Mr. Hamlin swallowed audibly. "I can't recall now."

"It was hers, wasn't it?"

Mr. Hamlin adjusted his spectacles. "I told you, I can't recall."

"You shouldn't protect her, Mr. Hamlin. She could be a murderer."

"She's not! She believes in justice, not revenge."

"What happens when there is no way to get justice for the death of her sister?" When Mr. Hamlin didn't respond, Harry continued to press him. "Miss Bolton seemed like a formidable and capable woman. I can't imagine she liked seeing the doctor who failed her sister continue to practice without repercussions. Did it gall her to see his clinic thriving?"

"Rose didn't kill that poor woman!"

Harry seemed to accept the answer—or accept that Duncan Hamlin wasn't going to give in—but I thought of one more point to make before giving up completely. "She telephoned you, warning you that we were on our way here to question you. At the very minimum, that call makes it appear as though you're colluding."

"I don't have a telephone."

"I'm sure one of your neighbors does. Are you aware the police can obtain call records from the telephone exchange company?" At his small gasp of surprise, I added, "Now, I'll ask again—are you very sure Rose Bolton isn't the killer, and you're not an accessory to murder?"

Mr. Hamlin's face became pale and waxy, and his hand began to shake. "Please, tell the police I had nothing to do with this. It's true that Rose telephoned me to warn me that you would be on your way here. She also told me not to say anything about our connection. She said it would look bad. But you're right, I have to admit the truth. Secrets just make us look guilty and we're not. I am quite sure Rose had nothing to do with the murder. She may be headstrong and rather cunning, but she had nothing against the deceased woman. She'd never even met her. If Rose blamed the doctor for my wife's death, she'd have killed *him*, not an innocent patient. Besides, I told you. Edith died of cancer. There was nothing he could do to save her."

"Perhaps she finds it difficult accepting that," I said gently.

His point about not knowing Isabel Kempsey was a good one, and it put an end to further questions. Without a solid motive to murder Mrs. Kempsey, it was unlikely Duncan Hamlin or Rose Bolton were the killer. While it was possible she was merely an innocent victim with a weak heart who'd been in the wrong place at the wrong time, and the killer had intended to punish Dr. Iverson with an elaborate plot to sabotage his clinic by sabotaging his machine, it was unlikely. It seemed overly complicated to me.

We left the workshop via the front office. Once outside, Harry asked me whether I'd been taken in by Rose Bolton. He sounded annoyed.

"I believed her entire story," I admitted as we walked. "The details were convincing, as was her behavior. Her father, the real agency owner, only hiring her because this job required a woman, and his reluctance to believe a woman capable of doing as good a job as her brother... It was all very plausible."

"I believed her when she spoke about the brother," he said. "She seemed genuinely sad."

"I think she was, but over the death of her *sister*, not a brother. She played us for fools, Harry."

"She told us what we wanted to hear. She flattered me by mentioning my successes, and even asking to join my agency."

"Her struggle as a young woman trying to be taken seriously in a man's profession had me sympathizing with her," I added.

He shook his head. "I can't believe I fell for her act. Am I so self-absorbed that a little flattery has me hoodwinked?

"You're not in the least self-absorbed, Harry. Don't blame yourself. We all like to be flattered sometimes. Besides, you told her that I solved the cases alongside you. Those are not the words of a self-absorbed man. Rose Bolton is simply a very good actress, and an expert at deflecting attention away from the truth."

"She certainly is," he muttered. "Do you want to return to Islington and confront her with what we know?"

"Not yet. She'll be expecting us to confront her again, so let's do the opposite. She can stew while she waits. It's unlikely she's the murderer anyway. I agree with Mr. Hamlin on that score. There's no strong motive for Rose to have killed Isabel Kempsey."

"It could have been an accident, given she couldn't have known about Isabel's heart, but I agree. We should wait. So, what next?"

I removed my watch from my coat pocket and checked the time. "I ought to get back for the meeting at the hotel. We're going to discuss what to do about Mr. Pierce's threat."

"Then I'll leave you here. I have another case that requires my attention, and I have to travel in the opposite direction. Until tomorrow, Cleo."

I stood on my toes and kissed his cheek. "Until tomorrow, Harry."

* * *

I WAS SOMEWHAT SURPRISED, and a little alarmed, to see Flossy talking to Mr. Lombardi in the foyer of the hotel upon my return. No other members of my family were present, although Mr. Hobart hovered nearby. Upon seeing me, he quickly approached. His usually cheerful countenance was nowhere in sight.

"Good afternoon, Mr. Hobart. Is everything all right?"

"I don't think so. Mr. Lombardi waylaid Miss Bainbridge a few moments ago, even though they haven't been introduced. It is most inappropriate. I wasn't sure what to do, but thankfully you are here now."

It was indeed rather inappropriate for a man to speak to an unchaperoned young woman, although the space was a public one, so it wasn't the worst thing in the world. "Do you think he knows she's the daughter of the owner?"

Mr. Hobart's lips flattened. "I think that's why he approached her."

"I see." Whatever Mr. Lombardi said turned Flossy to stone. No, not stone. Glass. She looked as though the slightest touch would shatter her.

I thanked Mr. Hobart and hurried toward them, a smile plastered on my face. "There you are, Cousin. I've been looking for you."

The points of Mr. Lombardi's moustache lifted as he gave me a more generous smile than I'd given him. "Ah, *la bellissima* Miss Fox." He took my hand and kissed the knuckles. "I have just met your cousin. She is very interested in a new pill made by my company."

Flossy held up some mail she'd been holding. "I was on my way to the post desk when Mr. Lombardi introduced himself. He suggested I sit in on his presentation on Saturday to hear all about the new pill." She blinked rather furiously as she lowered her gaze. She was on the verge of tears. What had he said to her?

With one eye on Flossy, I addressed Mr. Lombardi. "My cousin isn't a doctor or pharmacist. Why would she be interested in your medicine?"

"It is not a medicine. It is a pill, yes, but for the improvement of a lady's figure."

Improvement? Allowances could be made for language and cultural differences, but Mr. Lombardi's English was excellent, and I suspected telling a woman her figure needed improving would be equally as offensive in Italy as England.

Mr. Lombardi didn't seem to notice my horror as he barreled on. "Calling it a medicine is a good idea." He waggled a finger in the air. "No, not a medicine. A cure! A cure to make fat disappear." He clasped my hand between both of his. "Miss Fox, you are a genius. *Grazie mille.*"

I watched him cross the foyer to the front door, a bounce in his step, until Flossy made a choking noise beside me.

With a hand covering her mouth, she hurried toward the lift. When the door didn't immediately open, she gathered her skirts and took the stairs.

"Flossy, wait!"

She didn't slow down, so I quickened my pace. I finally

caught up to her on the first-floor landing. I wasn't surprised to see she was crying.

"Don't listen to him," I said, wrapping my arm around her waist. "He's loathsome."

"I know that, but he's right. I *am* fat."

"You are beautiful and lovely, Flossy."

"But compared to other women—"

"Do *not* compare yourself to others." I caught her by the elbows and gave her a little shake. "You are not them, and they are not you. Besides, most women we know starve themselves, or lace their corsets so tightly they feel lightheaded. I'm sure the lack of air prohibits their brains from forming sensible thoughts." Some women's waists were so tiny from years of extreme lacing as to distort their figure into an unnatural shape. Such measures must be unhealthy for both the mind *and* constitution.

"Flossy? Cleo?" Floyd came up the stairs, his smile fading when he noticed his sister's state. "What's wrong? Flossy, why are you crying?"

"Mr. Lombardi called me fat," she blurted out.

"The bloody nerve of him!" Floyd circled his arm around her shoulders. "How dare he."

"*You* call me fat all the time."

"Not fat. Plump. It's actually a compliment, you know. Most men like a woman with a little roundness."

"Ugh." She pushed him away. "Keep that talk for your chums and mistresses."

We three continued up the stairs at a more sedate pace. I was pleased to see Floyd indignant on Flossy's behalf. The siblings may bicker, but they were each other's advocate when required.

"Let's talk about nicer things," Flossy said when we reached the second-floor landing.

She sounded as though she'd shrugged off Mr. Lombardi's comments, but I decided to keep the conversation light. I didn't want to mention the upcoming meeting about Mr. Pierce's threat and worry her.

"Perhaps you can both help me," I said. "It's Harry's

birthday soon and I want to know what to get him. Any suggestions?"

"Nothing," Floyd growled. "He's merely your colleague, and you don't have to buy colleagues birthday gifts."

"Floyd's right," Flossy said. "Mr. Armitage is someone you work with from time to time. You don't have to get him anything. It's not as though you're going to his birthday party."

Floyd glared at me over the top of his sister's head. I returned it with an arch look of my own.

Unaware of the exchange, Flossy continued on. "Although if you do want to get him something, Cleo, I'm happy to go shopping with you."

I squeezed her arm. "Thank you, Flossy. We'll go shopping regardless."

She clapped her hands in delight. "Good. There's no better medicine for the soul than a little jaunt to the shops. I'd like to see Mr. Lombardi try to bottle *that*."

Floyd grunted. "If he could, he would."

* * *

My uncle's office was large, but, even so, it felt cramped with all the senior staff, as well as Peter the assistant manager, Floyd and Harmony in attendance. After Uncle Ronald informed them of Mr. Pierce's threat to disrupt Mr. Lombardi's presentation, I gave them a description of Mr. Pierce's appearance. At the conclusion of the meeting, Mr. Hobart and Peter were instructed to inform the rest of the front-of-house staff, particularly the doormen and porters.

Before they all dispersed, I asked them to wait and hear what I had to say. "I learned something troubling about the Bella Vita Company this morning."

Floyd crossed his arms over his chest. "It can't possibly be more troubling than Lombardi's exchange with Flossy."

Uncle Ronald frowned. "What happened?"

"He called her fat."

Harmony looked up from her notes with a gasp.

116

Mrs. Poole rolled her eyes and muttered "Idiot" under her breath.

Uncle Ronald grunted. "I hope you defended your sister's honor."

"He did," I assured him. "What I learned is different. It will affect the entire hotel. His company is in financial difficulty. The Italian newspapers are reporting that he overextended himself and now can't pay back his loans without closing several factories. I'm worried that he won't be able to pay for the Mayfair's services."

Uncle Ronald stroked his moustache in thought.

Floyd, however, thumped his fist on the desk. "That must be why he keeps changing the subject when I bring up payment. Father, we should cancel the presentation before more money is spent. If he leaves the country before he pays us, we'll never recoup it."

"Or we could ask him to pay up front," Mr. Hobart said. "We could present him with an invoice for what we've already spent and say we won't spend more until it's settled."

"And if he doesn't, *then* we cancel," Floyd added.

Uncle Ronald continued to stroke his moustache with his thumb and forefinger. "His presentation has led to an increase in guest reservations. We'll still be out of pocket if he doesn't reimburse us for the catering *et cetera*, but as an advertisement to other companies considering similar events, it could still work out positive for us in due course."

Floyd scoffed. "You're going to let him get away with it? Father, the man's a bounder! He doesn't deserve to even be allowed to set foot in the Mayfair Hotel, let alone do so for free."

Uncle Ronald would ordinarily have strong words in response when Floyd disagreed with him, but not this time. "The man is worse than a bounder, I agree, but this requires a delicate touch. I'll speak to him."

Floyd pushed himself to his feet. With a disappointed shake of his head, he walked out of the office. Uncle Ronald dismissed the rest of us.

As we exited, Mr. Chapman asked if he could speak to me

in private. Given my fractious history with the steward, I was intrigued. Once the others had left, I asked him how I could be of assistance.

"It's me who can help you. Possibly." He glanced around to make sure we couldn't be overheard, then lowered his voice. "Out of all the people I could speak to about this, you're the one I trust with the information." At my surprised look, he added, "I know. Ironic, isn't it?"

"Should I be flattered?"

A ghost of a smile touched his lips. Perhaps he had a sense of humor after all. "You may have guessed that what I'm going to tell you is very sensitive. If you pass it on, please don't tell anyone it came from me." He glanced up and down the corridor again before continuing. "I've heard the waiters say that Mr. Lombardi bothers the maids."

"Unfortunately, it's true. But that's not news."

"But this may be. Either his harassment of the *maids* is a ruse to throw everyone off, or he likes both."

"Both what?"

"Women and men," he whispered. "In fact, I have it on good authority that he does more than *bother* men."

I pressed a hand to my throat as a flush crept up it. "Oh. I see."

"I know this because I've seen him at the Café Royal."

I frowned. "I don't understand. The Café Royal is frequented by the artistic set. What of it?"

"Men who like men also go there, as do women who dress as men."

"Mr. Lombardi is new to the city. Perhaps he didn't realize it attracted that sort of crowd."

Mr. Chapman tilted his head to the side. Not a hair on his elegantly coifed head moved. "I didn't just see him having a drink, Miss Fox. I saw him kiss a man."

"Did he recognize you?"

"He wasn't kissing me! And no, I'm sure he didn't."

I recalled seeing men come and go from the Café Royal on the evening Harry and I had watched it from the other side of Regent Street. Our vantage point outside number fifty-nine had given us the perfect view of the door. Perhaps that was the entire point of that chosen meeting place. It had nothing to do with the jewelry shop located there, and everything to do with the Café Royal opposite.

Did the person who'd written that note to Dr. Iverson want to take him inside? Did Dr. Iverson have affairs with men as well as women? If he did, perhaps the author of the note didn't want to join him; perhaps they wanted to blackmail him.

What if Isabel Kempsey had been the author and the doctor discovered that? He may have decided to silence her before she ruined his reputation and spread the gossip. Killing her in his own consulting rooms wasn't a very good idea on the surface, but what if he thought he could get away with it? By hiring Harry, it made him *appear* innocent.

"Miss Fox? Are you listening?" Mr. Chapman prompted.

"I'm sorry, what did you say?"

"I said that you could use the information to ensure Lombardi pays the hotel now before he leaves London."

I frowned. "You mean blackmail him?"

Mr. Chapman winced. "It's such a dirty word, but yes. Blackmail him. I can try to get evidence if you need it."

"I'm not sure I want to go down that route. As much as I dislike him, I don't want to use someone's nature against them. Why are you doing this, Mr. Chapman? I would have thought you'd be reluctant, too."

He adjusted his tie, even though it was already pin-straight. "That's my business. Suffice it to say, the man needs to get his comeuppance, and I will be glad to play my part in serving it to him."

I watched the steward walk off. Whatever his reason for telling me, his information was more useful to me than he could know.

CHAPTER 9

$\mathcal{A}$rmed with the information learned from Mr. Chapman about the Café Royal, the first task for the day was clear—find out if Dr. Iverson had affairs with men as well as women. Harry informed me over coffee in his office that he'd heard the rumors about the Café Royal after Oscar Wilde's arrest five years prior.

"He used to hold court there. I thought it had changed after his arrest in ninety-five, when it suffered from the extra attention in the press, but apparently not. Did this information come from Chapman?"

I'd promised Mr. Chapman that I wouldn't divulge the source of my information, but Harry already knew about the steward's proclivities, so I didn't feel as though I was breaking that promise when I nodded. "He told me he saw Mr. Lombardi there, and suggested I use the information to blackmail him into paying his hotel bill. The news would be damaging to his business."

"I think his business is already financially damaged, but I see Chapman's point. So will you use it against him?"

I lowered my coffee cup to the desk. "It doesn't feel right. Not to get him to pay his bill."

"But for uncovering a murderer?"

"I wouldn't hesitate. If Dr. Iverson has withheld pertinent

information, he needs to be confronted about it. It's a motive. His practice would suffer if such proclivities were made public, so if Isabel Kempsey wrote that letter to him—or he *thought* she did—he might believe his only recourse to silence her was to murder her. If she was angry with him for ending their affair, she might have decided to get her revenge by anonymously drawing him to the Café Royal where he'd be exposed."

Harry wasn't entirely convinced with the theory, however. "I didn't get the feeling Iverson was hiding anything like that from me. I admit I could be wrong, though, and it's worth following up. Besides, I want to return to the clinic and find out more about the late Mrs. Hamlin's treatment. Both Duncan Hamlin and Rose Bolton could have been angry enough with Iverson's failure to diagnose her cancer to want to harm his practice."

We finished our coffees and returned the cups to Luigi. On the way to Dr. Iverson's rooms, we discussed ways to discover more about Dr. Iverson's possible proclivities, but none felt satisfactory. We settled on the direct approach. If asking him if he had affairs with men offended him, then so be it.

We didn't get the chance to ask him, however, as he wasn't there. According to Miss Wainsmith, he still hadn't returned to work after his ordeal.

She indicated the telephone on her desk. "I've just been notifying those patients who are due in today and also have telephones, but so few do." She sighed heavily. "I'll have to tell them when they arrive for their appointments. Some will agree to see Sister Dearden without the doctor present, but those who insist on seeing him will have to make alternative arrangements."

"That sounds inconvenient," I said.

"It is, particularly when Sister Dearden is more than capable." Miss Wainsmith pressed a hand to her chest. "Not that I'm complaining about the extra work, you understand. I'd never do that."

"Why not?" Harry asked.

"This is an excellent position. Sister Dearden and I are fortunate indeed to be working here."

"Dr. Iverson pays well?"

"Very well, but it's more than that. He's kind, and he doesn't demand I stay back at the end of the day. He and Mrs. Iverson were patient with me when I was still learning. Sister Dearden is happy here, too. As an advocate for women's health, she finds the work fulfilling. She's such a generous person when it comes to giving her time and expertise to women in need."

The consulting room door opened and Sister Dearden ushered a patient out, thanking her for keeping the appointment.

"Will Dr. Iverson be in again before my next appointment in two weeks?" the patient asked.

"I'm quite sure he will be," Sister Dearden said.

The patient looked pleased. "That's good to hear. Although you are an excellent substitute, Sister, I do miss the doctor's cheerful face. Please pass on my regards."

"We'd be happy to."

The patient left without paying, so presumably she had an account.

Sister Dearden greeted Harry and me as she stopped by the desk to pick up a pencil. "Miss Wainsmith has informed you the doctor isn't in?" she asked as she made a brief note in the patient's file.

"She has," Harry said. "We have some questions for the both of you, if you have a few moments to spare."

Sister Dearden looked pointedly at the empty chairs in the waiting area. "Alas, we do. The patients prefer the doctor, despite my best efforts." The two women exchanged subtle glances, which I took to mean the patients preferred the doctor because he flirted with them. If either of them was jealous, the look was too subtle for me to tell.

"I'm not sure how we can help any more than we already have, but we'll try," Sister Dearden went on.

Miss Wainsmith clasped her hands on the desk in front of her. "Yes, of course we will. What is it you wish to know?"

On the way in, we'd decided I should be the one to ask the question, but now that it came time for it, I hesitated. It was a terribly awkward topic.

Sister Dearden noticed my reluctance. In a brisk, no-nonsense manner, she urged me to continue. "I can see you're embarrassed, but I assure you we've heard all sorts of things here."

"Speak for yourself," Miss Wainsmith joked, somewhat nervously.

I cleared my throat. "Do you recall the anonymous letter we mentioned? The one Dr. Iverson threw out that was found in Isabel Kempsey's things after her death, along with love letters from the doctor?"

Both women nodded, giving me their full attention.

"The note said to meet at a particular address on Regent Street," I said. "Mr. Armitage and I went there at the appointed time, but no one showed up. It later came to our attention that the address was directly opposite a venue where men can meet in private."

"Do you mean a gentleman's club?" Miss Wainsmith asked. "The doctor belongs to one. What of it?" She blinked innocently back at me.

"It's not a gentleman's club."

The more worldly Sister Dearden understood my meaning. "Are you suggesting Dr. Iverson has relationships with other men?"

Miss Wainsmith gasped and her cheeks pinked. "What utter nonsense! Miss Fox, I can assure you, he is *not* that way inclined. Is he, Sister?"

"Indeed not. Not that I am aware of, at least." There was a note of amusement in Sister Dearden's response.

Not Miss Wainsmith's, however. She was furious on her employer's behalf. "That is a most offensive suggestion, Miss Fox. You ought to be ashamed of yourself for even thinking it. You've met him, after all. He is very masculine, and very popular with women. Indeed, I've never even seen him look at a man in the sort of way you're implying. Not even Mr. Armitage here, and he is a particularly handsome man. If the doctor were interested in men, Mr. Armitage would certainly be worthy of a longing gaze, but I didn't see anything of the sort."

Was her denial too vehement for a mere employee? Could she be defending her lover?

Harry cleared his throat. Suddenly realizing she'd exposed her own thoughts on Harry's looks, Miss Wainsmith flushed even redder. She busied herself with the paperwork on the desk.

A somewhat amused Sister Dearden turned to the filing cabinet to slip the last patient's file into a drawer.

Miss Wainsmith's protest may have been vehement, but I tended to agree with her. If Dr. Iverson liked men, he would have taken particular notice of Harry. Harry was a man worthy of more than one look. But there'd been no lingering gazes. Was the meeting place's proximity to the Café Royal important at all? More importantly, who had written the letter? Miss Wainsmith had claimed not to have seen it, but if the note was delivered to the clinic, it would have passed through her hands and into the doctor's, so perhaps it wasn't sent to the clinic at all.

I was about to press Miss Wainsmith again when Harry brought up the subject of the missing key. "You were right and it was the woman you saw return later claiming to look for her missing glove."

Sister Dearden closed the filing cabinet drawer with a bang. "I knew it! Did she make a copy?"

I removed the key Mr. Reid had given me from my bag. "She did, then returned your original key while pretending to search for her glove." I set the key on the desk.

Miss Wainsmith flipped the pages back through the appointment book. "Mary Linton, her name was. Very suspicious of her, we were. Weren't we, Sister? She just wasn't the typical sort of patient we get here."

"Have you informed the police?" Sister Dearden asked.

"Not yet," Harry said.

"Why not? She stole my key and *must* have come in and

tampered with the Electro Therapy Machine before Mrs. Kempsey died. You've solved the case, Mr. Armitage."

"But why would she kill her?" Miss Wainsmith asked. "Was she in love with Dr. Iverson, too? Was it jealousy?"

"That would be my guess."

"It would be an incorrect guess," I said. "The woman's name is not Mary Linton and she wasn't having an affair with the doctor, or wanting to start a relationship with him. She may blame him for the death of her sister."

"He hasn't killed anyone!" Miss Wainsmith cried.

Sister Dearden didn't deny it, however. "Who was her sister?"

"Mrs. Edith Hamlin," Harry said.

"I've never heard of her," Miss Wainsmith said.

"She died last year."

Sister Dearden's brow furrowed in thought. "I remember her. Her death rocked Dr. and Mrs. Iverson, but it wasn't unexpected. Mrs. Hamlin came to us looking for a cure for a delicate constitution, but it turned out that her fragility was the result of an underlying disease."

"Rose Bolton—the real name of the woman calling herself Mary Linton—blames Dr. Iverson for not detecting the disease."

"There was nothing anyone could have done for her. As I recall, she was prescribed a tonic to keep her comfortable."

"Nerve Elixir?" I asked. "It contains an addictive amount of cocaine."

"Only those with a weak constitution become addicted," Sister Dearden said. "Anyway, it was the disease that killed her. Let me look at her file."

I bit my tongue to stop myself responding. For now, we needed Sister Dearden and Miss Wainsmith to believe we were on Dr. Iverson's side. Accusing him of getting his patients addicted to the Nerve Elixir wouldn't help us. Besides, the nurse was right about one thing. In Edith Hamlin's case, the cancer had killed her.

While Sister Dearden searched through a drawer in the filing cabinet, I asked Miss Wainsmith about the note again.

"Dr. Iverson told us that he received the note along with his other mail, but you said you don't remember seeing it. Is that still the case?"

"I haven't lied, Miss Fox," she snapped. "I didn't see the letter."

Sister Dearden closed the filing drawer. "Here it is. Edith Hamlin." She rejoined us at the desk and opened the file.

We all crowded around, even Miss Wainsmith.

Sister Dearden pointed to the two-word diagnosis: nervous condition. Below that were a list of her symptoms, including anxiety, crying for no reason, and irregular womanly courses, which the doctor stated most likely led to her inability to conceive. The final symptom of weight loss was underlined and repeated three more times at three different appointments, a month apart. Her weight was recorded, as were other physical measurements. Finally, the doctor listed his treatments. They included sessions on the Electro Therapy Machine and doses of Nerve Elixir tonic as required. There was no mention of cancer.

Sister Dearden pointed to Edith Hamlin's weight measurements. "You can see she got thinner and thinner."

While the misdiagnosis was interesting, what interested me more was the penciled note scrawled on the first sheet of paper at an angle on the right-hand side. The handwriting was difficult to decipher at first, but when I did, I gasped. It said Edith Hamlin was *recommended by Isabel Kempsey.*

It was the connection we needed to the victim! The women knew each other.

Harry noticed the name, too. "Why is it written like that, off to the side?"

Miss Wainsmith also gasped as she read the note, and Sister Dearden pressed her fingertips to her lips. They, too, had realized the importance of it.

"It's Dr. Iverson's handwriting," Sister Dearden murmured. "He must have jotted it down during one of Mrs. Hamlin's appointments. It means Mrs. Kempsey recommended Dr. Iverson's services to her."

"He likes to know how the patients hear about him," Miss

Wainsmith added. "It helps to know who to thank if it was a personal recommendation. Good lord, does this mean Mrs. Hamlin's sister killed Isabel Kempsey because she recommended Dr. Iverson, whom she blames for not curing her sister?"

It was possible either Rose Bolton or her brother-in-law, Duncan Hamlin, did blame Mrs. Kempsey. Both were still grieving over Edith Hamlin's death, a year later.

A patient arrived and Miss Wainsmith and Sister Dearden set about convincing her to stay and be seen by the nurse instead of rescheduling her appointment. Harry and I left, but we were silent for some time, each of us lost in our own thoughts. It was Harry who finally spoke up when we reached the intersection.

"Do we confront Rose Bolton or Duncan Hamlin next about Edith Hamlin's connection to the victim?"

"Neither," I said. "I think we should speak to Isabel's husband and sister. They might know about the connection."

"In that case, we'll call at the Kempsey residence. I'm sure we'll find Miss Rowbottom there, too."

I smirked. "She may have already moved in."

* * *

UNLIKE PREVIOUS OCCASIONS, Mr. Kempsey was pleased to see us today. Indeed, the fact he showed any emotion at all was rather surprising. So far he'd seemed indifferent to his wife's death, but his eager greeting implied he'd been suppressing his emotions, after all.

"I'm glad you're here, Armitage. I telephoned your office but there was no answer, so I presume you have your own reason for calling on me." He invited us to sit on the sofa and was about to speak again when his sister-in-law appeared.

Miss Rowbottom stopped short upon seeing us. "I thought I heard voices, but I was expecting it to be acquaintances paying their respects. Mr. Armitage, I must protest most vehemently. Your timing is very insensitive. My brother-in-law is exhausted. You need to leave."

"Nonsense," Mr. Kempsey said. "I'm not in the least tired. Anyway, the timing is fortuitous. It saves me a visit to Soho. As I was just telling Armitage, I tried telephoning his office, but no one answered. Your assistant should stay there to answer it," he added with a flick of his wrist in my direction.

"Miss Fox is my associate," Harry said, yet again. "Why did you telephone me?"

Miss Rowbottom dismissed the hovering maid and sat in the chair closest to her brother-in-law. "Yes, Ian, why did you?"

Mr. Kempsey reached for a small leather-bound book on a side table. It easily fit into his palm as he fished a pair of spectacles from his pocket. "This is my wife's diary. Not her regular diary with her appointments, mind, but a secret one. At least, I don't think it was intended for anyone else to see. She jotted down her thoughts, some of them quite bleak and…private." He cleared his throat as he flipped through the pages.

Miss Rowbottom sat forward, craning her neck to see. "You didn't tell me about it. When did you find it?"

"This morning."

"Why were you looking through Isabel's things?"

He peered over the spectacles at her. "She was my wife."

Miss Rowbottom sat back. "Yes, of course. I merely meant it must be difficult for you to go through her things and read her secret thoughts. You should let me do it, so it's one less bother for you."

He stopped turning pages when he reached October. "Here! Listen to this. A week before her death, she wrote: 'Meet Will I. Tell him I know.'" Mr. Kempsey handed the diary to Harry. "'Will I' is Dr. Iverson. I don't know what she was going to tell him, but I believe the code in the pages leading up to it might give a clue. I can't decipher the code, but perhaps you can."

Harry lowered the diary so we could both read it and flipped back through the pages. Isabel Kempsey's jottings consisted mostly of a series of times beside what I guessed to be locations. Several were C Royal—Café Royal. It seemed likely she'd discovered the doctor frequented the venue. Other locations appeared to be public spaces such as parks. They were probably all places where she'd seen the doctor meet someone. Given the Café Royal's reputation, it was a reasonable assumption that she saw him meet men.

"There, you see," Mr. Kempsey went on. "Isabel *wasn't* having an affair with the doctor. She was gathering information about him, perhaps to blackmail him. I don't know why she would do that—she didn't need the money—but what other reason could there be?"

Jealousy sprang to mind, but I kept my opinion to myself.

His sister-in-law wasn't so kind, however. Miss Rowbottom reached across the gap and clasped his forearm. "My dear Ian, she *was* having an affair with him. She told me to my face that she loved him. It's most likely that when he broke it off with her, she was angry and sad, so she followed him around the city like a puppy. She must have learned something about him while doing so, something he wouldn't want made public."

Mr. Kempsey snatched his arm away. The familiar blank mask descended over his face, and he was once again the indifferent husband. Except now I realized it wasn't indifference. It was a way of protecting himself from not just the loss of his wife, but the truth of her infidelity.

"The entry in the week before her death states she was going to tell Dr. Iverson she knew whatever it was she'd found out about him," Miss Rowbottom went on. "You're right in that she probably wanted to blackmail him, but not for money. For his affections. Either way, it's a very good motive to kill her."

Mr. Kempsey indicated the diary in Harry's hand. "You may keep that, Armitage. Take it to the police."

Harry shook his head and held it out to him. "It must come from you, sir. But thank you for showing it to us. It's enormously helpful."

Mr. Kempsey accepted the diary. "You had some more questions for us, I presume?"

"Does the name Edith Hamlin mean anything to you?"

"No."

Harry looked to Miss Rowbottom, but she also denied knowing Mrs. Hamlin. "Who is she?" she asked. "And how is she important to the investigation?"

"We can't divulge that information."

I watched Miss Rowbottom carefully. Out of the two of them, I suspected she knew Isabel the best. "Are you sure your sister never mentioned her? Could she be an old friend Isabel bumped into? Or a new acquaintance?"

Miss Rowbottom shook her head. "The name isn't familiar to me, but I'll go through Isabel's secret diary to see if there's any mention of an Edith Hamlin." She reached for the small leather-bound book, but Mr. Kempsey kept it away from her.

"*I'll* look through it," he muttered.

Miss Rowbottom's hand recoiled as if he'd slapped it.

We left the Kempsey residence and I presumed we'd make our way to Duncan Hamlin's workshop next, but Harry suggested we take stock of the investigation in a tea shop first.

"I have an idea," he said.

"Does it involve you flirting with Dr. Iverson in order to discover once and for all if he's interested in men?"

"It does."

"It's a dreadful idea! You are not flirting with anyone, Harry, male or female."

His dimples flashed with his grin. "Jealous?"

"Of course not. I'm objecting on the grounds that you'd be upset if the situation was reversed, and I was the one flirting with a suspect."

"I'd be upset because I couldn't stand seeing you flirt with another man, whether it was an act or not. In other words, I'd be jealous. Admit it, Cleo, you've got a jealous streak in you. It's not a bad thing, by the way. In fact, I quite like it. It makes me feel as though I'm special to you."

I slowed my pace and turned to him. "If you don't realize you're special to me yet, then clearly my kissing needs work."

His lips twitched with his wicked smile. "Your kissing is perfect already, but I'm always available for more practice."

I nudged him with my elbow and laughed. If my kissing was indeed perfect, it was only because he'd taught me. Prior to Harry, I'd kissed only one other man and it had been a disappointment. Harry, however, was experienced.

"Something the matter?" he asked quietly.

"I've come to the somewhat unnerving realization that I am capable of jealousy when it comes to you."

He blew out a relieved breath. "Is that all? I was worried you were beginning to panic about being in a relationship."

"Harry," I chided as I took his hand. "You must stop thinking it'll come to an end."

He studied our clasped fingers. "I'm sure I will, in time."

Spotting a deep recessed doorway, I led him to it and proceeded to push him back against the door. "Will a little practice help convince you?"

He looped his arms around my waist and pulled me against him. "Definitely."

* * *

ALTHOUGH WE'D DISCARDED Harry's plan to flirt with Dr. Iverson, we stopped in a tea shop anyway to discuss our next move. First of all, I wanted to know if Harry believed the clinic's staff or not.

"Miss Wainsmith and Sister Dearden could be lying to protect the doctor," I said. "They both say they like working for him, and he pays them well, so they'll be more inclined to ensure that continues."

"By covering up the murder of his patient?" Harry shook his head. "If just one of them lied for him, I could believe it, but not both. If he did do it, I doubt either of them know."

I waited as the waitress brought tea and sandwiches to our table, then continued after she left. "In that case, we should take their word for the fact that the doctor isn't interested in men."

"Not necessarily. They could be lying about that, and that alone, to protect his reputation."

I poured tea from the pot into the white cups, then

selected an egg and cress sandwich finger. "I didn't get the feeling they lied, did you?"

"No. But they could be good actors, or he could be hiding his true nature from them, too. Aside from the doctor himself, the one person who would truly be aware of his…interests would be Mrs. Iverson." Harry watched me over the rim of his teacup. "Do you want to ask her?"

I considered the implications while I chewed, eventually shaking my head. "Not yet. I think we should talk to Duncan Hamlin first and confront him about his late wife's connection to the victim. How did Mrs. Kempsey know Mrs. Hamlin? If they were particularly close friends, and Isabel Kempsey blamed Dr. Iverson for not diagnosing Edith Hamlin's cancer, the doctor may have killed her to silence her."

"Or one of the staff did," Harry added. "To protect their employer and their good jobs."

"Indeed." I suddenly lowered my half-eaten sandwich. "Could Mr. Kempsey have been right? Could Isabel Kempsey's affair with Dr. Iverson have been a lie on her part? Could she have started it in order to destroy him as revenge for her friend's death?"

"Miss Rowbottom, seemed to think Isabel loved him. She claims Isabel told her as much. She also said Isabel didn't know Edith Hamlin."

Had Miss Rowbottom lied about Isabel's depth of feeling for the doctor as part of her scheme to win over Mr. Kempsey now that her sister was out of the picture? It seemed a disloyal thing to do, but it was obvious the sisters hadn't gotten along. "Siblings can have such complicated relationships," I murmured. "I see it in my own family. Flossy and Floyd can be at each other's throats, then the next moment he's protective of her. Aunt Lilian felt inferior to my mother to the point that it affected her well into adulthood, years after my mother died. And yet she loved her, too."

"My father and Uncle Alfred are each other's best friend, but that may not have always been the case. Aside from them, I don't have much experience with siblings either."

I reached across the table and clasped Harry's hand. "Perhaps that's why we're drawn to each other. We understand what it means to feel alone in the world."

He rubbed his thumb along my knuckles. "It may be one reason," he said quietly. "But there are many others."

The waitress passed our table and Harry withdrew his hand. He picked up his teacup but didn't sip. "Isabel Kempsey's family had never heard of Edith Hamlin. We should ask Edith Hamlin's husband and sister again about if they knew of Isabel Kempsey before her murder, now that we have proof that there was a connection between Edith and Isabel."

I sipped my tea in thought.

"You don't agree," Harry said.

"I do, but I consider them our main suspects at this point. If one or both are guilty then they'll lie to save themselves. We can't believe anything they tell us, so I don't think we should ask." I regarded him over the teacup. "I think we should try to find out answers another way."

"You have a mischievous twinkle in your eye, Cleo. Should I be worried?"

"That depends on how you feel about breaking and entering."

CHAPTER 10

*H*arry wasn't against breaking and entering the premises of our suspects, but he didn't want me to be the one doing it. He wanted me to keep watch outside Duncan Hamlin's office while he searched through the late Mrs. Hamlin's personal effects, but there was one problem standing in the way of that plan. Duncan Hamlin didn't leave the premises.

By three o'clock, I'd grown impatient. I came up with a new plan that involved Harry distracting Mr. Hamlin with technical questions about electricity and his inventions. He agreed, albeit reluctantly. "I don't want you up there for more than ten minutes, Cleo. It will be difficult to keep him talking for much longer without him growing suspicious. It's a small place and Mrs. Hamlin's effects will have been put away by now, so I suggest searching a cupboard. In exactly ten minutes, you have to leave. Understood?"

"Perfectly."

He removed my watch from my jacket pocket and checked it against his, then slipped it back into the pocket. "Meet me around the corner afterward. Ten minutes begins now."

"I think it should begin once you're in the workshop."

Harry was already crossing the road and didn't respond.

I watched through the window from a safe distance while he spoke to Duncan Hamlin. The inventor's face went from tired to enthused in a moment as he invited Harry into his workshop. Whatever Harry had said worked. I suspected his own enthusiasm had been genuine, and Duncan had picked up on it. It was the reason I'd suggested Harry be the one to talk to him.

I slipped into the office then up the staircase to the room above the office and workshop. It was a small space, barely big enough for a bed, dressing table, two armchairs, and a cupboard. An even smaller kitchenette contained the bare essentials. Duncan Hamlin wasn't one for cleaning the dishes. They were piled up in the sink, the remnants of previous meals congealing on them.

I looked through the four dressing table drawers first, expecting to see only masculine items. But two of the drawers contained embroidered handkerchiefs bearing the initials E.H., as well as scarves, jewelry and a woman's underthings. There were no diaries, letters or address books, however.

I softly closed the drawers and tiptoed across the floor to the cupboard, only to step on a loose board. It creaked under my weight. I froze. Listened.

When I heard no one charging up the stairs, I continued on, my heart pounding. Once safely at the cupboard door, I searched through the hanging and folded garments inside. As with the dressing table, Edith Hamlin's effects were alongside her husband's, as if she'd simply stepped out for the day and was expected to return later. If it wasn't for the dirty dishes in the kitchen, I'd have thought he still lived with a woman.

I rifled through coat pockets, but it was the reticules and bags that interested me more. There were only three. I quickly dug through each one, setting aside handkerchiefs, combs, pins and coins. I found one address book and one small note-book, the latter with a silver retractable pencil attached to a slim black ribbon that wrapped around the little book.

I quickly looked at the contents of each, but it was obvious I couldn't study them in any depth in the time I had left. I popped them into my bag and left, careful to avoid the creaking floorboard.

I hurried away from Mr. Hamlin's office and waited around the corner. Harry joined me moments later. "Did he suspect?" I asked.

"Only once, when he thought he heard something, but I distracted him with a question and he soon forgot about the noise. What about you? Any luck?"

I removed the notebook and address book from my bag. "If Edith knew Isabel, these should have some reference to her."

Harry glanced back the way he'd come. "How do you plan on returning them without being seen?"

"By post, anonymously after the investigation concludes."

We took a hansom to our next destination, reading through each book for any reference to Isabel Kempsey. We found none.

I slipped them back into my bag as the hansom drew to the curb a few doors down from Rose Bolton's detective agency.

The distraction technique Harry used on Duncan Hamlin wouldn't work on Rose Bolton, so this time we were forced to wait for her to leave. Fortunately she did a mere fifteen minutes after we arrived. She locked the office door behind her and strode away, head bent into the breeze.

I stood in such a way as to hide Harry from view while he used his lockpicking tools to unlock the door. He had the task completed in a much faster time that I would have, and we slipped inside, closing the door behind us.

Miss Bolton had drawn the curtains before she left, but there was enough light coming in around the edges to see by. The small office was sparsely furnished, reminding me of Harry's office space soon after he'd moved into it. There were no pictures of a personal nature, nor any decorative touches that a woman would add to her home. It was bland and businesslike. There were only two places to search—the desk and a crate that Miss Bolton used to store client files. There were very few, however. Her business wasn't doing well.

It didn't take long before we completed our search. We were just about to leave when the door opened. Rose Bolton stood on the threshold, her hand on the door handle, and gasped upon seeing us.

"What are you two doing in here?"

I couldn't think of an excuse. Nor could Harry, apparently. We both stood silently staring back at her.

She didn't ask again. "Get out this instant or I'll scream for the police."

"You won't scream," Harry said calmly. "If you do, we'll be forced to tell D.S. Forrester of Scotland Yard that you blame Dr. Iverson for not diagnosing your sister's cancer. We'll also tell him you stole a key to enter the clinic before the murder of Isabel Kempsey."

"They won't believe I'm guilty. Duncan and I blame the *doctor* for Edith's death, not Mrs. Kempsey. Neither of us would harm her to punish him."

There was no way to untangle ourselves from our predicament except to admit the truth. "We've learned of a connection between them," I said. "One that gives you a motive."

She frowned. "What connection?"

"Mrs. Kempsey recommended the doctor to your sister."

"Nonsense."

"Dr. Iverson wrote Isabel Kempsey's name on Edith's medical file."

The frown deepened. "That's not right. Edith first learned about the doctor when Duncan worked for the Medical Electrical Company. The company supplied that ridiculous revitalizing device to Dr. Iverson. Edith thought it was a marvelous invention that could cure her weak constitution. She didn't realize she had cancer. She made an appointment at Iverson's clinic specifically so she could try that infernal machine, but no one recommended the clinic to her. She went of her own accord." She folded her arms and arched her brows, challenging.

Could we have misread the writing on Edith Hamlin's file? It had been difficult to read, after all. But no, I'd read Isabel Kempsey's name, as had Harry. Perhaps Edith had given her sister a different story, keeping Isabel's name out of it altogether. But why?

"I can see what you're thinking, Miss Fox," Miss Bolton went on. "I can assure you, my sister wouldn't have misled me. We were close. She told me everything." She looked away, her lips pressed tightly together. After she composed herself, she turned back to me. "I suspect you won't believe me, and nor should you. It's your job to be suspicious of everyone and every piece of information. I suggest you speak to my brother-in-law and ask to see Edith's personal effects. He'll have kept it all, every scrap of paper and jotted note she left behind in her little notebook. If you can't find Isabel Kempsey's name in there, then you'll know I'm telling the truth and they didn't know each other."

I removed the address book and notebook from my bag. "We've already looked. Please return these to Mr. Hamlin."

"You stole them!"

"Borrowed," I said. "We would appreciate it if you didn't tell him. We don't want to upset him."

She snatched them off me. "You've got a nerve."

"As do you," Harry reminded her.

"Yes. Well. It seems we're alike." Miss Bolton stepped aside, inviting us to leave.

The moment I stepped out of the office, she intercepted Harry behind me.

"You believed me when I said I worked for my father," she told him. "Admit it, Mr. Armitage, I'm a good detective."

"You're a good actress," he conceded. "You had me fooled."

She smiled at his praise. "I may have lied about a few things that day, but I didn't lie about wanting to work for you. I can do whatever is required of me, from typing to accompanying you when you interrogate suspects."

"I have all the help I need."

Miss Bolton's smile froze as her gaze flicked to me and back. "Of course."

"You shouldn't give up yet." Harry indicated the office. "Your business may well take off."

She sighed. "Not unless I get some more interesting and high-profile cases, and who'll give a woman those?"

"Perhaps you could team up with a man," I said. "One you trust, who sees you as an equal partner and won't take all the credit when you solve a case."

"And where will I find that unicorn?" she bit off.

"I found one at a hotel, but good men are everywhere."

"Not in my experience. And anyway, Miss Fox, you seem to forget that you haven't received any public recognition for solving cases. Mr. Armitage has, but not you. It seems to me you're not a team of equals, after all."

"My situation requires me to stay in the background."

"And if it didn't?" she scoffed.

"If it didn't," Harry said tightly, "I would sing her praises loudly." He pushed past her and together we crossed the road.

Once we turned the corner, I took his arm. It was rigid with tension. "Don't let her bitterness bother you, Harry. I am perfectly happy with our arrangement. We make an excellent team, and she's simply envious of my good fortune."

The tension melted from his muscles. One of the good things about Harry's temper was that it rarely appeared and when it did, it faded quickly. "We *are* an excellent team, Cleo, but there's no denying you've been the one to solve most of our cases. Even if I can't tell the journalists that, at least I can tell you."

I hugged his arm. "Thank you, Harry. Perhaps one day I can have my name in the newspapers and on your door."

He laughed softly.

I rubbed his sleeve with my thumb. "I couldn't have solved the cases without your help."

"Yes, you could have. But you wouldn't have had nearly as much fun."

* * *

ACCUSING one's client of murder could be a disastrous business move, but if anyone could get away with it, it would be Harry. In his most diplomatic manner, he asked Dr. Iverson if Isabel Kempsey had accepted the ending of their relationship or if she'd been bitter.

The doctor hesitated before answering. "She took it well enough. Mr. Armitage, I don't understand how that matters."

Mrs. Iverson sat in her usual seat with the same stoicism I'd come to expect from her. Nothing seemed to faze her, not her husband being taken to Scotland Yard for questioning, not discovering he was having an affair with a patient, and not our continued interrogation when Harry was supposed to be on his side. Now she calmly explained why the question was being asked. "Because if she was bitter, and made threats, then you may have killed her to stop her following through on those threats."

"Good God, man!" Dr. Iverson exploded. "Why would I engage your services if I were guilty?"

"As a ruse to make it appear as though you're innocent," his wife continued.

"It's necessary to rule you out altogether," Harry added.

Dr. Iverson dragged both hands over his face, muttering something unintelligible as he did so. He still looked exhausted from his ordeal, his face somewhat ashen. Guilty or not, he was certainly anxious. "Isabel was sad that our relationship ended, but she agreed it was necessary after her husband found out. You have my word. Is that enough?"

"Were you in a relationship with anyone else?" Harry asked.

Dr. Iverson shot to his feet. "I fail to see how that is important."

"Do sit down," Mrs. Iverson said. "Mr. Armitage is your best chance of clearing your name. You know the truth won't upset me, so please just answer him." A measure of frustration crept into her tone, but I suspected it was frustration at her husband for hesitating because he was worried about her feelings rather than because of his guilt.

Dr. Iverson hitched his trouser legs and sat. "There were others before Isabel, but they weren't what I'd term a relationship. They were merely dalliances, and they were over by the time I began with Isabel. There has been no one since."

"Were any of the dalliances with men?" Harry asked.

The question earned quite a strong reaction from both the Iversons. The doctor once again shot to his feet, loudly protesting. His wife's reaction was rather different. After a small gasp, she laughed.

I was far more interested in her than her husband. She seemed genuinely surprised by the notion. To me, the response was rather telling. If she was surprised, it meant we were wrong. This smart, observant woman would have noticed if her husband liked men in that way. Despite their unconventional relationship, they'd been married a long time —long enough to have a son of university age. She must know him well.

Dr. Iverson shook his finger a mere inch from Harry's nose. "Who told you that? Whoever it is, they're lying! I've had dozens of women! A hundred, probably. I've *never* been with a man. Never even desired one. Not even you, Armitage, and Miss Wainsmith says you're very handsome."

Mrs. Iverson rolled her eyes. "How is that question relevant to your investigation, Mr. Armitage?"

Harry gently but firmly moved the doctor's finger away from his face. "It was merely a theory based on the location for the meeting place stipulated in that anonymous note to Dr. Iverson that was found in Mrs. Kempsey's things."

Dr. Iverson tugged on his jacket hem then sat again. "Ah. I see. Your theory is that you think I killed her because she discovered I...like men. Well, I can assure you that theory is quite wrong on several points, the strongest of which being that I am *not* of that persuasion. Further, my relationship with Isabel ended by mutual agreement. Neither of us had reason to be upset with the other."

"And yet you don't seem particularly distressed by her murder."

"Of course I'm distressed! Just because I'm not spilling tears doesn't mean it hasn't affected me. It has."

I tended to believe him, based on his appearance. Some of

the exhaustion could be attributed to his heartache over losing someone he cared about.

"Before you ask," Mrs. Iverson said, "I want to assure you that I also didn't kill her out of jealousy or concern that she was going to expose my husband's infidelity or ruin his reputation. I hope you believe me, Miss Fox."

Surprised to be singled out when I'd said very little so far, I blinked at her. "Me?"

"I sense you're quite intuitive when it comes to judging a person's honesty, or lack of."

"I don't think I'm particularly intuitive. No more so than Mr. Armitage, at least."

Her smile was rather dismissive. "May I also be so bold as to suggest that whoever killed Mrs. Kempsey wanted to make a statement about my husband by murdering her in his consulting room."

"I say," her husband protested.

His wife ignored him and continued to address me. "Perhaps the killer wanted to cause my husband's practice some difficulty. Who would do that? Not merely someone who feels wronged by him, but someone who was wronged *medically*. A former patient he couldn't cure, or the loved ones of a patient who died while under his care."

"I assure you, we have considered those theories," Harry told her.

"Good. That is why he hired you."

Dr. Iverson straightened. "Pierce! That fellow blames me for his wife's death, even though it was nothing to do with me. Her excessive anxiety caused her to waste away. I can't perform miracles, but he seemed to think I should have cured her."

"We spoke to him," Harry said. "He blames both you and the tonic you prescribed for his wife's nerves."

"The Nerve Elixir." The doctor sniffed. "There's nothing wrong with it. It's strong, yes, but it does wonders to revive a weak constitution. You should see my patients after a dose of it. It's like witnessing a wilting flower enjoy a fresh bloom. Isn't it, my dear? You've used it. I wouldn't prescribe it to my own wife if I didn't believe in it, and trust it was safe." In my opinion, his effusive protest was proof that he knew it caused addiction but refused to acknowledge it.

Mrs. Iverson leveled her gaze with mine. "I stopped using it when I no longer needed it. We don't have bottles in the house anymore."

I couldn't tell if she knew or suspected it had addictive qualities, but her direct gaze was unnerving. I'd planned to say a number of things to Dr. Iverson about the tonic, but the words withered on my tongue.

Harry, however, had no such qualms. "I think everyone in this room knows the reviving effects of the tonic are temporary. The Nerve Elixir contains cocaine, which scientists now believe is highly addictive. Something you would be well aware of, Doctor, since I'm sure you keep up with the latest medical journals."

Dr. Iverson cleared his throat. "Back to Pierce. He must be your strongest suspect, considering he barged into my clinic and caused a scene."

"We have doubts that he has the knowledge required to tamper with an electric device."

"Isn't he the caretaker for St. James's Hall? I recall his wife saying he managed it, but when I pressed her she admitted he was merely the caretaker. Most of my patients are married to nobility or wealthy businessmen, so the conversation stayed with me. I'm sure a caretaker of a music hall would have an understanding of electricity."

We'd dismissed Mr. Pierce because of the faulty light in his hallway that he seemed unable to fix, but perhaps he'd simply not got around to it in his grief-stricken state.

Or perhaps he'd deliberately steered us away from the truth because he knew it made him a suspect.

In light of the new information, we decided to call on him again.

* * *

As with the last time, Mr. Pierce looked and smelled worse than Floyd after a night carousing with his chums and other disreputable persons. He squinted reddened eyes at us, even though the sun was covered by a gray London miasma. I couldn't tell whether the redness was from excessive drink or grief, but it didn't matter. The excessive drink was a product of his grief.

Mr. Pierce took a moment to recognize us, but when he did, he stepped aside to let us in. He scrubbed at his stubbled jaw, as if embarrassed that he hadn't shaved. Ash fell from a cigarette clutched between the finger and thumb of his other hand onto the floor tiles. Even in the poor light I could tell they needed a good clean.

Harry flipped the switch to turn on the hall light. It still didn't work. "You haven't fixed it."

Mr. Pierce blinked up at the ceiling. "So?"

"You work as a caretaker at St. James's Hall."

Mr. Pierce rubbed the back of his head so vigorously I worried he'd make his hair fall out. "I've taken some time off. What of it?"

"I'm just wondering why you haven't fixed the light."

Mr. Pierce's shrug seemed to take considerable effort, as if his shoulders weighed heavily on him.

All of a sudden, a well of sympathy rose within me. Although I was very aware that this man planned to sabotage an event at the hotel in two days, I felt sorry for him.

"I'm going to make you a cup of tea," I said. "You're going to find a ladder to fix that light and have a chat with Mr. Armitage." I gave Harry a speaking look. Hopefully he understood I wanted him to talk Mr. Pierce out of his plan, as well as discover how much he knew about electricity.

I entered the kitchen at the end of the short hall with a hand over my nose to block the smell of rotting food. It quickly became clear there was no point making tea when there were dirty dishes piled up. Much like Duncan Hamlin, Mr. Pierce's grief had stripped him of his will to maintain hygienic standards.

I warmed up a pot of water on the range then poured it

into the trough. With a bar of carbolic soap and a brush, I set to work scrubbing at the dishes, leaving them to dry on the bench on a clean cloth I found in a drawer.

I'd barely begun when Mr. Pierce entered the kitchen and sat down on a chair at the table with a heavy sigh. He drew on his cigarette and stared directly ahead. Harry was nowhere in sight.

"Mr. Pierce?" I asked. "Have you fixed the light?"

He waved the cigarette in the direction of the hall. "He's doing it."

The entire point had been to get *him* to do it so we could tell if he had knowledge of electricity or not. I peered down the hall to see Harry on the ladder.

"Do you have any food in the house?" I asked. "Any fresh food?"

He waved the cigarette at a wall. "The neighbor brings me things from time to time." He plugged the cigarette into his mouth and sucked deeply.

I continued cleaning the dishes. "Last time we were here, you said you were going to ruin the Bella Vita Company's event at the Mayfair Hotel. I hope you've changed your mind."

"Of course I haven't! That quack takes advantage of the vulnerable. He needs to be exposed. *I'm* going to expose him. I'll punish him for murdering my wife!"

"He didn't murder your wife," Harry said from the doorway.

Mr. Pierce rested his elbows on his knees and lowered his head.

"The hall light is fixed," Harry said, joining me at the trough. "The empty bottles have been removed to the court-yard and the rubbish taken out." He handed me a dirty teacup and leaned closer. "Sir Ronald would have a fit if he saw you doing menial work," he said, keeping his voice low so Mr. Pierce couldn't hear.

"Then it's fortunate he doesn't see me help Harmony tidy my suite every morning." I swapped a washed plate for the dirty cup. "You are aware that I wasn't brought up with a silver spoon in my mouth, aren't you? I had to cook and clean when I lived with my grandparents."

"I know." The mischievous look in his eye had me watching him carefully.

"Go on. Out with it, Harry. Tell me I've turned into a duchess."

The mischievous look turned to mock innocence. "I was merely going to praise you for settling so well into your new life that no one would guess you'd ever set foot in a kitchen before."

I flicked water in his direction, but only a few drops landed on his sleeve. "And what evidence are you basing such an opinion on?"

He showed me the plate that still had something encrusted on it.

"You distracted me," I said pertly.

"Forgive me, Duchess, but I won't apologize for being *your* distraction."

I laughed.

It wasn't until Mr. Pierce got up and walked out of the kitchen that Harry and I realized how insensitive our playfulness had been. We hurriedly finished the dishes, made Mr. Pierce a cup of tea, and bade him good day without even giving him a warning to stay away from Mr. Lombardi and the Mayfair Hotel.

* * *

I'D ENJOYED the Saturday Pops at St. James's Hall three times since moving to London. Flossy was fond of the music played at the popular concerts, and even more fond of escaping her parents' suffocating scrutiny. The Saturday afternoon concerts held a short stroll from the hotel were an acceptable occasion for me to act as her chaperone, and it gave us both something to do in between our other social engagements and my investigations.

Harry and I accessed the building via the side entrance used by staff and musicians. From somewhere deep inside came the whine of violins tuning up, followed by the lower hum of the cello. We made our way toward it, only to be stopped by a middle-aged man with a pencil tucked behind his ear and shirtsleeves rolled to his elbows.

"May I help you?" he asked.

Harry introduced us as private detectives. "We're making inquiries about Mr. Pierce, an employee here."

"Former employee," the man said. "He was dismissed for drunkenness."

Dismissed! That must have been quite a blow coming after his wife's death. No wonder he was struggling.

"I see," Harry said. "Is it true he was the caretaker?"

"He was. I'm his replacement. I only started yesterday, so I'm afraid I can't help you if you want to know what he was like. Do you want me to find someone who did know him?"

"That's not necessary. Can you tell us what Mr. Pierce's job entailed?"

"That I can do. The caretaker keeps this whole place operating smoothly." He tapped his chest. "Without me, it would fall apart. I make sure everything's in working order, from the audience's seats to the stage, and everything backstage."

"Does that involve lighting?"

"It does."

"Do you get electricians in to fix the lights, or do you do it?"

"I do it all."

"So you have some knowledge of how electricity works."

The caretaker frowned. "I know how not to electrocute myself, if that's what you mean."

Harry thanked him and we left.

"I have renewed sympathy for Pierce," I said. "I'm glad I washed his dishes."

Harry agreed. "Dismissing him when he's already suffering from the loss of his wife isn't fair. It's no wonder he's angry with the world."

"You have more knowledge about electricity than I do," I went on. "Do you think Mr. Pierce's work as a caretaker means he would know how to tamper with the Electro Therapy Machine?"

"If he knew how *not* to electrocute himself, then he also knows how to tamper with the wiring to ensure it *did* electrocute when switched on."

Considering he was angry at the world, Mr. Pierce might not care who the device electrocuted. Also, he couldn't have known that the first patient to use it had a heart problem. He may not have *intended* to kill anyone, merely ruin Dr. Iverson.

Whether Isabel Kempsey's death was accidental or intentional, Mr. Pierce must be considered a suspect.

r. Hobart greeted me the moment I entered the hotel foyer. It was late in the afternoon, but not yet time for him to leave. He was all smiles as he asked me how my day had been.

"Productive," I said. "And yours?"

"Pleasant, thank you." The manager did enjoy his work, although I suspected he wouldn't describe it as pleasant if he was answering someone who wasn't related to the Bainbridge family. "I've been tasked with informing you about three things, Miss Fox. The first is to give you a message from Sir Ronald. You are expected to join the family at dinner tonight."

"Thank you. And the second thing?"

"There is a meeting tomorrow afternoon at four to discuss specifics for security at the Bella Vita Company's presentation. I thought you should be there, considering you know this Pierce fellow. Harry should, too. I'll telephone him before I leave to let him know."

"I'll be there. And the third thing?"

"Miss Cotton wishes to see you if you can spare the time. She's using my office to make some telephone calls."

"Thank you, Mr. Hobart." I was about to walk off when I thought of something. "Have you bought Harry a gift for his birthday?"

"My wife bought him a tie and matching handkerchief. She spent quite a bit of time last night embroidering his initials into the latter."

"I don't know what to get him. Do you have any ideas?"

"None. If we did, we'd buy something more interesting than a tie."

I sighed. "It's in three days and I can't think of a single thing."

"Your presence at his birthday lunch will be gift enough for him, I'm sure."

"You're too kind, Mr. Hobart, but I must arrive with something. His mother will think poorly of me if I don't."

"Ah. If the gift is to impress my indomitable sister-in-law rather than Harry himself, then may I advise something that proves you know him well. Nothing ostentatious or expensive, but shows you care enough that you want to give him something that reflects his character." The corners of his eyes crinkled with his smile. "Not a tie or handkerchief. I hope that helps."

I thanked him and walked off, feeling more anxious about what to get Harry than before.

Harmony was just hanging up the telephone earpiece when I entered Mr. Hobart's office. I indicated the desk, the telephone and papers. "This suits you, Harmony."

"Getting my own office is a long way off, Cleo, but thank you. I've finished here, and Mr. Hobart will be requiring his office back. Shall we go up to your suite?"

"All right, but what did you need to talk to me about?"

"I thought you might want help doing your hair for dinner tonight."

"You're not my maid at the moment. You don't have to do my hair."

She rounded the desk, clutching a folder full of papers. "I want to."

"Don't be silly, Harmony. I'll ask Jane or one of the other maids."

"I insist."

"This isn't about my hair, is it? You want to talk to me."

She sniffed. "Very well, I admit it. I've missed our chats after you've spent a day investigating."

We'd had breakfast together that morning, but I didn't remind her of that. I looped my arm through hers. "I've missed them, too. But you can chat to me of an evening without doing my hair. You don't need an excuse."

"I'm doing it anyway. Jane isn't as good, and neither of us will be as carefree with our conversation with her around." She had a point.

Once in my suite, I put in an order to the kitchen through the speaking tube for tea to be sent up. After it was delivered by one of the footmen, we both took off our shoes and sat on the sofa with contented sighs.

"Tell me what you learned today," Harmony said. "Have you narrowed down your list of suspects?"

"We'll discuss the investigation in a moment, but first, I have to ask you something more important."

"More important than solving a murder?"

"Perhaps not quite, but it is tying my stomach in knots just thinking about it."

"You poor thing. Is it Mr. Lombardi?"

"It's Harry's birthday present. I don't know what to get him."

"A tie? Handkerchief?"

"It's the first birthday gift I'll ever get him, and there'll never be another first. It needs to be special."

"You could embroider the handkerchief yourself."

"Aside from the fact that Mr. and Mrs. Hobart are giving him that exact thing, I do not think my embroidery skills are up to the task. I'm adequate, at best."

"You'll think of something, Cleo."

I sighed. She was even less help than Mr. Hobart.

"You will," she insisted. "You have good instincts."

I pulled a face. "Not always. For instance, Mr. Lombardi likes men as well as women, but I would never have guessed. Possibly Dr. Iverson, too, although he vehemently denies it. That's two men in a matter of days, and I was quite oblivious. I can't always trust my instincts."

"Men who like men are very good at hiding their nature. They have to be. You *can* trust your instincts, Cleo. They're right about most things."

I studied her over the rim of my teacup, but she seemed quite serious. "Are you forgetting that I accused Harry of murder last Christmas, based on instinct?"

"That doesn't count. It was your way of flirting with him."

"Hardly. I wasn't interested in him at that time."

"Ha!"

"Also, it's a terrible way to flirt with a man. 'Excuse me, sir.'" I playfully batted my eyelashes at her. "'You're far too handsome and charming to be true, so you must be guilty of poisoning the guest.'"

She laughed softly. "I didn't say you were a *good* flirt."

I giggled. "At least I didn't pretend to eat food I don't like to flirt with one of the cooks."

"I do like Victor's cooking!"

"I saw you stuff the results of his experimental flourless cake into your apron pocket."

"I was saving it for later."

"You took a bite first and told him it was delicious."

She flashed a grin. "It was truly awful. Fortunately, we're now at a point where we don't have to flirt anymore or try to impress one another."

I sighed again. "Unfortunately, Harry and I are not at that point. I have to buy him something special for his birthday."

"Trust your instincts, Cleo. They *are* good. You'll think of something to get him. Now, drink up then let's choose you something to wear to dinner."

* * *

IF I'D KNOWN who we were dining with, I might not have gone out of my way to look nice. The last person whose attention I wanted to attract was Mr. Lombardi. Unfortunately, he and I were the first to arrive at the table.

Mr. Lombardi took advantage of being alone and trapped

my hand in his. He drew it to his lips but didn't kiss it. "It is a pleasure to dine with a beautiful lady."

"Two ladies. My cousin will be joining us any moment." I tried to remove my hand, but he held it tightly. I was glad I was wearing gloves so I couldn't feel the hair of his moustache or his breath on my bare skin.

"Of course, of course. Miss Bainbridge is a flower, but you, Miss Fox, are a gem. A diamond, if I may be so bold." He finally kissed my hand.

I whipped it away. His smile didn't waver, however. He moved his chair closer to mine.

"I am very glad that we can speak alone, Miss Fox. I think you and I understand each other, yes?"

"No, I don't think we do."

"Ah, but I sense you are a woman of great spirit. I think you like adventure, and I am a great traveler." Was he suggesting I run away with him? "You were an orphan, and I did not have my family's support."

"Our situations are not the same, Mr. Lombardi."

His hand whipped out and grasped mine again, catching me unawares. "I worked hard to be successful, but now I can enjoy my success." His tongue darted out beneath the moustache like a woodland creature inspecting its surroundings. "I would like to enjoy it with *you* while I am in London, Miss Fox. I am a generous man. *Very* generous."

Harmony told me I had good instincts. I was going to trust them now and be rude to a guest. I snatched my hand out of his grip, shifted my chair away, and grabbed the fish fork. "Touch me again and I will stab you in the thigh."

He tipped his head back and laughed.

Floyd approached, frowning. "Did my cousin say something amusing?" He may have addressed Mr. Lombardi, but he watched me closely.

"She is a diamond, Mr. Bainbridge. Exquisite. I cannot believe she is not married. In Italy, she would have been snapped up by now." He snapped his fingers. "Women of such passion are rare jewels, particularly in England I have found."

Floyd's frown deepened. "Passion? Cleo?"

I set the fork down beside the others. "Mr. Lombardi was telling me how he is a very successful businessman. I was about to respond by asking if that's due to the popularity of the Nerve Elixir."

"Yes, it is." Mr. Lombardi straightened his shoulders, puffing out his chest. "I do not want to boast, as I know you English do not like that, but my tonic is the best in Europe. Perhaps the world!"

"I thought you didn't mean to boast," Floyd said, his smile hard.

"Ah! But it is not me who says this. It is everyone. The actress Sarah Bernhardt, the writers Rudyard Kipling and Jules Verne. Even your queen says it is fortifying!" Mr. Lombardi emphasized the statement with raised arms, as if he were an evangelist preaching to his disciples.

"I have read the advertising material, Mr. Lombardi. It is quite the list of testimonials you've acquired. As a fellow businessman, I admire your promotional endeavors."

Mr. Lombardi attempted to look humble but failed. "It is only because the tonic is so very good at curing all manner of ills. Have you tried it, Mr. Bainbridge?"

"No. I'm not ill."

"I will give you a bottle tomorrow. I have been wanting to give one to your mother, but I have not seen much of Lady Bainbridge in the hotel. I think she suffers from her nerves, yes? She will benefit from my tonic, I guarantee. The entire world cannot be wrong."

Floyd's fingers skimmed over the silver cutlery. I hoped he had enough control not to pick up the fork and threaten the guest the way I had. I doubted Mr. Lombardi would report me to my uncle, given it would mean revealing the reason I wanted to stab him, but I doubted Floyd could get away with it. To alleviate some of the tension I sensed Floyd was feeling, I was about to mention the article in the Italian newspaper that discussed the closure of Mr. Lombardi's factories but decided against it. I didn't want to reveal all the cards in my hand yet.

At the restaurant entrance, Mr. Chapman greeted Uncle Ronald and Flossy. They all looked at us before my uncle and cousin approached our table. While my uncle stopped to speak to a guest, I put a smile on my face and asked Mr. Lombardi a question that I hoped would unsettle him. "The Nerve Elixir is your bestselling product, is that right?"

He looked pleased that I was taking an interest. "It is, because it is so powerful, so good. Many people suffer from melancholy, particularly women, but my tonic revives them. It gives them energy." His hands gestured to his torso with a lifting motion.

"So your marketing materials say. What I want to know, however, is what happens if it stops selling?"

He tilted his head to the side. "I do not understand the question."

"If sales of the Nerve Elixir fall significantly, does your business fail?"

Floyd stood as Flossy arrived at our table, having left her father behind.

Mr. Lombardi didn't stand. He continued to stare at me. "Sales will not fall, Miss Fox. There is nothing wrong with the ingredients in my tonic."

"I didn't say there was." I turned to my cousin. "Flossy, dearest, you're here. Come and sit down. No, not beside Mr. Lombardi. He wants Uncle Ronald to sit on his other side tonight so they can more easily discuss business matters." I may be stuck with him, as it was impolite to swap places now, but I could save Flossy. Hopefully, the horrid man wouldn't dare flirt with me—or try anything else—after I'd threatened him with the fork.

The dinner was surprisingly, and blessedly, short. Mr. Lombardi excused himself before dessert and left. Uncle Ronald ate his vanilla blancmange quickly, then got up to mingle with hotel guests, leaving me with my two cousins.

Flossy pushed her trifle away, untouched. "Pretending to enjoy listening to that man is the absolute worst. The sooner he checks out, the better."

Floyd leaned across her to speak to me, forcing her to sit

back. "What were you and Lombardi talking about when I arrived, Cleo? I want the truth this time."

I was going to lie, but decided there was no point. Besides, Flossy needed to be warned. "His flirtation crossed a line."

"That bloody cur. Just say the word and I'll call him out."

Flossy screwed up her nose at him. "Don't be silly. You couldn't duel with a fly, let alone a man."

"It wasn't anything I couldn't handle," I said. "Do not cause a scene, Floyd. Not until after his event is over, and, even then, wait until he has left the hotel altogether if you must say something to him."

Somewhat mollified, he sat back and finished his dessert.

I ate mine, too, but hardly tasted the ice cream. I couldn't stop thinking about all the famous people who'd endorsed the Nerve Elixir. "Do you think Lombardi personally knows the people who've given testimonials praising his tonic?" I asked Floyd.

"He told me he sent them all free samples of the tonic and asked them to write back endorsing it if it worked. He says he has thousands of positive reviews, but only uses the most famous people in his advertisements."

"It must have been expensive to send free samples all around the world," Flossy said.

"It's ingenious. Think about it, Flossy. If you needed a new medicine, would you try the one endorsed by the queen or the one that fellow over there says cured him?" He pointed to a man at a far table.

"The queen, of course."

"It may have been expensive sending all those bottles, but it was a successful endeavor."

Flossy didn't seem to be listening anymore. She longingly eyed her dessert.

Floyd followed her gaze. "Are you going to eat that?"

She shook her head, and he swapped his empty bowl for her full one.

"Aren't connections interesting," I murmured. "Those important and well-known people trusted Lombardi enough to try his tonic. He must have met them before."

"He claims he hadn't," Floyd said.

Perhaps the connection was fleeting, a few moments at a gathering, an encounter in a hotel foyer...

Was Isabel Kempsey and Edith Hamlin's connection fleeting? An introduction at a luncheon, a shared interest that led to paths crossing? It was odd that neither spouse nor sister of each woman had heard of the other, but not entirely impossible. They may not have been friends as I'd thought, but mere acquaintances.

Or their relationship had been a secret one.

Once our desserts were finished, we three left the restaurant together. Mr. Chapman bade as goodnight as we passed him and we entered the hotel foyer. Floyd excused himself and headed to the post desk to pick up a newspaper. The desk was unmanned, Terence having gone home hours ago, but looking at the pigeonholes behind where he would usually stand got me thinking. I pictured him going through the mail after it arrived, sorting it into the holes, ready to be collected by guests. Mail for the hotel itself was set aside for the appropriate senior member of staff. All the mail to the hotel came through Terence, and he was very good at making sure it got into the right hands.

Usually. There'd been an occasion when the mail had been sorted incorrectly. Flossy had received post meant for her brother because Terence read the name incorrectly.

The letter setting up the meeting outside the Café Royal that had been discovered in Isabel Kempsey's things after her death may not have been intended for Dr. Iverson at all. Without the envelope, and with no name on the letter, we couldn't be sure. Nor could he. He'd simply assumed it was meant for him because it was among his other mail.

Assumptions could cause mistakes in investigations. They could lead to the wrong paths being taken and incorrect conclusions being made. Despite our experience, Harry and I had made a fundamental mistake and assumed the same thing as Dr. Iverson.

* * *

DR. IVERSON WAS BACK at work the next day, much to Miss Wainsmith's relief. "I wasn't looking forward to spending another day turning patients away." She kept her voice low so that the women in the waiting area couldn't hear. "Although Sister Dearden is a marvelous substitute, and I would personally be happy to be seen by her, most prefer the doctor. It's not just his professional knowledge, it's his manner." Her gaze turned wistful. "He can be so understanding, his calm temperament is like a soothing balm for fragile nerves." Her cheeks flushed as she busied herself with the appointment book. "So the patients tell me." She cleared her throat. "Do you need to speak to him, Mr. Armitage?"

"Actually, it's you we came to see."

"Me? Oh. How can I help?"

"We have more questions about the anonymous letter found in Isabel Kempsey's things, the one setting up a meeting on Regent Street."

"I already told you. I don't remember it at all."

"But you must have received it from the postman and given it to Dr. Iverson along with his other letters."

"I know I must have, but I honestly don't remember it."

"Wouldn't it be a thing you remembered?" I asked. "An anonymous letter suggesting to meet at a particular place at a particular time. It's all rather clandestine. I think I'd remember it if I saw it."

Miss Wainsmith chewed on her lower lip. "I suppose." Her lips parted with a gasp. "Oh! Perhaps it arrived on a day I wasn't here. I've been a little unwell off and on for a few weeks. When did the doctor say he received it?"

"Five days before Mrs. Kempsey's death."

She counted back on her fingers. "That was Wednesday. Yes, I was ill that day. Mrs. Iverson filled in for me. She's familiar with how things work here, so it's easy for her to slip into the role rather than get a temporary girl in. In fact, she used to be a receptionist years ago at a different practice. That's where she met Dr. Iverson. I'm sure she'll remember the letter. She's very clever." Her brow suddenly furrowed. "Wait a moment. Wasn't she there when you asked me about it the first time? I think she was. I wonder why she didn't say anything at the time. Perhaps she didn't remember seeing it, after all."

"It would seem so," Harry said, his tone easygoing. "Thank you, Miss Wainsmith. You've been very helpful."

Miss Wainsmith smiled. "I'm so glad. I do want to help the doctor. Having this sword hanging over his head is a terrible burden to carry."

Her metaphors may have been mixed, but the resulting imagery was clear.

The consulting suite door opened and a patient emerged. She thanked the doctor and expressed her pleasure at seeing him again. "I'm sure this nasty business will all be over soon. I engaged the services of Mrs. Cook, the medium, and she spoke to her spirit guide right in front of me. The guide assured Mrs. Cook that your name would soon be cleared of all wrongdoing, Doctor."

Dr. Iverson touched the patient's elbow. "That's very comforting to know."

Sister Dearden walked out of the consulting suite with the patient and closed the door behind her. "Perhaps you could ask this Mrs. Cook to speak to her spirit guide again and speed up the process of finding the murderer." She shot a glare at Harry. "That would be most helpful."

The patient's smile froze as she seemed to be trying to gauge whether Sister Dearden was being sarcastic or not.

Harry and I left the clinic ahead of the patient who remained to make another appointment. "That was enlightening," Harry said as he placed his hat on his head.

"Indeed. If Mrs. Cook's spirit guide believes the case will be solved soon, then we're on the right path this time. She's a very famous medium."

He'd been looking back at the door, but his gaze now slid to me. "You believe in spirit mediums?"

Watching him struggle not to show any signs of disapproval was rather amusing, so I couldn't help teasing him a little longer. "I can see you're a skeptic, but is it a problem if I do believe in ghosts and mediums?"

"I, er… No, it isn't. If you believe, Cleo, then it doesn't bother me. I accept everything about you."

"Even if you think I'm a crackpot? That is sweet of you, Harry."

His smile was uncertain. Like the patient with Sister Dearden, he couldn't tell if the remark was serious or not.

I decided to put him out of his misery. Besides, I could no longer contain my laughter. "While I don't have any strong opinion about the existence of ghosts, I do think spirit mediums like Mrs. Cook are frauds. You can rest assured I won't be seeking the services of one."

"Was that a test?"

"No, but if it had been, you'd have passed with flying colors."

"Good. I think." He indicated we should walk on, and I fell into step beside him. "If *I* believed mediums could really communicate with spirits, would you still want to be with me?"

"Of course," I said. "It would solve the issue of what to buy you every birthday. I'd simply pay for a session with a medium and be done with it."

He laughed softly. "You know you don't need to buy me anything. Your presence at my family lunch will be gift enough for me."

"So you and Mr. Hobart keep saying."

"Uncle Alfred said that? How did you respond?"

"Never mind that. But if you do have any gift ideas, please give me a very large hint." We rounded the corner, heading in the direction of the Iversons' house without having discussed our destination. "Why do you think Miss Wainsmith didn't tell us Mrs. Iverson replaced her on the day Dr. Iverson read the anonymous letter the first time we asked her about it?"

Harry shrugged. "Perhaps she simply forgot. Or she didn't match the day of the letter's arrival with the day she wasn't there. The more important question is, why didn't Mrs. Iverson tell us? She must have been the one to pass it on to him, and we mentioned it to her husband in front of her."

"For the same reasons as Miss Wainsmith, I suppose. She didn't realize it was that day." Even as I said it, I didn't believe it. Mrs. Iverson must have been the one to handle it, so why not say so? "Harry, I think we need to seriously consider Mrs. Iverson is the killer."

His pace slowed. "I agree, except for one thing. If we presume the anonymous letter is from a lover, either male or female, why would she pass it on to her husband? Why would she want him to carry on the affair?" When I didn't respond, he answered his own question. "Because she doesn't love him. Not even a little. She hasn't shown any feeling toward him, neither anger nor sorrow, despite learning some rather shocking things about him. I can accept she's not an emotional woman, but to show absolutely nothing is very odd."

I wasn't convinced, however. "There's something about her that I can't put my finger on. I feel uneasy in her presence and I'm not entirely sure why, but what if it's because I'm sensing she's lying? Perhaps she's faking indifference about her husband's affairs so that we'll *think* she doesn't have a motive to set him up for Isabel Kempsey's murder."

Harry stopped walking altogether. "You make a good point. All right, let's assume she's faking a lack of emotion and she is in fact jealous or vengeful. We can't be certain she has any electrical knowledge yet, but we do know she had access to her husband's key and the appointment book, so she knew when Isabel Kempsey was due in."

"Did *you* feel uneasy in her presence?" I asked.

"No, but I believe you when you say you did. You have good instincts, Cleo."

Either he and Harmony were colluding, or they were both right. I would trust my instincts about Mrs. Iverson, although I wished I could put my finger on why I felt uneasy in her presence.

"As much as I'd like to confront her about the letter to see her reaction, I don't think we should," Harry went on. "She's not going to blurt it all out.

"Not without proof," I agreed. "Before we confront her,

we need to be sure about her feelings, or lack thereof, for her husband. I think we should get a third opinion."

"From whom?"

"I have someone in mind." I set off along the street at a brisk pace. "I'll tell you on the way."

CHAPTER 12

Given the last time we spoke to Rose Bolton had been a rather tense affair after we broke into her office, I expected to be met with opposition to our suggestion. She agreed immediately, however, right after Harry offered to pay her. At first he'd protested against my suggestion of hiring her to approach Mrs. Iverson since she was also a suspect, but I managed to convince him after reminding him that Rose had proved she was an excellent actress, fooling us both, and Mrs. Iverson had never met her. The day Rose stole Sister Dearden's key while pretending to be Mary Linton, Mrs. Iverson hadn't been there.

Between the three of us, we settled on a ruse that would hopefully get Mrs. Iverson talking, giving Rose a thorough idea of her character and feelings—or lack thereof—for Dr. Iverson. She was going to pretend to be a journalist writing a piece about how the murder had affected Dr. Iverson's wife. The viewpoint of the wife was one that a female journalist working for a women's periodical would be more likely to take than a male reporter. We suggested some questions she could ask, but it was Rose herself who said she'd try to get Mrs. Iverson to admit she'd do anything for her husband. It wouldn't be considered a confession, but it would be a small crack that we could widen if we applied pressure.

Rose was enthusiastic about the scheme. She seemed to like playacting. I said as much to Harry as we waited around the corner from the Iversons' house. "Do you think we can trust her, when she's so good at putting on an act?"

He hesitated before answering. "I'm not sure. I believed her when she said she knows of no connection between her sister and Isabel Kempsey, but it's possible she was acting then, too."

"But you don't think she was," I finished for him.

He leaned against the side wall of the last townhouse in the row and crossed his arms. "Did you believe her?"

"Yes, but I feel as though my instincts can't be trusted on this case, despite what you say. I would never have guessed that Mr. Lombardi had a predilection for men, for instance." I pulled a face at the mention of his name. "Horrid man, but not for that particular reason. There are many other reasons, though."

"You have that look in your eye, Cleo. I'd be worried if I were him."

"He should be. I almost stabbed him in the thigh with a fork at dinner."

Harry stilled. "What did he do?"

"Nothing a firm poke with a fork couldn't resolve."

He cupped the side of my face and his thumb gently stroked my cheek. "Are you sure you're all right?"

I placed my hand over his and nodded.

I was about to speak when Rose Bolton rounded the corner. She sported a smug smile.

"Did Mrs. Iverson admit she'd do anything for her husband?" I asked.

"No. I don't think she cares a whit for him. I pretended to empathize with her, telling her that as a woman whose husband had also been wrongly accused of a crime, I understood what she was going through. I mentioned my suffering, *et cetera*. She remained emotionless throughout."

"Then why do you look like the cat that got the cream?"

"Because you may be the detective who solved all those

murders, Miss Fox, but *I've* discovered something about Mrs. Iverson that *you* did not."

"What?"

"She's a sapphic."

I stared at her. Beside me, Harry shifted his weight from one foot to the other.

"It means she likes to have relationships with women," Rose went on.

"I know what it means." I thought back through my encounters with Mrs. Iverson. It all began to click into place. My unease in her presence wasn't because she was lying to us or because she was guilty—although she may very well be—it was because she'd taken a sapphic interest in me.

Rose Bolton's lips tilted with her wry smile. "You're blushing, Miss Fox. Does that mean she *did* look at you in a way that only men have before?"

"Her gazes did linger," I admitted. "And she showed an uncommon interest in me."

"She flirted with you," Harry said flatly.

"I suppose it was flirting, but I didn't realize it at the time. I thought she was playing some sort of strange game with her husband, encouraging *him* to flirt with me." It sounded ridiculous now that I thought about it, but it had never occurred to me that *she* was attracted to me.

Rose made a miffed sound through her nose. "Don't consider yourself special. She flirted with me, too."

"Did you let on that you guessed she was sapphic?" I asked.

She scoffed. "Of course not. I'm not a fool. Do you know, I'm not entirely sure she realized she was flirting."

"What do you mean?" Harry asked.

"I think she was admiring me without being aware of what she was doing."

"So she didn't intend anything to come of the admiration," he clarified.

"I suppose not. Do you have any more tasks for me, Mr. Armitage?"

"That's all. Thank you for your assistance."

"Don't thank me. Pay me. I apologize if that's too forward coming from a woman, but we don't all have the luxury of working for free because we live in a luxury hotel owned by our uncle."

"Well done, Miss Bolton," I said smoothly. I was determined not to let her ruffle my feathers. "When did you work it out?"

"I knew I'd heard your name somewhere, so I spent most of yesterday scouring old newspapers, focusing on the social pages. You were mentioned a few times in connection to the Bainbridges of the Mayfair Hotel, most recently when you attended a ball a few weeks ago."

I acknowledged her investigative endeavor with a shallow bow. "Congratulations."

Her lips pinched, perhaps in irritation that I wasn't more upset at being found out.

Harry broke the awkward silence. "You have my card with my office address. Come tomorrow and I'll pay your fee. If I'm not there, I'll leave it with Luigi in the Roma Café below."

Rose gave a curt nod, tugged on her jacket hem, and strode away.

"Well," I said, blowing out a breath. "That was enlightening."

"But not too surprising."

I frowned. "Why do you say that?"

"It stands to reason Mrs. Iverson found you attractive if she's that way inclined." His fingers skimmed mine. "You are lovely, Cleo."

"Oh. Uh. Thank you." When I realized I was touching the hair at the nape of my neck I dropped my hand to my side.

Harry smirked. "Come on. Let's confront her."

"Mrs. Iverson?"

"Yes."

"Now?"

"If you're too embarrassed—"

"I'm not embarrassed. I'm flattered and somewhat nervous, if I'm honest. What if I blush when she looks at me?"

"She'll think you're even prettier than she already does."

"That's not helpful, Harry."

"You'll be fine, Cleo. Just relax and follow my lead."

* * *

Now that I was aware of Mrs. Iverson's interest in me, the signs were obvious. I was somewhat used to the lingering gazes of men, the coy smiles, and their efforts to give the best impression of themselves, but I'd misunderstood those same cues from a woman. The meeting wasn't as unnerving as I thought it would be. Indeed, I felt quite flattered.

That is, until the tone of the encounter changed when Harry brought up the topic of the anonymous note. "Why didn't you tell us you were working the day it arrived in the clinic when we first mentioned it?"

"Was I?"

"Miss Wainsmith was ill. You worked at the reception desk last Wednesday in her stead."

"Did I? Goodness, I quite forgot."

"Come now, Mrs. Iverson. You don't expect us to believe that."

She bristled. "Are you calling me a liar?"

I decided to step in. Perhaps Mrs. Iverson's interest in me would work to our advantage and soften her a little. "When we mentioned it, you sat where you are now, and almost said something when we brought it up with your husband. But you didn't. It makes it seem as though you have something to hide."

Her long, bony fingers clasped together in her lap. It wasn't the softening I'd hoped for, but she remained silent, which I took to mean we were right.

"You received the letter along with the regular mail," I went on. "You placed it with your husband's other correspondence, knowing it was from a would-be lover."

"That's absurd. Why would I want him to meet a lover?"

"Because you have no interest in your husband."

She studied her interlocked fingers a moment before

lifting her gaze to mine. "You're right, Miss Fox. My husband and I are merely friends now. Intimacy ended when we realized we couldn't have more children after our son was born." She lifted her chin, challenging. "I'm not jealous of his lovers, so why would I murder one, if that's what you're suggesting? Let's assume I did want to murder Isabel Kempsey for some reason, why would I do it in my husband's clinic? His success is my success. Ruining his reputation and business would be an utterly stupid thing to do. Come now, Miss Fox. You're better than this."

Her rebuke stung, but I hadn't played my trump card yet. "Perhaps you wanted to murder Mrs. Kempsey because she discovered your nature and planned to expose you."

"My what?"

"Was she blackmailing you?"

"Of course not. Why would she?"

"You like women, in the sapphic sense."

The knuckles on her interlaced fingers turned white.

"Don't bother denying it. My instincts tell me it's true and apparently my instincts are very good. Also, the journalist who was just here told us you flirted with her."

The muscles in Mrs. Iverson's jaw bunched with the clenching of her back teeth. She remained silent, however, so I continued.

"As to the point about punishing your husband, I'm presuming you don't care what happens to him. If the police arrested him for the crime, it was of no consequence to you."

"How dare you! I may not love him, but we are married. I made a vow. That means something to me." It was telling that she responded to that accusation, but not the one about being sapphic.

"The murder of Isabel Kempsey was deliberate. Until now, we'd been assuming the location was also deliberately chosen, to cause Dr. Iverson problems and perhaps even damage his reputation. But perhaps the location was merely chosen for convenience because the killer had easy access to the consulting room and the Electro Therapy Machine. Perhaps it wasn't a personal attack on your husband at all."

Mrs. Iverson leaned forward to get her next point across. "I didn't kill her, Miss Fox." She sat back and unclasped her fingers. "As for my sapphic nature, I haven't told anyone. I haven't acted on it, nor do I intend to. I have a reputation as the wife of an eminent physician to uphold."

"Isabel Kempsey may have guessed. We did." It was a lie, but I wasn't going to admit that I'd failed to detect her interest in me. "Was she blackmailing you, Mrs. Iverson?"

She squeezed her eyes shut and rubbed her forehead. Her former composure was nowhere in sight.

"Regarding the anonymous letter," Harry prompted. "Do you remember the envelope it came in and whether there was a postmark."

She suddenly stopped rubbing and stared directly ahead at the wall. She pressed a hand to her stomach. "It wasn't for him."

"Pardon?"

"I've just realized… It may not have been intended for my husband at all. I simply *assumed* it was for him, since it was clearly from someone making a rendezvous with a love interest, and he has had numerous lovers over the years." Her face had gone pale when I made my accusation, but it flushed with color again as she became more animated. "Not only was the letter unsigned, but it wasn't addressed to anyone, and it didn't come in an envelope."

"No envelope?" I echoed.

"It was just a piece of folded paper among the other mail."

"Where did the other mail come from?" Harry asked. "Did you place it on his desk after the postman handed it to you?"

"I did. It sat there for at least an hour before I was able to sort through it. I saw the note, read it, and added it to the mail that my husband needed to attend to personally." She turned to me. "How is the letter tied in with Mrs. Kempsey's murder?"

"It may not be," I said. "But we won't know for certain until we find out who authored it, who it was meant for, and whether the rendezvous was innocent or not."

"I see." She rose, signaling time for us to leave. "If that

letter wasn't intended for my husband, after all, then it seems you'll have to look elsewhere for your suspects. Poor Mrs. Kempsey didn't die by my hand, or his."

We saw ourselves out and didn't get far before we began to speak over each other. Harry stopped to let me continue first.

"So, if the letter wasn't intended for Dr. Iverson, it must have been intended for Miss Wainsmith. She's the one who usually sorts through the mail, and the author of it would probably know that."

"Or the author knew Mrs. Iverson was there that day and it was intended for *her*," he said.

"We should check the appointment book for a list of patients who would have been in the waiting room at that time on the day it was received. Any one of them could have slipped it into the pile on the desk." It would be a time-consuming task to then question each patient, but hopefully a name stood out.

I set off in the direction of the clinic and Harry fell into step beside me. "It may not be a patient," he said. "The author could have handed it to the postman outside and asked him to include it with his delivery. They may never have entered the building."

My pace slowed as I considered that. "If the anonymous author didn't go inside, he or she wouldn't know Miss Wainsmith wasn't there that day. It may have been intended for her, after all." I stopped when we reached the intersection with Harley Street. "You try to chase down the postman and ask him whether someone handed him the note while I'll look at the appointment book. We'll meet back at your office." I checked the time on my watch. "Then we'd both better head back to the hotel for the final security meeting about Mr. Lombardi's event."

"Meet me at Roma Café after you've finished at the clinic," Harry said. "I'll need a bowl of Luigi's pasta by then."

A few minutes later, I re-entered Dr. Iverson's clinic. Miss Wainsmith looked up from the desk with a smile. It slipped when she realized it was me and not a patient, before returning brighter and quite fake.

She peered past me. "You are alone, Miss Fox. No Mr. Armitage?"

I indicated the appointment book. "May I take a peek?"

She hesitated before inviting me around to her side of the desk. She slid the book toward me. "What are you looking for?"

"The names of patients waiting here on the day the anonymous letter arrived." I flipped back to the relevant page and quickly scanned the names. None were familiar. *Drat.*

"You think one of them saw it?"

I thanked her and returned the book. I was about to leave but paused. Miss Wainsmith was pretty. If I were interested in women, would I desire her? Did Mrs. Iverson?

The consulting room door opened, and Sister Dearden emerged. Like Miss Wainsmith, she seemed surprised to see me so soon after my last visit. "Hello again, Miss Fox. Do you wish to make an appointment?"

"No. Why do you say that?"

"You're here without Mr. Armitage."

"Oh. I see. I needed to look at the appointment book while he does something else."

I smiled at them both, studying each through a different lens than I had on previous occasions. Did they know about Mrs. Iverson's preference for women? Had she flirted with either of them? Would either be offended if Mrs. Iverson took an unconventional interest in them?

Miss Wainsmith was the prettier and younger of the two, and the more naive. Mrs. Iverson called the receptionist silly and seemed to have little respect for her. Was that all a ruse to throw us off the scent that she actually liked her? Could they be lovers?

As for Sister Dearden, she may be a little frumpier and older, but there was a confidence and intelligence about her that the receptionist didn't possess. As a nurse at a medical practice whose patients were mostly women, would she be worried they'd stop going if they thought she was sapphic after seeing Mrs. Iverson flirt with her?

Had either one killed Isabel Kempsey because she'd somehow found out and threatened to spread gossip about the doctor's wife? Protecting reputations was a strong motive.

Yet both women liked working for Dr. Iverson. Their positions were secure and he paid well. By murdering a patient at the clinic, they risked it all by making him look guilty.

"Miss Fox?" Sister Dearden waved a hand in front of my face. "Are you all right?"

"I am."

She smiled, relieved. "I was worried we'd have to give you a dose of Nerve Elixir."

Miss Wainsmith opened the top drawer of her desk and pulled out a bottle. "You can use mine."

I thanked them both and left the clinic without taking her up on the offer.

* * *

WHEN I ARRIVED at the Roma Café, I didn't enter immediately. I stood on the opposite side of the street and stared at the painted sign above the door. Roma *Café*.

Café Royal.

I suddenly knew who the anonymous note was meant for.

Harry wasn't there, so I ordered a cup of tea and sat at the table by the window. After a moment, I got up again and approached the two elderly men on their stools. I greeted them and inquired after their health in Italian. I didn't remember much from the lessons my father had given me, but I did remember that.

The leathery faces of both men folded into twin winces as they shrugged. The movement encompassed more than just their shoulders, making the answer clear without a single word being uttered. Like most men their age, the years were taking their toll.

I indicated the newspapers on the counter within their

reach. "Have either of you read anything more about Mr. Lombardi's Bella Vita Company since I was last here?"

They may not have understood the entire sentence, but they repeated the company name and its owner clearly back to me. They spoke over each other in Italian, but it was the shake of their heads that gave me the answer I was after.

Luigi set a teapot and two cups on a tray on the counter. "Your muddy water is ready, Miss Fox. Just in time." He nodded at Harry as he entered. "Would you like me to bring you pasta? I made a large batch."

Harry and I ordered a bowl each, then he picked up the tray and carried it to our table. "You look like you stumbled upon a clue," he said. "Did you recognize a patient name in the appointment book for the day the letter arrived?"

"No, although I *have* realized something. But you first. Did you speak to the postman already? That was fast."

"I intercepted him on his rounds not far from Harley Street. He's adamant no one has ever directly handed him a letter to deliver to Dr. Iverson's clinic."

"Could he have accepted an unofficial payment to do it and keep quiet about it?"

"Possible, but I don't think so. He seemed offended that I'd even suggest he'd deliver an unstamped piece of mail."

I sighed into my teacup.

"You seem disappointed," Harry said.

"If no one handed him the letter then it could be a patient, and I was hoping not to have to call on them all."

"Tell me the thing you've realized."

Luigi brought over bowls of pasta and placed them in front of us. It smelled delicious, and I was momentarily distracted as I picked up my fork.

"Cleo?" Harry prompted.

"The anonymous note wanted the rendezvous to occur on Regent Street, opposite the Café Royal. We've been wondering if the location had any significance, and I believe it does. Mr. Chapman told me men meet men at the Café Royal, but he also said *women* who dress as men go there.

Although my experience of these things is limited, I believe women who dress as men often have sapphic tendencies."

Harry lowered his fork and met my gaze. "You think Mrs. Iverson was the intended recipient then, not Miss Wainsmith or the doctor?"

"She is sapphic. If the postman didn't accept a bribe to deliver the anonymous note then it must have been placed with the other mail by someone *inside* the clinic. They'd see Mrs. Iverson working there and know she would sort through the mail before anyone else saw it. Therefore it *has* to be meant for her. Given we know she likes women, and the rendezvous was near the Café Royal, it's very likely the note was written by another woman."

"Excellent deduction, Cleo. Dr. Iverson's patients are almost all women. Any one of the patients in the waiting room that day could have placed that note there. I know it's a long list, but at least it's a definitive one."

We mulled that over as we ate our pasta, discussing which women in our investigation may have written the note to Mrs. Iverson. The victim was among them, but not Edith Hamlin. She'd died a year ago, and the letter had been received only last week.

We'd just finished eating when the door opened and one of those women rushed inside, her face flushed and carrying her hat. She didn't carry her usual bag, however. Spotting us, she rushed over.

"They've arrested him," Rose Bolton blurted out. "They've arrested Duncan!"

CHAPTER 13

*H*arry agreed that I should be the one to speak to
D.S. Forrester on the telephone. While the
sergeant may no longer be bruised from my obvious preference for Harry, he was still likely to tell me more than he
would Harry.

After waiting several minutes, Forrester's voice finally
crackled down the line. "I wondered how long it would be
before you telephoned, Miss Fox, although I admit I didn't
think it would be this soon."

"I heard about Mr. Hamlin's arrest from a member of his
family," I said. "We met him as part of our investigation. Do
you have evidence that points to him?"

"Of course I do."

"My apologies, I didn't mean to imply you would arrest a
man with no evidence."

"You know I can't tell you anything."

"I do, but Harry's client will appreciate no longer being
the focus of your attention, Sergeant. Is there anything we can
tell the doctor to give him hope?"

He paused, which was better than an outright refusal.

"Please, Monty." Hopefully using his first name would
work in my favor and not strike another mark against me.
"We both have the same objective. In fact, perhaps we can

help gather more evidence for you while you interrogate Mr. Hamlin. We've made some solid contacts while investigating this case, including people close to him. They trust us and might open up to us more than to the police." I chewed my lower lip as I waited for his response. While I hadn't completely lied, it was certainly an embellishment of the truth.

He gave in with a sigh. "Very well. We were given a letter he wrote some time ago to his former employer threatening to destroy him by sabotaging his device, the Electro Therapy Machine."

Mr. Reid had told us Mr. Hamlin had been upset at his dismissal, but he'd not mentioned a letter. "Why did it take Mr. Reid until now to give it to you?"

"He only just found it."

"How convenient."

"I thought it was coincidental, too, but Hamlin hasn't denied writing it, so I can only assume he did."

"What *does* Mr. Hamlin say about it?"

"Nothing. He's refusing to talk."

I wondered if Forrester knew Edith Hamlin had been a patient of Dr. Iverson's, and the doctor had failed to diagnose her cancer. If he didn't yet, he would soon. It would seal Mr. Hamlin's fate, and I didn't want to be the one to tell him. Not yet. It didn't feel right. There were pieces of the puzzle missing, most notably the reason Duncan would kill Isabel Kempsey.

"Thank you, Sergeant. You've been a great help, and I'm sure you'll crack him soon. You're a marvelous investigator." I hung up the receiver.

Harry stood on the opposite side of his desk to me, his arms crossed over his chest. "That was a little much at the end."

I pushed myself to my feet and rounded the desk. "Probably, but I feel as though I need to bolster his confidence a little. It took a bit of a dent after...you know." I clasped his jacket lapels and stood on my toes to kiss him.

He unfolded his arms and circled them around me, kissing

me back. When I finally pulled away, he resisted. "We don't have to go just yet, do we?"

"A man has been arrested, Harry. I feel sorry for Duncan Hamlin, but I know that doesn't mean he's innocent. Even so, if he is, we need to find the real killer quickly, because Forrester can build a strong case against him. Hamlin has motives to destroy the doctor in abundance."

"Perhaps he's *not* innocent."

He tried to kiss me again, but I placed a hand to his chest, warding him off.

He sighed. "Very well. From what I overheard of the conversation, it sounded like Reid is involved."

"He found an old letter written by Hamlin threatening to destroy the Electro Therapy Machine. It seems suspicious that he never mentioned its existence before today."

Harry glanced at the clock on the mantel. "We'll call on him now, but we shouldn't stay too long. We have the meeting at the hotel, and I don't want to miss it."

"I'm not sure our presence is entirely necessary. We've given the best description of Pierce that we could. We can't do more than that."

"Sir Ronald has asked me to go, and I don't want to disappoint him. Not now when I'm trying to stay on his good side." He stole a kiss, then fetched my coat from the stand.

I glanced at the clock, too. "We'll make sure we're not late."

* * *

MR. REID INVITED us into his office with enthusiasm, but not because he was pleased to see us. "I've been meaning to contact you, Mr. Armitage. You promised to clear my device of any fault in causing the death of that woman at Iverson's clinic, but there's been no retractions in the newspapers. They continue to mention the Electro Therapy Machine in a negative light every time they report on the police investigation."

"I promised no such thing," Harry said, his voice calmer than mine would have been. "I was hired by Dr. Iverson to clear *his* name. In doing so, I *suspected* I'd be proving your device was sabotaged. But I didn't promise."

Mr. Reid rested his elbows on his desk and buried his hands in his hair. "This is a nightmare. My reputation is ruined a little more each day this isn't resolved."

"Is that why you faked a note from Duncan Hamlin?"

"It's not a fake! He did write it."

"Then why not mention it earlier to us? Or the police? Why wait until now?"

"Because I forgot about it. I found it this morning among my paperwork." He indicated his office with its cluttered desk and workbenches. "I received it in the mail shortly after I dismissed him last year. It wasn't signed but it's written in his hand. I provided the police with a copy of notes he took when he worked here so they could compare the writing."

"They arrested him a short time ago," Harry said.

Mr. Reid swallowed. "Good. The sooner this is over with, the better."

It was easy to believe a piece of paper got lost in the large, untidy office, but not for an entire year. "What did it say?" I asked.

"He accused me of not paying him appropriately for his design. If I didn't compensate him, he would ruin me."

Although I had sat, Harry remained standing. He now wandered around the office, his hands clasped behind his back. "*Did* you use his design without adequately compensating him?"

"He was employed by me at the time. Any design he worked on was owned by me." He pointed at the door. "I'd like you to leave."

"We're not finished." Harry finally sat. "Let's presume Hamlin did design the Electro Therapy Machine during his employment here."

"He has no claim!"

Harry put up a hand to stop him. "I'm not interested in whether that's true or not. It only matters if Hamlin *believes* it. Ever since his dismissal, he's been something of a thorn in your side. Not only does he think he ought to have been compensated better, he established his own company to create a device that will rival yours."

Mr. Reid sniffed. "It won't be as good."

"The reputation of your device is currently suffering. You just told us your reputation is being ruined a little more each day this isn't resolved. By having your rival arrested, you remove the man who has been bothering you for some time."

Mr. Reid shot to his feet. "Now listen here, Armitage. I did *not* fake that letter. Hamlin wrote it. I dare him to deny it in a court of law."

That was the part that niggled at me. According to D.S. Forrester, Duncan hadn't denied it. He wasn't talking at all. If he were innocent, why not say so?

"You once described Duncan as a good employee," I said. "You even said you treated him like a son."

"He betrayed me by taking my designs with him. I owe him nothing."

"That letter could be enough to convict him. He'll hang for murder, Mr. Reid. Is that what you want?"

He lifted his chin and peered down his nose at me. I peered back, unblinking.

After a moment, he sat again. "The death of Hamlin's wife changed him. She was ill for quite some time before she finally passed. The disease weakened her, made her tired, and she could spend all day in bed. Apparently, she used a tonic and powders that eased the pain and enlivened her enough so he would come to work, but the effects never lasted long."

Her file at the clinic said she was using the Nerve Elixir, which would explain her brief periods of revitalization. The cocaine's effects were strong but temporary, and she would have required more and more of it to achieve the same result.

"I was very patient with him during that time," Mr. Reid went on.

"You say her illness changed him," Harry said. "Do you think he became a man capable of murder?"

"He adored her. If he blamed the doctor..." Mr. Reid shrugged, as if that answered the question.

"If he blamed the doctor, why kill Mrs. Kempsey?" I asked.

"It may have been an accident. I don't know. That's for the police to determine now."

It may well have been an accident. Isabel Kempsey had complained of an erratic heartbeat. Dr. Iverson may have cleared her of a problem, but that didn't mean it hadn't existed. It was entirely possible the person who tampered with the machine never meant for her to die. They presumed the doctor would switch the device off immediately. She would be seriously hurt, but most likely alive.

Taking all the evidence into account, as well as the motive, it was looking very likely that Duncan Hamlin was guilty.

* * *

I INSISTED we arrive separately at the hotel, just in case Uncle Ronald or Floyd were in the foyer and grew suspicious if we arrived together. They weren't, and I found them in the ballroom. The large space was set up for Mr. Lombardi's presentation with chairs placed in rows in front of a low platform where he would stand to speak. Tables were arranged behind the chairs with bottles of the tonics and pills his company manufactured, as well as glassware for the participants to sample each one. Brass plaques declared the name for each medicine—Soothing Syrup, Toothache Drops, Paralyxia Pills, Snake Oil Liniment, and Hair Restorer Quinine. Beside the plaques were stacks of leaflets extolling the virtues of the medicines.

Harry arrived shortly after me. We spoke briefly, as it would look odd if we didn't talk at all, then he joined Peter and Goliath. Unlike the last meeting, this one did not contain just the heads of each department, although some where present. It was for the front-of-house staff whose job it would be to stop Mr. Pierce entering the hotel.

I stood near the back as Harry described Mr. Pierce's appearance. After he finished, Harmony went through the details of the extra security she'd hired, and where she wanted everyone to stand and which part of the foyer they ought to monitor. Finally, she made sure everyone knew what to do if Mr. Pierce did show.

Since it didn't directly involve me, I found my attention drifting back to the investigation. Once it was over, I joined Peter, Frank and Goliath as they headed to the staff parlor for a short break. A nice cup of tea would do wonders to help me sort fact from fiction, but going over the evidence with them would be even better.

They wanted to know my personal thoughts on Mr. Pierce first, however. "Do you really think he'll storm in here and cause a scene?" Peter asked as he handed me a teacup.

"I do, yes. He's angry, sad and a drunkard. I believe he feels he has nothing to lose."

"A volatile combination indeed."

Frank cracked his knuckles. "I dare him to try and get past me."

Goliath rolled his eyes. "It's me he won't get past. No one can beat the giant of the Mayfair."

"Nobody calls you that."

"People do."

"No, they don't."

Peter made a good point, however. "You could be elsewhere at the time, Goliath, moving guests' luggage. You might not be in the foyer when Pierce arrives."

Goliath looked disappointed at the possibility of missing out on the excitement. "If there's luggage to move, I'll send the other porter." He selected a biscuit from one of the tins and placed it on his palm then dipped his hand back into the tin to get another. "It's better if I stay downstairs on account of being a big man." He added another two biscuits to the pile and went to get more.

Frank slapped Goliath's hand away from the tin. "You've had enough."

"You calling me fat, Frank?"

Frank looked pointedly at Goliath's stomach region, which seemed flat to me.

"Enough, you two," Peter growled.

"You're not in charge of us," Frank snapped back.

"Actually, I am. Besides, Miss Fox doesn't want to hear you bickering."

"That's true," I said.

Peter shot me a grateful look.

"I have a question for you all," I said before the bickering resumed. "Actually, it's more of an opinion. If I apprise you of our investigation, can you tell me what you think we should do next? We've come to a bit of a dead end."

All three gave me their full attention as I laid out the evidence against Duncan Hamlin. "Although we have other suspects with motives, he has the greatest knowledge of the device, and a motive for revenge against both Dr. Iverson *and* Isabel Kempsey."

Goliath nodded along, but Frank shook his head. "Being the one to recommend Mrs. Hamlin visit the doctor isn't a strong enough reason to kill Mrs. Kempsey. Seems to me he should have killed the doctor."

"Miss Fox said he wouldn't have known about her heart condition," Goliath pointed out. "So maybe he didn't intend to kill anyone, just cause a lot of bother."

Peter was yet to give his opinion. He studied his biscuit as he dunked it into his cup of tea. When he lifted it out, tea dripped back into the cup, the biscuit forgotten. "The husbands and sisters of both Mrs. Kempsey and Mrs. Hamlin deny a connection between the women."

"They stated they didn't know of one," I said, "but one or more could be lying."

"I think you need to know for certain if they were acquaintances."

"The doctor wrote Isabel Kempsey's name on Mrs. Hamlin's file, so they must be."

"Did you see it?"

"Yes." I sat up straighter. "But we didn't *verify* it. What if Dr. Iverson added it later, *after* the death, to make it appear as though there's a connection?

"Or someone else did," Goliath added. "Someone could have faked his handwriting."

"Thank you, all of you. I now have a plan."

The door opened and Harry entered. "I thought I'd find you in here, Cleo."

"Good timing." I indicated the teapot. "Pour yourself a cup of tea and sit down. I have a plan."

Peter, Goliath and Frank returned to work, leaving Harry and me alone in the staff parlor. Although it was an odd place for a family member of the owner and a former employee to meet, at least it wasn't in the privacy of my suite. If caught in there, my reputation would be damaged and Harry would incur Uncle Ronald's wrath.

Once Harry was seated with tea and a biscuit, I told him my plan for the evening. He put up the usual level of resistance to my involvement in nocturnal sleuthing—which was to say it was halfhearted—then finally gave in with a sigh. He knew I wouldn't be excluded. We agreed to meet at the kitchen service entrance of the hotel at midnight, me with a lamp and he with his lockpicking tools.

"Make sure none of the staff see you," I told him. "I don't want anyone reporting to Uncle Ronald that you and I snuck out of the hotel together."

He grunted. "At least then he'd know we're together and we could end this pretense. I know I agreed to it, but it's already becoming wearisome."

"It will end when the time is right," I said gently. "When he realizes you are my equal."

"I know, but…what if that day never comes, Cleo?"

"It will." I collected his empty teacup and placed it on top of mine. With my free hand, I caressed his jaw. "It will."

* * *

BY THE LIGHT of a portable oil lamp, we inspected Edith Hamlin's medical file. The untidy handwriting referencing Isabel Kempsey matched some of the medical notes on the rest of her file, but not all. The initial personal information was written in one hand, the diagnosis in another, and monthly updates on her weight and other measurements were noted in a third style.

"The receptionist wrote the name and address," I said, pointing to the relevant lines on the first page. "I presume Dr. Iverson wrote the diagnosis and what he prescribed, and Sister Dearden must have written Mrs. Hamlin's weight and other comments during each appointment. The individual letters of Isabel Kempsey's scrawled name matched the doctor's handwriting."

Harry removed another file from the cabinet at random and opened it. "The handwriting also matches the doctor's diagnosis in this one." He returned the file and put out his hand to accept Edith Hamlin's.

I shuffled the papers together to re-pin them with the Gem paperclip but couldn't find it. I must have dropped it. By the light of the lamp, I searched the vicinity, but it wasn't on the desk surface or the floor. One of us must have accidentally kicked it under the desk.

When I still couldn't find it, Harry suggested getting another one. "Miss Wainsmith probably keeps a box in the desk drawer."

I opened the top drawer and moved aside some medical bottles and paper packets to search for the clips.

Harry joined me and picked out one of the bottles. He read the label. "Laudanum." He picked up another bottle and one of the packets. "This tonic contains gentian root and some other herbs. This powder contains sodium bicarbonate."

"Is Miss Wainsmith ill?"

Harry returned to the filing drawer and searched through them. "She has a file."

I peered over his shoulder and read Dr. Iverson's diagnosis. "'Stomach complaint'. That's rather vague."

Harry pointed to the symptoms. "Abdominal pain, occasional vomiting after eating, weight loss and pale complexion."

"She is very thin and looks tired," I said.

"According to these notes, she has been losing weight

every week for the past several weeks. The vomiting began three months ago and the abdominal pain shortly after that."

"I've noticed she often touches her stomach. Sometimes it's just a little flutter of her hand near her abdomen. She has had time off work recently, too. It seems the medicines aren't working."

We returned the bottles and packets and found a box of spare Gem paperclips. Slipping one onto the top of the papers, we returned both Edith Hamlin's and Miss Wainsmith's files to the cabinet. Moments later, Harry relocked the clinic door and we slipped away into the crisp autumn night.

"The handwriting *is* the same as Dr. Iverson's," I said as we walked.

Harry didn't respond. His head was tilted down, as if he was studying the pavement at his feet, but I couldn't see his face well under his hat. I suspected I knew the direction of his thoughts, however.

"You think Miss Wainsmith blames Dr. Iverson for not curing her," I said.

He looked sharply at me. "We don't know if she's dying."

"I truly hope she isn't, and that it's simply a complaint she'll recover from. But the signs aren't good, Harry. The dramatic weight loss, the inability to keep down food, stomach pains so terrible she needs several tonics and powders to get her through and yet she still takes time off work. I don't know what it could be, but it has been going on for months."

We walked on in silence, each with our hands buried in our coat pockets, collars up to protect our necks from the breeze whipping along the empty street.

After several moments, Harry broke the silence. "You're right. There's a very good chance she blames Dr. Iverson for not curing her. That's a motive to ruin him."

"And the connection to Isabel Kempsey?"

He shrugged. "I can't see one, except that she was the doctor's lover and Miss Wainsmith might think that killing her would punish him. Or she didn't know about Mrs. Kempsey's heart condition and didn't think tampering with the machine would do anything to her other than give her a nasty jolt."

"It's unlikely she has any electric knowledge," I pointed out. We'd meant to ask her but forgot. If she were guilty, she would have lied anyway.

"True. But we have to consider her as a suspect. We'll interrogate her tomorrow morning. It's Saturday and she won't be at work. We can call on her before Lombardi's presentation begins."

I could tell from his tone that he wasn't looking forward to the conversation. Neither was I. Nor did I want Miss Wainsmith to be the murderer, because she was dying and blamed the doctor for not helping her.

But if she was dying, then perhaps she didn't care what happened to her now. Perhaps she was prepared to risk being hanged to get revenge on Dr. Iverson by murdering the woman she thought he loved.

CHAPTER 14

$\mathcal{N}$ow that I knew about her illness, I saw Miss Wainsmith differently. She wasn't merely pale, she was deathly pale. She wasn't just slim, she was gaunt. Although she put on a smile in greeting, it was tight at the edges, as if she were in pain.

It was early and she'd come from the dining room where she must have joined the other lodgers for breakfast. She carried a teacup with her. It didn't contain tea, however, just milk.

"Does that help?" I asked, indicating the cup as we sat in the parlor.

She blinked huge eyes at me. "Pardon?"

"Milk is sometimes given to sooth diseases of the stomach."

She pressed a hand to her middle, only to quickly move it away again. "It helps a little. How did you know?"

We weren't prepared to tell her we broke into the clinic, so we didn't answer. Instead, Harry continued with the line of questioning I'd begun. "How long is Dr. Iverson going to continue with your current course of treatment?"

She simply shrugged.

"Perhaps that's a question you should ask him," I said.

"I don't understand. If a different course of treatment is

required, he hasn't said as much to me. I'm sure he'll mention it if it becomes necessary, but hopefully it won't. The laudanum in particular is helping."

"It's merely masking the pain," Harry went on. "It's not curing you."

She swallowed and glanced at the doorway.

"Have you discussed this with anyone else?" I asked. "Your family or friends?"

"I don't have any good friends here in London, and I'm not close to my family."

"What about Sister Dearden?"

She glanced at the doorway again. "She's been very good to me. She answers all my questions and advises me on medicines and so forth. It was she who told me not to bother with the Electro Therapy Machine."

"Why not?" Harry asked.

Miss Wainsmith placed her fingers to her lips and cast another guilty look at the doorway. "I probably shouldn't say, so please don't tell anyone I told you, but she claims the machine doesn't cure anything. It simply gives the patient a nice tingling sensation at the point where the discs touch the skin. The patient feels as though the machine is doing something, but it really isn't."

"Has she ever said that to Dr. Iverson?" I asked.

Miss Wainsmith shook her head vigorously. "She'd never say anything like that to him! She regards him very highly in all other things. The device is merely one treatment he offers. I should also add that she values her position too much, and he is such a nice man. She only said it to me because she didn't want me wasting my time."

"You believe her?"

"I do. Sister Dearden is very caring and an extremely dedicated nurse."

"And yet she works for a doctor whose treatments she doesn't believe in," I said.

"I told you, it's just the *one* treatment. Don't think poorly of her for not telling him her thoughts on the machine. She simply doesn't want to upset him. A harmonious working environment is best for everyone. Sister Dearden enjoys her work at the clinic. The good wages and easy hours allow her to see unfortunate women in her spare time without charging them. If she were in a hospital, she'd be overworked and underpaid, and those poor souls who come to see her wouldn't have anyone."

"They come here?" I asked.

"Mostly, although sometimes she visits them. One is with her now."

A thought struck me, but I needed to discuss it with Harry before I went upstairs to confront Sister Dearden. Harry's mind was on something else, however.

"I'll find a new doctor for you," he said to Miss Wainsmith.

"I don't need a new one. Dr. Iverson is one of the best. If he can't cure me, no one can."

"Perhaps so, but a second opinion can't hurt. I don't have a name yet, but I'll get it by the end of the weekend."

"Very well, but I don't think anything more can be done for me. Dr. Iverson is doing everything he can. Anyway, the laudanum helps..." Her bony fingers twisted in her lap and she looked away.

Once outside, I asked Harry if he planned to ask Mr. Hobart for a name. The hotel manager knew everyone of note in the city, including the names of the best doctors, not just the ones everyone thought were the best.

Harry confirmed it but added a grim point. "Miss Wainsmith may need a surgeon. Sometimes the only way to find out what's going on inside a body is to take a look."

It was a troubling thought. She was so young.

Harry looked over his shoulder at the lodging house door. "What do you think about Sister Dearden's opinion on the Electro Therapy Machine?"

"It makes me wonder if she thinks the doctor's other treatments don't work, which leads me to wonder if he has ever misdiagnosed a friend of hers. Perhaps she wants revenge for that misdiagnosis. I wonder if Edith Hamlin or Mrs. Pierce was that friend. Just because we don't know of a connection between her and either of them doesn't mean there isn't one."

Harry clicked his fingers. "What if her *lover* died as a result of Dr. Iverson's malpractice?"

I gasped, as the implication struck me. "You think she's sapphic, too? That *she* wrote the anonymous note to Mrs. Iverson?"

Harry looked at the lodging house again. "Do you want to ask her?"

I gave it serious consideration before shaking my head. "Not yet. If she's guilty of tampering with the machine to get revenge on Dr. Iverson, we won't get a straight answer from her. She's not going to admit she killed Isabel Kempsey, even if it was an accident. Nor do I think it's a good idea to let her know we're fishing for more information. Let's ask the doctor if Sister Dearden has ever questioned his methods. If they've argued over the death of a patient in the past, and if we can prove that patient was her lover, *then* we have solid evidence. It might be enough to convince Forrester to release Hamlin and arrest her."

Harry checked the time on his watch. "We'll need to be quick."

* * *

WE FOUND Dr. Iverson strolling along a path strewn with fallen leaves in the garden square near his house, his hands clasped behind him. He seemed to be deep in thought. I was glad he was alone. The previous discussion we'd had with his wife had been awkward, and I didn't want to bring up the possibility of Sister Dearden's sapphic tendencies in front of her.

Harry had no such qualms mentioning it to Dr. Iverson, however. "Has she ever recommended a particularly good friend see you, and that woman subsequently became your patient?"

"No. Never. Why?"

Not put off, Harry tried a different question. "Was she close to any of your patients?"

"Close?"

"Lovers."

"Good lord, no! That would be highly unethical. Besides, she isn't like that. She doesn't have relationships with women."

"Are you sure?"

He gave Harry an arch look. "I know when a woman is interested in me, Mr. Armitage."

"Are you implying she has flirted with you?"

"I am and she has." Dr. Iverson rocked back on his heels, seemingly rather pleased to tell us he'd captured another female heart. "It was at the end of a particularly trying day, after Miss Wainsmith had gone home. I was tired and frustrated, and Sister Dearden cheered me up. She was very flattering about my…" He cleared his throat as he glanced at me. "My attributes. She invited me for a drink, but I turned her down. She's my employee. It wouldn't be appropriate."

Apparently it was quite all right for him to have a relationship with his patients, however.

I was somewhat disappointed that our theory was extinguished so soon after we'd come up with it, but Harry wasn't giving up yet. "Has she ever confronted you over a diagnosis, accusing you of making a mistake?"

"No."

"She has never disagreed with you over a patient's treatment?"

"Never. Mr. Armitage, what are you getting at? Do you think Sister Dearden has something to do with Isabel's murder?"

"We're exploring a theory."

"Then I hope my answers have proved it to be wrong, because she isn't a murderess. Nor is she sapphic. Sister Dearden may be somewhat unfeminine in nature, but it's not fair to paint her as a lover of women simply because she's unwed and plain."

Harry's jaw firmed. "I assure you, we weren't."

Weren't we? Perhaps we had tried to fit her into that particular mold. Perhaps we'd believed the cliché that a direct woman lacking feminine qualities must not be interested in romance with a *man*. Although I liked to think of myself as an unprejudiced person, making assumptions about people was a necessary part of being a detective. I just needed to be more aware of making judgments that weren't clichéd.

If Harry felt similarly chastised, he didn't show it. He forged on with his interrogation. "We know Miss Wainsmith has been taking time off from work because of her illness."

Dr. Iverson frowned at Harry then me. "Did she happen to tell you what she believes is the cause?"

Since he was still looking at me when he asked the question, I answered. "She doesn't know the cause, and assumes you don't, either. Are you suggesting you do, or that she should?"

"Ah. This is awkward. Patient confidentiality and all that."

"I don't understand. Why haven't you told Miss Wainsmith the name of her disease?"

"Because I don't believe she has a disease. I believe she may be with child and doesn't want to admit it."

I drew in a sharp breath. It was not something I'd considered. Out of the corner of my eye, I saw Harry rub his jaw. "Are you saying you don't know?" I asked the doctor.

"I did examine her, but it would have been very early in the pregnancy as she'd only just begun to have symptoms. There's a good chance she didn't even know herself. That was a mere three months ago. Some women don't show until four or five, particularly with their first."

"But she's losing weight, not gaining it," Harry said.

"Some expectant mothers do lose weight at the start, when they can't keep anything down. The weight gain will come later as the baby grows. I believe she's one of those unfortunate women who gets very ill during pregnancy. I told her she needed to rest, but she refused. She said she couldn't afford to stay in bed all day."

The woman we'd seen a mere half hour earlier hadn't

mentioned being with child. She hadn't even hinted at the possibility. "What did she say when you asked her if she was?"

"She denied it. Unwed girls often do."

"Not to their doctor."

"When her doctor is also her employer, it's a difficult predicament. Miss Wainsmith needs her wages, particularly now, and will want to work for as long as possible. She'll try to hide the pregnancy until it becomes too obvious. Naturally, I haven't mentioned it to her again, as I didn't want to upset her. Her situation is difficult enough, and I want to do every-thing in my power to care for her and the baby."

Was that because he was the father?

The thought felt rather insidious and I couldn't shake it. It stayed with me all the way back to the hotel.

* * *

OUR ROLES HAD BEEN ASSIGNED at the previous day's security meeting. Harry was stationed at the front entrance alongside Frank and Goliath, while I stood beside one of the enormous floral arrangements in the foyer. If Mr. Pierce managed to slip past Harry unnoticed, I'd identify him and alert Peter.

It was not a plan I liked. It didn't use me to best advan-tage. As the only two people who'd met Mr. Pierce, Harry and I were in a unique position to stop him before he entered the building, but the hotel had *two* entrances—the front one for guests and the service one for staff and deliveries.

Mr. Pierce wouldn't get past Harry's keen eye, so placing me in the foyer was pointless. Uncle Ronald had dictated where to put me and Harry hadn't disagreed. They wanted me kept safe, but doing so meant I wasn't useful. It also meant the second entrance to the hotel was manned by staff who'd never met Mr. Pierce. Although Harry and I had given them a thorough description, there was a very good chance he would come in disguise. At the service entrance, he could pose as a deliveryman and slip past them. At least I'd have a better chance of recognizing him.

I informed Peter that I was going to join the staff at the entrance near the kitchen. He protested, but I wouldn't be swayed.

Some of the attendees were heading into the ballroom for Mr. Lombardi's first session. As I passed, I overheard them gossiping about Dr. Iverson's predicament. None seemed particularly worried for their colleague, although one did voice his concern that electric revitalizers could be so easily turned into killing machines.

I headed down the service stairs to the basement area. From the main corridor, staff could head to the larders, scullery and kitchen, the laundry and steam room, and beyond to the maintenance room, coal cellar and boiler room. The latter two I'd visited on my very first tour of the hotel but never been back. I was more familiar with the kitchen. The hum of voices was much calmer under Mrs. Poole's captaincy compared to when the previous *chef de cuisine* oversaw the domain, but the clang of lids and pots was the same.

I glanced into the kitchen and spotted Victor standing over a large pot, inspecting its contents. He looked up as I passed and nodded a greeting. I nodded back.

The two footmen lounging against the wall at the base of the short flight of steps that led up to another corridor straightened upon seeing me.

"You two are supposed to be out there." I pointed at the door at the top of the stairs that led to the laneway.

They exchanged glances then mumbled apologies. They climbed the stairs ahead of me then entered the lane. Usually employed to attend to the needs of guests, including acting as valet to the male guests who hadn't brought their own, they cut fine figures in their suits. They weren't used to watching for undesirable arrivals and I didn't blame them for worrying about a confrontation.

I engaged them in idle chatter while I kept my gaze focused on the lane entrance where it joined Piccadilly. The cobblestones were damp from recent rain and the air felt cool from lack of sunlight. I wished I'd worn a coat. I folded my arms, but it did little to ward off the chill.

An hour later, two new footmen took over guard duty. I decided to fetch a warmer coat for myself and re-entered the hotel. I took the stairs to my suite, collected a thick woolen coat, and returned to the basement.

As I got there, the door to the laneway opened, and a deliveryman carrying a large pot entered. I didn't like the way he kept his face averted as he walked toward me. His cap was pulled low so I couldn't get a good look at him, but he was the right height and build to be Mr. Pierce.

"Good morning," I said.

"Morning," he mumbled under his breath. "Crayfish delivery."

I blocked his path. "May I see?"

"Got to get 'em to the kitchen." He tried to push past me, but I continued to block him. As I drew closer, the smell got stronger. Not of crayfish but of unwashed man.

I knocked off his hat.

Mr. Pierce glared back at me. "You! What are you doing here? Never mind. Just get out of the way!"

"He's here!" I shouted to the footmen.

No one came.

"This isn't for you, Miss! Move aside!"

I shouted again, louder.

Mr. Pierce swore, then removed the pot lid. He tossed it aside and swung the pot to throw its contents over me. I covered my head with the coat to protect it from whatever was in that pot. The sound of a thick liquid sloshing was followed by splashing as it fell on the floor.

Then came a loud grunt. The pot crashed, followed by thuds and more grunts.

I lowered my sodden coat and saw Victor wrestling with Mr. Pierce on the floor. Victor had the upper hand, but Mr. Pierce put up a good fight. One or both of them were badly injured—there was blood everywhere.

No. Not blood. There was far too much, and the smell of paint fumes replaced the odor of my attacker. He'd thrown red paint on me. My coat had borne the brunt of the attack, as had the wall and floor, but some had also splashed on my skirt.

Victor managed to subdue Mr. Pierce before the two footmen reached them. His chef's uniform was smeared with red paint too. He got to his feet, shoving Pierce into the arms of one of the footmen, and looked down at his uniform.

He seemed more concerned about me, however. "You all right, Miss Fox?"

"I am, but my coat is ruined, as is your uniform." My skirt wasn't quite as bad, so hopefully it could be salvaged. "Thank you, Victor. You were marvelous."

"What do you want to do with him?"

"We'll take him to one of the storerooms and keep watch until the police arrive. Can one of you footmen let Mr. Hobart or Peter know that we caught our saboteur. I'm in no fit state to be seen in the foyer."

One of them hurried away while the other helped Victor wrestle a struggling Mr. Pierce into a nearby storeroom. I followed a few paces behind, holding my coat away from me in such a way so as not to damage the clothes I wore. Mr. Pierce refused to go quietly and protested loudly the entire way. Staff going about their duties gave us a wide berth. I handed the laundresses my coat in the laundry room and asked them to try to remove the paint if they could, and throw it away if they couldn't, then rejoined the men.

Victor pushed Mr. Pierce onto a stool in the storeroom where every shelf was crammed with labeled jars of varying sizes. I wasn't sure it was a good idea to keep Pierce in a room full of potential projectiles, but when Victor directed one of the footmen to fetch him a length of rope, my mind eased a little.

"You ruined everything!" Mr. Pierce spat at me. "I was going to destroy Lombardi's life like he destroyed mine. Now he'll get away with murder because of you!" He directed a string of expletives at me until Victor threatened to punch him in the mouth.

"Disrupting Lombardi's presentation won't achieve anything," I said.

"It will draw attention to the poison in that tonic he peddles. The newspapers will get wind of it and print the truth about his so-called medicines. He'd be ruined by the time I finished with him."

"You'd be in prison, Mr. Pierce."

"I don't care," he snarled. "What does it matter anymore?" He lowered his head and his shoulders slumped. "If the doctor got what he deserved like she promised, I wouldn't have to come here and punish the tonic maker."

The footman returned carrying the rope, then Harry rushed in behind him.

"Cleo! You're hurt!" He grasped my shoulders, his worried gaze scanning my face.

I took his hands in mine. "It's just red paint. The only thing hurt is my coat and my skirt." I squeezed his hands then released them.

I stepped back as Floyd entered with Peter and Goliath. I signaled for them to stay near the door but was ignored. Goliath stood over Mr. Pierce as Victor tied his hands behind his back with the rope.

"Cleo?" Floyd asked. "Why weren't you in the foyer like you were supposed to be?"

"Someone who knew what he looked like needed to be at the service entrance."

He scowled, but fortunately didn't scold me further.

Peter indicated the paint on my skirt. "Whose blood is that?"

"It's paint. There's quite a lot of it in the corridor just beyond the kitchen. It should be mopped up before someone slips."

He departed to find Mrs. Short, the housekeeper.

"Has someone telephoned the police?" I asked.

"Mr. Hobart is doing it now," Floyd said. "They'll come to the service entrance." He glared at our captive. "You'll pay for the cleaning up."

Speaking of paying for things...

Victor had tied Mr. Pierce's hands together behind his back and was in the process of tying his legs to the stool, so I felt comfortable getting close. The angry man who'd spat nasty things at me was nowhere in sight. Instead, Mr. Pierce looked utterly defeated. He must feel as though he had nothing left now. Even his revenge had been taken from him.

I spoke gently but firmly. "What did you mean when you said, 'If the doctor got what he deserved like she promised?' Who promised to ruin the doctor, and how?"

"I won't say another word."

He didn't have to. I'd worked it out. "It was Sister Dearden, wasn't it?"

Mr. Pierce's head jerked up in surprise. It was the only answer I needed.

"Cleo?" Harry prompted.

"Do you remember when we were told Mr. Pierce caused a scene at the clinic? He calmed down only after the nurse spoke to him. We all assumed she merely had a soothing way about her, but perhaps her words were more of a warning not to ruin what she had planned for the doctor."

Harry turned to Mr. Pierce. "Did the nurse tamper with the machine that killed Dr. Iverson's patient?"

"I don't know," Mr. Pierce mumbled.

"You could be charged with being an accessory to murder."

"I don't know! All I know is she must have failed because he's still treating patients, and no doubt still advising them to take Lombardi's poison. That's why I had to come here. Seems Iverson can rebound from an assault on his reputation, but Lombardi has further to fall. It's *his* tonic, after all."

Mr. Pierce may not be able to confirm whether Sister Dearden had tampered with the Electro Therapy Machine, but I was now quite sure she had. I suspected I also knew why she wanted to ruin Dr. Iverson. What I didn't know was why she wanted to kill Isabel Kempsey.

Without knowing the link, I wasn't yet prepared to confront Sister Dearden, but the path forward was clearer than it had ever been.

CHAPTER 15

Floyd directed the two footmen to remain in the storeroom and watch Mr. Pierce until the police arrived to take him away. He then shook Victor's hand before sending him back to the kitchen.

I received no praise for my part, nor did I expect any. As far as my cousin was concerned, I'd placed myself in danger. He did, however, advise me to rest in my room with a cup of tea.

I regarded him levelly. "Come now, Floyd, you know me better than that."

His lips flattened. "Do *not* tell my father you were involved." He went to walk off, only to return. I'd never seen him so angry before. My usually blithe cousin looked cross enough to have steam rising from his ears. "And definitely don't tell Mother."

"I wasn't going to."

He jabbed a finger at Harry. "And you, Armitage..." He lowered his hand to his side and tugged firmly on his cuff. "Your fee will be waiting for you by the end of the day."

Harry nodded, but he didn't appear to be listening. I suspected his mind was on the investigation, as was mine.

We didn't have a chance to discuss it, however. Floyd escorted us both back to the foyer, at which point he said goodbye to Harry. Harry returned the farewell then stood there, waiting for me.

"Cleo is needed here for the rest of the day," Floyd growled.

"Why?" I asked.

"To make sure Lombardi's presentation continues to run smoothly."

"Harmony will ensure that."

"Your presence is required to show Lombardi and his attendees that the Mayfair Hotel is better than our rivals because of our family values."

"Pishposh. You and your father are here for that, and Flossy, too." I indicated his sister, chatting to some guests. "Although keep her away from Lombardi."

"*Cleo,*" he ground out.

I gave him a little wave before heading off with Harry. Once we were outside, I glanced back at the door, expecting to see Floyd storming after us. Although Frank held the door open, it was a guest who emerged, not my cousin.

"We now know who the murderer is," I said to Harry. "We just need to know why Sister Dearden wanted Isabel Kempsey dead and Dr. Iverson blamed."

Harry clasped my elbow, stopping me. Deep furrows connected his brows and his eyes were hooded. It was as if a mask he'd been wearing until that moment slipped away, no longer necessary now that we were alone. "I was going to lecture you, too, but I think Floyd covered everything I needed to say."

"Harry," I said gently. "You know me better than he does and wouldn't dare lecture me, nor tell me to rest." I touched his jaw where the muscles tensed beneath my gloved fingers. I didn't like being the cause of that tension, but sometimes it couldn't be helped.

He blew out a ragged breath. "A cup of tea would settle *my* nerves right now." He took my hand in his. "Cleo, when I saw that red paint on you..." He drew my hand to his lips and kissed the knuckles before releasing me. "We'll take a cab to Sister Dearden's residence. It'll be faster than the omnibus."

* * *

ACCORDING TO MISS WAINSMITH, we'd just missed Sister Dearden. After my initial disappointment faded, I began to think her absence could work in our favor. Speaking to Miss Wainsmith alone could give us the answers we needed—*if* she wasn't a co-conspirator in the murder.

On previous occasions, we'd chatted to the two women in the communal front parlor of their lodging house. This time, however, the parlor was being used by other lodgers so we retreated to Miss Wainsmith's room on the second floor. It worried me to see her face looking waxy by the time she reached it.

Harry took her elbow and guided her to the faded green armchair by the fireplace. He shoveled extra coals into the grate from the tin scuttle, while I retrieved Miss Wainsmith's shawl from the back of a wooden chair positioned with a small round table by the bed. She accepted it with a weak smile.

"It's fortunate today is Saturday," I began. "Otherwise you'd need another day off work."

She settled the shawl around her shoulders, clasping it tightly across her chest. Like the armchair, it was also faded and some of the fringing was missing. "I'm fortunate Dr. Iverson is so good to me. I've taken so many days off these last months, yet he hasn't dismissed me. He and Mrs. Iverson have been a great support. Sister Dearden, too."

Seeing her thin frame shrouded in the shawl and sinking into the large armchair made me doubt the theory I'd formed, but I decided to continue on the path Harry and I had discussed in the hansom cab. We'd agreed it would be better for me to question her. The matter was delicate. So much so that I'd told Harry he shouldn't join us, but he refused to leave me alone with someone who could have helped Sister Dearden.

"When we spoke to you this morning, you said you'd gone to Dr. Iverson regarding your illness. We then spoke to him, and he told us he didn't think you were ill. He thinks you're with child."

Her nostrils flared. It was the most irritation she'd shown toward him, or anyone. "He asked me during my initial consultation if that could be true, and I told him it's impossible. I'm still…" A blush pinked her pale cheeks and I got the distinct feeling she was trying very hard not to glance in Harry's direction. "I know how babies are made, and I can assure you with absolute certainty that I'm not carrying one. I wondered if he didn't believe me, but he didn't let on."

With that part of my theory shattered, I only had one aspect left, and I'd doubted its veracity all along. Even so, I broached it with her. "Did Sister Dearden have any friends or family who were treated by Dr. Iverson?"

"Not that I am aware."

"Has she ever blamed him for the death of a patient?"

She frowned. "No."

Edith Hamlin had been a patient before Miss Wainsmith worked for him, but there was one other patient who'd died more recently, *and* her husband blamed the doctor. "What about Mrs. Pierce?"

She blinked at me. "The wife of the man who shouted abuse at the doctor? No, of course not. Unfortunately, not every patient can be saved. No one knows that better than a nurse, Miss Fox."

"Have you ever heard Sister Dearden and the doctor clash? Perhaps over a patient's treatment. Perhaps over yours."

"No!"

"But *she* was the one who told you to take the tonics and powders, not him. *He* thought you were with child, but she realized something else was causing your illness and went behind his back."

The fingers clasping her shawl at her chest tightened, bunching the knitted wool in her fist. "What are you implying?"

"Mr. Pierce informed us that Sister Dearden told him the doctor would 'get what he deserved.'"

She gasped. "Surely that's a lie to throw suspicion onto someone else. *He* blames Dr. Iverson for the death of his wife; Sister Dearden doesn't. *She* has no reason to kill Mrs. Kempsey or ruin him."

"We think she blames him for persistently misdiagnosing patients," Harry said. "She wants to harm his business in retaliation."

"That's absurd. And if it is true, why would she kill Mrs. Kempsey to punish him?"

"That may have been a mistake on her part. Mrs. Kempsey complained of a heart condition, but the doctor found nothing wrong. If Sister Dearden also believed there was nothing wrong, she may have merely intended to injure her, not kill her, to punish the doctor."

Miss Wainsmith's features pinched, either in pain or horror, or perhaps both. She didn't protest again, however. Was that because she believed her colleague *capable* of murder? Having lived and worked in the same building together for a year, she must know the nurse very well. It was a positive endorsement of our theory that Sister Dearden was guilty, but we still lacked a strong enough motive.

"Where is her room?" I asked.

Miss Wainsmith pointed at the wall to her left. "Next to mine."

Harry and I exchanged glances. I could tell he was thinking the same thing as me. The problem was the woman in front of us. She wouldn't allow us to break into Sister Dearden's room and I doubted we could sneak in without her realizing.

I was still considering how to proceed when Harry spoke up. "I hope she isn't guilty. Helping poor women with their medical needs is an admirable thing to do, and we'd like her to continue her work. But she won't be able to unless we prove her innocent. I think we can do that here and now."

She narrowed her gaze. "You want to look through her things, don't you?"

"You can be there the entire time, watching us. We'll be careful and put back everything we touch. She'll never know we were in there. She'll never know we suspected her."

Miss Wainsmith seemed to be wavering, so I added my weight to Harry's argument. "If we can't rule her out, I'm afraid we'll have to report everything to the police. They won't be as discreet when they search her room."

She gave in with a sigh. "I'll fetch the spare key from our landlady."

"There's no need," Harry said, most likely because he didn't want the landlady involved. It would only require further explanations and delays.

Miss Wainsmith followed us into the corridor and kept watch with me as Harry picked the lock on Sister's Dearden's door. She was quite amazed when he had it open in moments, and bent to inspect the lock to ensure it wasn't damaged.

Harry and I wasted no time. The room was identical to Miss Wainsmith's in size, although it wasn't as sparsely furnished and the furniture was of better quality and in newer condition. There was something missing, however.

"You told us Sister Dearden sees patients in here," I said to Miss Wainsmith.

"Yes."

"But there's no table long enough for a patient to lie on, just the small round one." The table was hardly large enough for two people to enjoy a cup of tea and slice of cake, let alone conduct a medical examination.

Miss Wainsmith indicated the bed, pushed up against the wall. "I presume she conducts her work there." She wrinkled her nose at the thought of sleeping in the same bed where medical procedures were conducted.

I quite agreed with her assessment. Perhaps Sister Dearden wasn't as put off by it as we were, or she placed a cloth over the bedcovers to protect them. I wouldn't condemn her based on the lack of an examination table.

I couldn't find a cloth large enough for that purpose, however. Nor could I find the sorts of things I'd expect in a medical consulting suite that exclusively treated women, such as suturing threads, and equipment for either aborting or delivering babies. There were no bandages and nothing that could be used as an antiseptic to clean wounds, not even a bottle of spirits. Nurses may not have received the formal education of a doctor, but the role germs played in causing infection had been known for decades. Even I understood it, in theory.

Harry signaled for me to join him at the glass-fronted cabinet. Some curios were positioned on the shelves, alongside a photograph of four men. Harry wasn't interested in them. "She has a number of medical texts, but this book caught my eye." He showed me the one he'd removed.

It was a book explaining how electricity worked.

A small gasp behind us had us both turning toward Miss Wainsmith. She held a book, too. It had a cloth cover and was small enough to fit in her palm. "That anonymous letter the doctor received mentioned a rendezvous opposite the Café Royal, didn't it?"

I accepted the book from her. It was an appointment diary with one week spread across two pages. Miss Wainsmith pointed to the entry for four days prior.

C. *Royal 9.*

It had a line through it, crossing it out.

"The Café Royal at nine PM," I said, showing Harry. "*She* wrote the note and added a reminder in here."

"Why did she want to meet Dr. Iverson?" Miss Wainsmith asked.

"Not him. *Mrs.* Iverson."

It was all beginning to make sense. Sister Dearden's motive had nothing to do with patients and misdiagnoses. It was linked to her sapphic love for another woman—the doctor's wife. After Dr. Iverson told us Sister Dearden had shown interest in *him*, we'd believed she wasn't sapphic, after all. His high opinion of his appeal to the opposite sex had led him, and us, to the wrong conclusion.

"Where did you find this?" Harry asked Miss Wainsmith.

"On the bedside table beside that spoon."

I crossed back to the cabinet while Harry looked through

the drawers. I bent to take a closer look at the photograph. It didn't show four *men*. It was four *women*, dressed as men. The one on the left was Sister Dearden. I didn't recognize the others. It wasn't definitive proof that she was sapphic, but it was a strong clue.

But why cross out the appointment in the diary?

I thought back through the previous days, and to that day in particular. If the note was intended for Mrs. Iverson, was the date significant? Four days ago, her husband had just been released from Scotland Yard, so Mrs. Iverson wouldn't have been able to slip out of the house without him noticing. Was that why Sister Dearden knew the rendezvous couldn't go ahead? But why make it that particular night in the first place? The note was written days before the murder. Was he due to be somewhere? Somewhere without his wife? A work appointment, perhaps…

Then I remembered. Mr. Lombardi entertained guests at the hotel that night. He'd invited his best customers from the medical profession to join him for dinner. Dr. Iverson was probably meant to attend, but having just been released, and with a cloud hanging over him, he'd canceled.

The day and reason didn't really matter. What mattered was whether Mrs. Iverson was Sister Dearden's co-conspirator, or an innocent bystander.

I studied the photograph again, but was quite sure none of the women dressed as men were Mrs. Iverson. I showed it to Miss Wainsmith. "Do you recognize any of the women with Sister Dearden in this?"

"Those aren't women." She went to hand it back, but I asked her to take another look. She did. "Oh! Well, that is curious. I'd never have noticed they were all women without a proper look. I do recognize one, as it happens." She pointed to the figure next to Sister Dearden, dressed in loose fitting trousers and jacket, a bowler hat in her hand. "She's one of Sister Dearden's patients who comes here from time to time." Miss Wainsmith handed the photograph back to me. "She's not a patient, is she? She's Sister Dearden's lover. Good lord…

all those so-called patients who come here are her lovers, aren't they?"

"Most likely."

Harry had been on his hands and knees, looking under the bed. He now stood and inspected a crumpled piece of paper. I peered at it, too, and read.

It was addressed to 'My Dearest Margaret' and signed 'Your lovingly enslaved Tuppence.' Margaret was Mrs. Iverson's name and Tuppence was Sister Dearden's. In it, Sister Dearden called Margaret 'an exceptionally rare jewel' with 'an ethereal quality' who'd captured Sister Dearden's heart so completely that she couldn't eat or sleep. She finished by writing, 'You must relieve me of this misery and consent to be mine or I'll go mad with longing. If you don't, I may do something even more drastic.'

More drastic than murder?

"She never sent it," I said. "She had second thoughts and threw it away. She must have decided it was too much, or that Mrs. Iverson would never leave her husband."

Harry removed a bottle from the bottom drawer of the bedside table. "Or she decided to speak to her in person." He showed me the bottle label. Nerve Elixir. "The spoon on the bedside table is still wet. I think she just took a dose before she left. The cocaine in it would give her energy. And courage."

We strode toward the door.

"Where are you going?" Miss Wainsmith called out.

"Stay in your room," Harry said. "If Sister Dearden comes back, don't speak to her. Pretend to be asleep."

I'd not thought it possible, but her face paled even more.

We relocked Sister Dearden's door then raced out of the lodging house and hurried in the direction of the Iverson residence. Neither of us spoke. There was nothing to say, and discussion might only slow us down. Although I had questions, and Harry probably did, too, we didn't have all the answers yet.

We just knew we had to get to Mrs. Iverson before Sister

Dearden committed the drastic action she alluded to her in her unsent letter.

The housekeeper answered our knock. "Dr. Iverson is not at home."

"It's not him we came to see," Harry said. "Is Mrs. Iverson in?"

"She's not receiving any more callers."

Harry tried to peer past her. "Is Sister Dearden with her?"

The housekeeper's lips thinned. She refused to answer.

Every delayed moment could prove fatal for Mrs. Iverson. Or give the co-conspirators time to hatch a new plan. I wasn't sure how close the two women were, or to what degree the doctor's wife was involved in the murder.

Mrs. Iverson's high-pitched cry came from inside. "What are you doing?"

Harry pushed past the housekeeper and raced up the stairs in the direction of the voice. The housekeeper and I picked up our skirts and hurried after him. We caught up to Harry at the sitting room door, but he wouldn't let us enter.

"Step away," he ordered.

Beyond him, Sister Dearden had her back to us as she stood over Mrs. Iverson, sprawled on the sofa. At Harry's command she jumped aside and thrust a knife to Mrs. Iverson's throat.

Mrs. Iverson hissed as the blade bit into her skin. She didn't try to push it away, or her attacker. She held her side. Blood dampened her fingers.

The housekeeper screamed.

Harry surged into the room, but Sister Dearden ordered him back.

"Don't come any closer, or I'll slice her open."

CHAPTER 16

"*B*ut you love her!" I cried. "Don't hurt her."

Sister Dearden bared her teeth. Her face was so twisted with rage and the effects of the cocaine in the Nerve Elixir that she looked nothing like the woman we'd first met a few days prior. "*She* has hurt *me*! Do my feelings mean nothing? Am I not deserving of love, too? Or is that reserved only for those who are *normal*?"

I moved up alongside Harry. "You *are* normal. I know it's been hard for you—"

"You *don't* know! You can never understand what it's like for me. Or her. You are not like us, Miss Fox. You are free to love whomever you choose." Tears welled in her eyes and her jaw shuddered as she struggled not to shed them. "But we must hide our love. We have to tell lies, even to our families. We are always pretending to be something we are not, always keeping secrets. It's exhausting."

I almost told her that I did understand, but held back. Harry's and my situation was not quite the same as hers. "Yet you found a way," I said gently. "You had a life."

"I did, but she ruined it all." She jerked her head at Mrs. Iverson.

Mrs. Iverson peered up at the woman looming over her. "How did I?"

"You denied your true nature. I poured my heart out to you, and you called me and people like me disgusting."

"I-I'm sorry. Truly. It's not how I feel. I-I was scared. Scared of uprooting my life, scared of the unknown, and the strange emotions you produced in me."

Her words caught Sister Dearden's full attention. So much so that Harry inched forward unnoticed.

Mrs. Iverson stared unblinking into the nurse's eyes. She reached one bloodied hand up and touched the wrist holding the knife at her throat. "Forgive me, Tuppence. I love you. I do. And I want to be with you. But if I don't get medical attention soon..." She winced in pain, not from the knife biting into her skin but from the gash in her side.

Sister Dearden eased back to inspect the wound.

Mrs. Iverson pushed the hand holding the knife away, but that only antagonized Sister Dearden. "You lied!" She plunged the knife downward.

Mrs. Iverson turned her face away.

The housekeeper screamed again.

Harry lunged and grabbed Sister Dearden, wrenching her backward. They tumbled to the floor, and the knife fell out of her hand. I grabbed it as they wrestled. The cocaine-fueled rage bolstered the nurse, but I suspected Harry was reluctant to use his full strength on a woman.

To save his sense of gentlemanly honor, I stepped in and kicked Sister Dearden's ankle. The act achieved no reaction from her. Thanks to the cocaine, she couldn't feel the pain.

She punched Harry in the face. He grunted but managed to catch her wrist before she punched again, then caught her other hand, too. Pinned to the floor, she could only kick out and use her voice. She shouted at him, calling him vile names.

"Fetch something to tie her with," he ordered.

The housekeeper raced off, just as Dr. Iverson arrived. "What the devil? Margaret?" He went to his wife's side. "You're bleeding!"

"Tuppence stabbed me," Mrs. Iverson said.

Dr. Iverson pressed down on the wound. "Miss Fox, go to my study, next floor up, first door off the landing. In the middle drawer of the desk is a medical kit. Fetch it for me, please. Quickly now."

I found the kit where he said it would be and hurried back. Thankfully, Mrs. Iverson didn't look any worse. She breathed heavily and was pale, but not deathly so. She would live, if the wound stopped bleeding soon.

Her husband set about tending to it with clinical indifference, as Harry tied up Sister Dearden with similar professionalism. She'd closed her eyes and gone quiet, but I could see her eyeballs moving beneath her eyelids. Her breathing was rapid, shallow, and her facial muscles twitched. I recognized the signs of cocaine-induced stimulation.

I still wanted answers, but she was too clever to admit anything in court. Although there was no doubt she'd be found guilty after this attack, she might close up on the details. If I ever wanted those answers, I had to get them now while the tonic gave her a feeling of invincibility.

Her skirts had risen to reveal her shins. I knelt and pulled them down to cover her as Harry helped her to sit up. "Was Isabel Kempsey your lover?" I asked.

Her eyes flew open and her gaze darted around the room, taking in her surroundings. Or perhaps not taking in much at all. It was impossible to tell. She didn't answer me. She didn't even acknowledge me.

"Did she reject you, too?" I went on. "Is that why you killed her?

"Isabel?" Dr. Iverson said from the sofa where he was bandaging his wife. "No, of course not. Sister Dearden was in love with *me*. If she's the one who killed Isabel then she must have done it to remove my existing lover out of jealousy, not knowing we'd already ended our affair."

Sister Dearden burst out in screeching, wild laughter. "Me, in love with you? You're a mad, deluded, arrogant *fool*." She spat each word in his direction with such violence that her entire body shifted forward with the effort. "I never flirted with *you*. That was merely being friendly. I was interested in your wife."

The housekeeper gave a small gasp. I sent her off, asking her to get word to D.S. Forrester at Scotland Yard.

Mrs. Iverson blinked back tears. "I've suspected for some time that she liked me in that way, that she guessed my nature. I suppose I guessed hers, too, and that's why we became friends. I never wanted more than friendship. But she did. I suspected as much when I received the note on the day I filled in for Miss Wainsmith. I guessed who it was from. I could tell by the way Sister Dearden looked at me that she was...interested. But you found it, my dear, and thought it was meant for you."

Dr. Iverson cleared his throat. "Yes. Well. It seems I am not always the focus for a woman's attentions. You'd think I would know better by now."

"The rendezvous mentioned in the letter never came to pass because she came here the night before it was due to happen and declared her love for me."

"Where was I that night?"

"Scotland Yard."

"Ah."

"You rejected her," I prompted Mrs. Iverson.

She nodded. "I've been avoiding her ever since."

"Why did you kill Isabel?" Dr. Iverson asked Sister Dearden. "What did my wife's rejection have to do with her?"

Sister Dearden lifted her chin, defiant. "You ended your relationship with Mrs. Kempsey and she was angry about it."

"It's true that she was upset, but it had to end. Her husband found out. I didn't want their marriage to falter. Isabel and I had no future, you see, as I didn't intend to leave Margaret."

"She was more than upset. She was distraught. And livid." Sister Dearden made a sound of disgust low in her throat. "It's so *typical* of you not to notice what a woman is feeling. Not unless it's amorous."

Dr. Iverson bristled. "She told me she was fine."

"Arrogant *and* an idiot," the nurse muttered.

Harry interrupted before the doctor could retaliate. "Did

Isabel Kempsey threaten to tell the doctor about you? Is that why you killed her?"

Sister Dearden regarded him with lips curled into a sneer, as if she considered herself superior to him even though she was still on the floor with her hands and feet bound. "She suspected I liked women and began following me to prove it." That explained the various notes about locations and times in Isabel Kempsey's secret diary. "She told me she would take the information to the press. She was going to make up a story that I touched her inappropriately during consultations, and that the doctor knew and did nothing to stop me. She was going to use me to ruin the clinic."

Mrs. Iverson gasped.

Dr. Iverson sniffed. "Ruin *me*, you mean. Isabel wouldn't have followed through on her threat. She was all bluster. She just needed to get a few things off her chest."

"She was going to destroy everything we'd built!" Sister Dearden cried.

"We? *I* built that place, not you. The patients come to see *me*."

"They come to be *cured*. You use it as your personal brothel."

"That is *not* true!"

"Those patients who don't succumb to your overtures are told they have a nervous condition. All you do is talk to them, or subject them to electric shocks, which are as pointless as giving them a pat on the back. You don't cure anyone! It's *me* who often advises which medications they should take, which treatments will revive them. I could run that practice much better than you." She jerked her chin in Mrs. Iverson's direction. "Margaret could work at reception, and I'd see the patients. We'd be a superb team."

"Women can't be doctors," Dr. Iverson pointed out.

"I'd dress as a man. I've done it before and no one at the Café Royal has known otherwise."

He barked a laugh. "That's absurd. It's nothing to do with looking like a man. It's to do with education, capability, intelligence."

"Enough." Harry's firm tone cut through Sister Dearden's protests. "With an ignorant attitude like that, Doctor, it's no wonder the women around you have taken advantage. I don't have the time to list all the women who've achieved great things, despite being denied a formal education, but I urge you to do some research." He looked to me. "Any more questions, Cleo?"

"Just one," I said. "Sister Dearden, did *you* write Isabel Kempsey's name on Edith Hamlin's file that day we asked about her?"

"It was easy. Neither of you were watching me, and I've been forging the doctor's handwriting for so long that it's second nature to me now."

"I say!" Dr. Iverson growled. "This is news to me."

Sister Dearden cackled, the sound bitter and brittle. "I knew you were looking for a possible link between Mrs. Hamlin and Isabel Kempsey, so I created one."

I had no more questions, but we didn't want to leave until D.S. Forrester arrived. Dr. Iverson asked if he and his wife could withdraw to a different room, and Harry agreed.

"I'll make tea," I said, following them out.

Dr. Iverson put his arm around Mrs. Iverson's shoulders to support her. "You know it's all right with me if you want to act on your…nature with other like-minded women. If you find love, you should accept it, Margaret."

She blinked damp lashes back at him. "But I love *you*."

"And I love you. But you know I'm talking about a different kind of love."

She shook her head. "I won't. It's disgusting."

"It isn't, because *you* are not disgusting. You are a good woman who has hidden herself away too long. Don't worry, Margaret. I'll protect you if necessary."

Mrs. Iverson leaned into her husband a little more. It was enough for them both, for now.

* * *

By the time D.S. Forrester arrived, Sister Dearden was no longer willing to talk. She'd closed up entirely and refused to even look at anyone. He ordered his constables to take her to Scotland Yard and for Duncan Hamlin to be released, while he remained behind to gather witness statements. Once finished interviewing Dr. and Mrs. Iverson and the house-keeper, he joined Harry and me in the sitting room.

"You deserve congratulations," he said flatly. "Both of you."

"Thank you," Harry said.

"It's good of you to acknowledge our efforts," I agreed. "Although I can see why you thought it was Mr. Hamlin. We did, too. If it wasn't for Mr. Pierce telling us that Sister Dearden had assured him the doctor would get what he deserved, I doubt we'd be here now. So you see it's quite by chance that we solved it at all."

"I know you're saying that to be kind, Miss Fox, but we both know I could have managed this investigation better. D.I. Hobart would reprimand me if he were still my superior officer."

"My father wouldn't have been too harsh," Harry said. "He understands that hurt feelings can cloud judgment."

"Hurt feelings?" The sergeant glanced sideways at me beneath his furrowed brow. "I meant I should have taken more notice of the Electro Therapy Machine before I asked the manufacturer, Mr. Reid, to look at it. He put it back the way it was supposed to be, after informing me it had been tampered with. I should have taken more notice of the way the wires were rearranged, to help determine the level of electrical understanding required. If I'd known a woman could do it, I might have cast my net wider."

"Is that so," I said coolly.

"I've put in a request for my own portable camera. That way this won't happen again. If I forget how the crime scene looked, I can simply refer back to photographs rather than relying on memory and notes."

I tilted my head to the side and regarded him.

He narrowed his gaze. "Is everything all right, Miss Fox?"

"Oh, er, yes. I hope we can work on another case together soon, Sergeant."

"Not too soon, given the circumstances in which we always meet. And hopefully I'll have a camera by then, although I don't know if my superiors will grant me one after I made a poor account of this case." He held out his hand to me. "Until we meet again, Miss Fox." He shook my hand then Harry's. "Armitage."

"Forrester," Harry intoned.

We waited until he was gone then went in search of the Iversons. We found them in Mrs. Iverson's bedchamber, where she was sitting up in bed with a cup of tea.

Her husband sat beside her but stood upon our arrival. "I'll fetch your fee from my study, Armitage, if you'll be good enough to wait here."

"Before you do, I have a request," Harry said. "I'd like you to reduce my portion."

Dr. Iverson glanced at me. "With the rest going to Miss Fox?"

"No," I said, firmly. "I didn't become involved to receive financial compensation."

"Then why?"

"For something interesting to do?" Mrs. Iverson suggested.

It seemed right to confess now that it was all over. Besides, I wanted a favor and he ought to know the reason behind it. "My aunt is Lady Lilian Bainbridge."

"My patient?" Dr. Iverson regarded me anew. "I see the resemblance between you now. Does she know about..." He cleared his throat as his gaze flicked to Harry.

"My sleuthing? She does, although not about this case specifically. By the way, she is no longer your patient. She's seeing a new doctor now. One who is helping her overcome her addiction to cocaine."

Dr. Iverson stiffened.

"You know the Nerve Elixir you advised her to take was making her addicted," I went on.

"The tonic works wonders to revive the constitution of the anxiety ridden."

"Temporarily, yes. But once its effects wore off, her anxiety was worse than ever." I suddenly felt so very weary. He and many others in the medical profession *must* know what cocaine did to the body, yet they continued to deny it. "She had suffered for months and continues to suffer. You are very aware of this, Doctor. It will all be in her file."

"I say, this is an ambush!"

"Is this true?" Mrs. Iverson asked her husband. When he didn't answer, she grabbed his hand. "Is it true?"

"The research into addiction is quite new." At her urging, he added, "But from my own observations, it appears so."

"Is that why you threw out all of our bottles? If it's so terrible, you must stop telling your patients to take it!"

"But—"

"No! You must warn every one of them about the research into cocaine addiction. If they are already addicted, you will help them recover." She turned to me, a determined set to her jaw. "As for Lady Bainbridge, can we do anything for her?"

"I don't think so," I said, "but there is something you can do to discourage others from thinking the Nerve Elixir will cure them."

"Go on."

"Dr. Iverson, I want you to telephone as many newspapers as you can and inform them you want to state publicly that the cocaine in the Nerve Elixir causes addiction."

"I can't do that!" the doctor cried. "My good name and reputation are everything! If I publicly decry a leading brand, my professionalism will be questioned in all the medical circles."

Mrs. Iverson glared at her husband. "Miss Fox and Mr. Armitage *saved* your reputation. You *will* do this for them. Today, Miss Fox?"

"Today," I said firmly.

"If it's any consolation," Harry added, "by coming out now, you will protect your good name into the future. I believe the tide will turn against medicines containing cocaine and other addictive substances. You may receive some backlash now, but you'll eventually be lauded as the doctor who led the charge against such substances."

Dr. Iverson pursed his lips as he considered his predicament. At least he didn't seem quite so against the idea. His relationship with his wife may be an unconventional one, but he certainly respected her. "The fellow who owns the company that manufactures the Nerve Elixir is currently in London. In fact, he's running a presentation today at your family's hotel, Miss Fox. I was supposed to be there. Won't they be upset to see their guest's name dragged through the mud in the newspapers?"

"I doubt it, given Aunt Lilian's situation. Anyway, it won't make this evening's papers, and Mr. Lombardi is checking out tomorrow. The hotel won't suffer from the negative publicity."

"Unlike Lombardi. If other doctors follow my lead, this will ruin him."

Mrs. Iverson laughed wryly, only to wince when the act pained her side. "Very neat, Miss Fox. Very neat, indeed." She touched her husband's elbow. "My dear, you were going to fetch Mr. Armitage's fee."

Dr. Iverson left. Once he was gone, Mrs. Iverson invited me to sit on the chair beside the bed. I did, while Harry moved to the window, giving us some privacy.

"I wanted to apologize for my part in all this," she said to me.

"Did you play a part?" I asked, quite seriously.

"I suspected Sister Dearden's interest in me. I didn't connect it to the murder, but I should have told you that I suspected she'd written that anonymous letter to me. I'd simply dismissed it, you see, not thinking she was the one who tampered with the Electro Therapy Machine. If there's anything more I can do to show my gratitude to you both, please let me know."

"My only request is that you look after Miss Wainsmith. She's very unwell. Harry is going to give her the name of a new doctor, and I hope you'll support her and encourage her to see him. She has no one here in London, and I think she needs a friend."

"I will."

Her husband returned and handed Harry an envelope. "You've done me a great service, Armitage. While my practice has suffered, thanks to Sister Dearden's actions, and will continue to suffer, at least I am a free man. I will do as Miss Fox asks and draft a statement about the addicting nature of the Nerve Elixir, then personally deliver it to every newspaper on Fleet Street this afternoon. You're right, Miss Fox. It's time for the medical profession to take a stand against medicines containing cocaine."

I shook his hand. "Thank you, Doctor. I appreciate you taking this risk."

Harry accepted the envelope and shook Dr. Iverson's hand, too. "I have one more request to make, Doctor. This one won't take up any more of your time."

* * *

HARRY OFFERED to escort me back to the hotel, but I declined.

"I have some shopping to do on the way," I said. "I'll see you tomorrow for lunch at your parents' house."

His fingers skimmed the bare skin of my wrist above my glove. "I look forward to it, Cleo."

I smiled. "As do I."

We parted, and I caught an omnibus to Piccadilly Circus. From there, it was a short walk to the toy shop on Regent Street. It felt odd buying a grown man a gift there, but the sales assistant assured me many of the customers for the product were adults.

With my purchase in hand, I returned to the hotel. I greeted Frank amiably, receiving a grunt in response before he remembered to ask me how the investigation was progressing.

"It's solved," I told him. "Isn't that marvelous?"

He grunted again, which I interpreted to mean, 'Well

done, Miss Fox, you and Mr. Armitage are a formidable team with a tenacity that will get you far in life.'

"Thank you, Frank," I said. "That's very sweet of you."

The bewildered look on his face implied my interpretation was off, but I didn't care. I was in a good mood.

Instead of heading up to my suite on the fourth floor, I decided to slip into the ballroom and see how Mr. Lombardi's event was faring. The attendees weren't there, however, nor was Mr. Lombardi. I checked my watch. They must be at lunch in the restaurant.

Two maids and a footman were tidying the tables in the ballroom, replacing used glassware for clean, and realigning chairs to ensure they once again formed neat rows before the attendees returned. I greeted them by name and was about to leave when Harmony entered.

"I thought I spotted you come in here," she said. "Is everything all right?"

"Marvelous. And here?"

She sighed as she looked around at the tables with their sample bottles of medicines. "It's all going swimmingly."

"That is good news."

"Is it? It doesn't feel like it. I never thought I'd say this, but part of me wants this event to fail. Unfortunately, the doctors and pharmacists are all having a good time. Many of them seem to already know each other and are enjoying meeting again. It's like an all-day social event, particularly since they're in a luxury hotel and being treated like royalty."

"That is such good news, Harmony. Continue to give them the famous Mayfair Hotel personal service. We want them leaving here with wonderful memories that will encourage them to return again, and to tell their well-heeled patients and customers about us."

"I understand your intention, but it galls me they'll leave here with wonderful memories of Lombardi and his medicines, too."

"Don't worry about that."

"Why are you smiling?"

"You'll find out tomorrow. Will you be working?"

"I have the day off. Cleo, what have you done?"

"All will be revealed in the newspaper."

"Which one?"

"Hopefully all of them."

The door opened and Mr. Lombardi entered ahead of his attendees. I said goodbye to Harmony and went to leave, but he moved to block my path.

"Miss Fox, what a delight to see you." He pressed a hand to his chest while his gaze lowered to *my* chest. "Have you come to watch me perform on the stage?"

I waited for his gaze to lift to my face before responding. "I came to see how the event was proceeding. Have you been happy with the hotel's service?"

"Very much. Miss Cotton has made sure all is smooth sailing, as you English say." He chuckled. "I almost wish I did not have to leave so early in the morning, so I could enjoy the hotel even more."

"How early?" I asked.

My question caught him by surprise. Was that because he hadn't meant to tell anyone that he hoped to slip out of the hotel while the night staff were still on duty and the check-in desk wasn't manned? If he timed his departure well, he could leave the hotel without the night porter noticing, and without paying. "I cannot recall the precise time," he said. "I think it is not so early, after all." He smiled brightly and clasped one of my hands between both of his. "Would you like to try some of my medicines?"

"Which ones contain cocaine?" I asked loudly.

His eyes pinched at the corners. "Most do."

"Then I'll pass."

Several of the attendees frowned at me then murmured to their colleagues. Mr. Lombardi quickly released my hand as if it burned him. Without another word to me, he walked off to speak to the attendees, most likely to reassure them that my comment was made by a silly female who didn't know good medicine from bad.

I left the ballroom, almost bumping into Uncle Ronald and Floyd in the vestibule. They stood by the fireplace, chatting amiably to some of the attendees before they returned for the afternoon sessions. I waited until they were free, then joined them.

"How is Aunt Lilian?" I asked Uncle Ronald.

"I haven't seen her since this morning, at which point she was still asleep. Perhaps you can look in on her, Cleopatra. She likes your company."

"Of course. Floyd, have you managed to get any money out of Lombardi yet?"

"He'll be presented with a final bill when he checks out. Are you still worried he'll try to get away with not paying?"

"I am, particularly if he reads the morning newspapers before he sneaks off."

"Why?"

If I told them about Dr. Iverson's plans, I'd have to admit that I knew about them because I'd helped Harry on the case the doctor hired him to solve. Although I wasn't forbidden from working with Harry, my uncle wouldn't like it.

Well, so be it. I told them. Before Uncle Ronald could scold me for working on an unladylike investigation with a man he didn't approve of as a friend for me, I finished by once again advising Floyd to ensure Mr. Lombardi paid his account this evening. "He informed me he will be leaving very early in the morning. I don't think he meant to, most likely because he doesn't intend to pay if he can get away with it."

Uncle Ronald turned his glowering expression from me onto the doors leading to the ballroom, while Floyd muttered a few words under his breath.

I shifted the package from the toy shop from one arm to the other and was about to head off, when Uncle Ronald stopped me. I braced myself for the lecture.

It never came.

"We're going to have a lunch tomorrow as a family. Your aunt needs a little cheering up. It'll just be the five of us. That way it won't be overwhelming for her, and she can leave early if she needs to."

"Tomorrow lunch? I can't. I have a prior engagement."

"Cancel it."

"Can't we change it to another day?"

"No. Sunday is the quietest day for all of us."

"Could it be for dinner instead of lunch?"

"I have plans for dinner at my club." He looked down his pudgy nose at me. "You will be there, Cleopatra. Nothing's more important than family."

I suspected he remembered it was Harry's birthday tomorrow and guessed that I planned to celebrate it with him. My uncle wasn't giving me a lecture because he knew I would probably throw his prejudice back at him. His tactic of blocking me from celebrating Harry's birthday was a way to avoid an unpleasant confrontation yet still achieve his aim of keeping me from seeing Harry.

I was still thinking how I wanted to respond when Uncle Ronald entered the ballroom, Floyd on his heels. Mr. Lombardi's bombastic voice as he addressed the attendees carried clearly through the open door before it closed behind my uncle and cousin.

I walked back into the foyer, the gift suddenly feeling heavy. But it was my conscience that weighed me down. Who should I choose to disappoint? My family or Harry?

CHAPTER 17

I made sure I was in the foyer at dawn the following morning to see Mr. Lombardi leave. I wasn't the only one. My entire family had the same idea. Although I suspected Floyd hadn't yet been to bed, my aunt and uncle exited the lift along with Flossy. While Aunt Lilian was pale and thin, she didn't look tired. Perhaps she was enthused by the prospect of having Mr. Lombardi out of our lives.

"Did Lombardi pay?" I asked my uncle.

"He did." Uncle Ronald rocked back on his heels, a smug smile in place. "Floyd had a word as he handed over the bill of account, and Lombardi agreed to pay immediately."

Floyd's smile matched his father's.

"What did you say to him?" I asked.

"I simply have a naturally persuasive manner," Floyd said.

Uncle Ronald went to fetch the early editions of the newspapers from the night porter. I waited until he, my aunt and Flossy were out of earshot before stepping closer to Floyd.

"You blackmailed Lombardi, didn't you?"

"As I said, I'm persuasive."

"You discovered he frequented the Café Royal, where he had liaisons with men, and you used that as leverage to force him to pay."

Floyd's eyes widened. "How do *you* know about that?"

"Haven't you learned you can't keep anything from me? What I don't know is how you found out. Did someone tell you or did you see him?"

"I received an anonymous note. I wasn't entirely sure I could trust it, but it served its purpose. Lombardi settled his account when I asked if it was true. I didn't need to resort to blackmail, so you can stop casting a censorious glare at me, Cleo."

"You may not have used the term blackmail, but it was implied."

It seemed Mr. Chapman had realized I might not use the information he'd given me, and found a way to make sure someone else did. He'd gone to the right person. While Uncle Ronald was ruthless, he had a gentlemanly manner in his business dealings. He wouldn't use blackmail.

Floyd confirmed my suspicion by asking me not to tell his father.

"Very well," I said. "But you have to do something for me in return."

"That depends on what it is."

"I'm going to propose the family's celebratory luncheon be moved to a different time. You're going to go along with me."

"Moved to when?"

I didn't get a chance to answer him. Uncle Ronald handed each of us a newspaper. My heart did a little flip of joy when I found the article about the Nerve Elixir on the front page of *The Daily Telegraph*. I quickly scanned it and was pleased to see that Dr. Iverson had held up his end of the bargain.

"Here it is!" Flossy showed me a similar article in *The Daily Mail*.

The others also found reports on the negative effects of the high level of cocaine in the Nerve Elixir and other products manufactured by the Bella Vita Company in *The Daily News*, *The Morning Post*, and *The Times*. All quoted Dr. Iverson. Although the mentions were buried in articles covering the arrest of Sister Dearden for the murder of his patient, I was glad to see it appearing in all five of the dailies, and on the front pages, too. I doubted they'd have been as interested in his medical opinion if it wasn't for the sensational nature of the murder. I didn't care why they'd quoted him, just that they had.

I was equally pleased to see that D.S. Forrester was noted as the investigating officer whose doggedness had led to the arrest of the murderess. Harry's final request to the doctor had been to ensure the journalists gave glowing accounts of the detective sergeant. Hopefully it would give Forrester's confidence a boost after the bruising it had received from my rejection. Harry's agency was also noted as assisting Scotland Yard. He'd get yet more work from the publicity. He might even get a pat on the back from Uncle Ronald. It was a point in Harry's favor to bank for when it came time to announce our relationship to my family.

The lift door opened and Mr. Lombardi exited carrying two suitcases. The night porter went to assist him. Mr. Lombardi's steps slowed when he saw us, standing side by side. I wasn't sure if it was the show of unity that unnerved him, or the fact we were all smiling, but he looked unsettled. He tried to hurry past us, but Uncle Ronald blocked him.

He handed Mr. Lombardi his copy of *The Times*, folded to display the article about the murder. "You may be interested in this. I believe the doctor involved has given glowing testimonials about your Nerve Elixir in the past. Seems he's no longer a supporter."

Mr. Lombardi read the article, drawing in a sharp gasp when he got to the mention of his tonic. He said something in Italian that I couldn't translate, but its nature was clear from the guttural tone.

I held out my copy of *The Daily Telegraph*. "You may also want to read this one."

"And this," Floyd said, adding his copy of *The Morning Post*.

Flossy stepped up and stabbed her finger on the article in her copy of *The Daily Mail*. "This reporter writes so eloquently that the editor gave it two columns. What makes it particularly ironic is the appearance just below of an advertisement for one of your rivals' tonics."

Mr. Lombardi's shirt collar suddenly seemed much too tight as the veins on his neck bulged in anger. The wicked side of me thought it would be fitting for Flossy to point out that his neck had become too fat.

Aunt Lilian peered sympathetically at Mr. Lombardi. "You poor man. You don't look at all well. Shall we get you something to revive you for your journey home? I would have suggested some of your tonic to get you through the ordeal of the travel ahead, but after reading these articles, I'm not sure that would be safe." She added her copy of *The Daily News* to the other newspapers he held. "Some more reading to help while away the hours on your journey."

Mr. Lombardi's nostrils flared, and for one dreadful moment I thought he was going to berate her. Then Uncle Ronald grabbed one of Lombardi's arms and Floyd took the other. Between them, they escorted him from the hotel, the night porter trailing behind with a somewhat confused expression on his face.

Flossy put an arm around her mother's waist. "You were marvelous."

"I was, wasn't I?"

I put my arm around her waist, too. "Aunt Lilian, you are delightfully wicked. I love it, and I love you."

"Thank you," she said. "Both of you. I couldn't ask for a lovelier and braver pair of girls."

Floyd and Uncle Ronald rejoined us, the former dusting his hands off as if he'd just thrown out the rubbish. "Right then," Floyd said. "I'm off to bed."

"Let's have breakfast," I said. "Why wait to celebrate at lunch when we're all together now?"

Floyd glared at me from beneath heavy eyelids covered with red spidery veins. "Now?" he growled.

"Why not? We're all wide awake with nothing much to do, and it *is* breakfast time. We can have the restaurant opened up just for us."

Floyd heaved in a huffy breath as he glared at me.

"Besides," I went on, "I'm so relieved that Mr. Lombardi paid his account after being worried he'd leave before doing so. Aren't you pleased, too, Floyd?"

"We could postpone luncheon until dinnertime," he said with an arch look at me.

Uncle Ronald repeated his excuse that he had a dinner engagement at his club this evening. He made no comment about breakfast, however.

Aunt Lilian glanced from me to Floyd. Even suffering as she was from her addiction, she was more aware of the subtle cues than her husband. "I think breakfast is an excellent idea, Cleopatra. Don't you agree, Florence?"

"Oh, yes," Flossy said. "Confrontation makes me hungry. I'm going to have extra bacon today, in honor of the man who called me fat getting what he deserved."

Not even Floyd had the heart to disagree with that. He flung an arm around her shoulders and kissed the top of her head. "I'll join you in the feast of bacon. But first, I need coffee."

"Breakfast it is," Aunt Lilian declared.

Uncle Ronald clapped his hands together. "Capital idea, Cleopatra. The cooks are already in the kitchen. I'll see them now and put in orders for five of everything. Floyd, you open up the restaurant. We'll get underway before Chapman gets here and insists on turning it into a formal occasion." He looked so pleased that I dismissed my previous opinion. He didn't realize I planned to meet Harry for his birthday, after all.

"Quite right, dearest," Aunt Lilian said. "This can be an indoor breakfast picnic. No need for tablecloths and silverware."

"Steady on, my dear. We're not barbarians."

She laughed, much to his confusion.

* * *

THE HYPOCRISY of going to church with my family after our celebratory breakfast, then lying to them about where I was going afterward wasn't lost on me. I told them I was heading to the Tate Gallery for an exhibition and would be gone for some hours. Perhaps if Floyd had been there, he'd have challenged me, but Uncle Ronald, Aunt Lilian and Flossy all seemed to believe me.

I caught a train to Ealing then walked from the station to Harry's parents' place. D.I. Hobart welcomed me into his home with enthusiasm. As did his wife. When I'd first met Harry's mother, she was somewhat curt with me. She'd blamed me for getting him dismissed from his position at the hotel. Since I *was* to blame, I'd accepted her frostiness.

Recently, however, she'd been more pleasant. Today, she even smiled in greeting. "Harry tells us you helped him solve the murder at the doctor's clinic. Your name should be in the newspapers alongside his." She indicated the stack of newspapers on the table in the sitting room. There were even more than had been delivered to the hotel.

Mr. Hobart was there with his wife. As Harry's aunt and uncle, and childless themselves, they were a very close family. The more I came to know them all, the more I realized they'd needed Harry in their lives as much as he'd needed them. Aged thirteen when they'd taken him in, it couldn't have been easy for anyone, but they'd gotten through those difficult years and managed to raise an incredible young man.

I was suddenly feeling as fortunate to have found him as they were. My face must have expressed my feeling of good fortune because Harry suddenly flushed, embarrassed.

Remembering my gift, I held it out to him. "Happy birthday, Harry."

"I told you not to get me anything," he chided.

"I couldn't resist. I first got the idea when I saw it in the toy shop window in Regent Street. Then something D.S. Forrester said decided it for me."

"Toy shop?" Harry's mother asked. "What on earth did you find in a toy shop that a man would want?"

Her sister-in-law sat forward as Harry unwrapped his gift. "Is it a spinning top?" Mrs. Ann Hobart asked.

"Why would Harry want a spinning top?"

"Why would Forrester mention one?" D.I. Hobart asked, as he too leaned forward.

Only Mr. Hobart, the hotel manager, had an inkling. Even though he didn't say, I could tell from the way his eyes twinkled that he might be on the right path. As someone used to guests asking where they could find the perfect gift, I wasn't surprised he'd heard of the Kodak Brownie box camera, even though they were quite new.

Harry's face lit up as he unwrapped the box. "A portable camera!" He removed the device, which was also box shaped, along with a roll of film I'd included. "I've wanted one ever since reading about them." He blinked at me with childlike wonder. "Thank you, Cleo."

His enthusiasm was infectious. I grinned back. "My pleasure."

He opened the instruction leaflet, the rest of us already forgotten.

"Why are they sold in toy shops?" his aunt asked.

"I don't know," I said. "I saw one in the window the other day, but it wasn't until D.S. Forrester spoke about getting a camera for his investigations that I realized Harry would like one too."

"The manufacturer marketed them to children when they first came out earlier this year," her husband said. "They've only just started selling them in England.

"It looks expensive," Harry's mother said.

"Not at all. That's the beauty of them, and why they've become so popular in such a short time."

Harry inserted the roll of film into one side of the compartment, then threaded the loose end of the roll onto the empty spool on the other side. He turned the knob to wind it and closed the compartment panel. "Line up and I'll take a photograph."

Harry's aunt declined, while his mother declared she needed to take her apron off, and she wasn't going to do that before lunch was ready. She headed toward the delicious smells coming from the kitchen.

"Can I help you?" I called after her.

"No, thank you," she tossed over her shoulder. "My sister-in-law is all the help I need."

Harry's aunt leapt up from the sofa and hurried after his mother.

While we waited, Harry photographed his uncle, father and me, then I took the camera and photographed him with his father then his uncle. We then sat to discuss the investigation. D.I. Hobart insisted on knowing every detail, and asked many questions, while his brother listened. Afterward, Mr. Hobart asked me to describe Mr. Lombardi's reaction when he read the newspaper articles mentioning his company.

"How do you know we saw him before he checked out?" I asked.

He simply smiled that knowing smile of his. The smile turned satisfied when I described how Mr. Lombardi couldn't get away from us fast enough.

Lunch was declared ready a short while later, and we moved to the dining table. Although the food wasn't as rich or lavish as that served at the hotel, it was delicious and hearty. The wine flowed freely. All talk of the murder was set aside in favor of more pleasant conversation.

When the four members of the older generation fell into a discussion about politics, I found my concentration drifting. I wasn't sure when my gaze focused on Harry, but at some point it did, and he noticed. He lifted his wineglass in salute. I picked up my glass and saluted back.

When the afternoon's shadows grew long, I bade them all farewell, and thanked my host and hostess for luncheon. Mrs. Hobart kissed my cheek while D.I. Hobart looked like he wanted to kiss the other, but wasn't sure if it was appropriate or not. In the end, he simply shook my hand.

Harry escorted me to the front door. Before opening it, he took my hand. "Thank you for coming, Cleo. It means a lot that you'd risk Sir Ronald's ire. By the way, did I mention he finally asked me yesterday whether I would return to work at the hotel?"

"What did you say?"

"I refused. I told him my business was too successful to abandon it, and that I had grand plans for the future."

"Was he disappointed?"

"Actually, no. I thought he would be." Harry shrugged. "Seems he wasn't so set on the idea, after all." He leaned down to kiss me, but I put a hand to his chest.

I glanced past him along the corridor. "They'll see."

He chuckled softly. "Cleo, they know we're together."

"When did you tell them?"

"Officially, a week or so ago. Unofficially, I've been hinting for some time that you were going to feature more in my life."

"Some time?"

"After things ended with Miss Morris."

"That long ago?" I circled my arms around his neck. "That explains your mother's acceptance of me. I'm glad she has softened her stance and hasn't thrown me out for being a wicked influence on you."

He smirked. "If only she knew how wicked."

"Harry," I chided.

"Cleo," he murmured back.

I teased the thick dark hair at the back of his head, my gaze locked on his. Having told his family about us some time ago, most men would pressure their girl into telling hers. But not Harry. He was giving me the time I needed.

That day would come. I knew we couldn't stay in limbo forever, more than friends yet not publicly a couple, but for now, it felt right. Indeed, it was a relief not to have to contend with my family and their prejudice. I was enjoying our stolen moments, our secret rendezvous. They felt special, and completely ours.

"Happy birthday, Harry. Now, for your other gift." I leaned against him, stood on my toes, and kissed him thoroughly.

Available 2nd June 2026:
MURDER AND THE MISSING TREASURE
The 12th Cleopatra Fox Mystery

A legendary pirate's treasure is at the heart of a murder where a beloved member of the hotel staff is the main suspect. Read on for a description of MURDER AND THE MISSING TREASURE by C.J. Archer.

ABOUT: MURDER AND THE
MISSING TREASURE

A pirate's treasure, lost for decades, lures the greedy and adventurer alike. Did someone commit murder to get their hands on it?

When the celebrated biographer of the infamous pirate Blackheart takes a suite at the Mayfair Hotel to live out his final months, Goliath the porter is desperate to ask the one question that has haunted treasure hunters for decades: Where is the loot buried? Forbidden to disturb a guest, he instead visits the man writing the author's own life story, only to discover him dead at his desk. Accused of the crime, Goliath turns to Cleo and Harry to clear his name.

As they investigate, the danger escalates when a description of Goliath is splashed across the front page of the newspapers. It's only a matter of time before someone connects the hotel porter to the manhunt, and to Harry, who is secretly hiding him.

The hotel is already under siege from the press, as word spreads that Blackheart's biographer is in residence. The tantalizing link between the treasure and the murder fuels a frenzy, disrupting the hotel and driving away high-profile guests.

With suspects including a titled heir and a man claiming to be Blackheart's secret grandson, can Cleo untangle fact from fiction before Goliath is discovered and the hotel's reputation is ruined? And, more importantly for some, will the location of the hidden treasure finally be revealed?

Available June 2026 :
MURDER AND THE MISSING TREASURE
The 12th Cleopatra Fox Mystery

A MESSAGE FROM THE AUTHOR

I hope you enjoyed reading MURDER ON HARLEY STREET as much as I enjoyed writing it. As an independent author, getting the word out about my book is vital to its success, so if you liked this book please consider telling your friends and writing a review at the store where you purchased it. If you would like to be contacted when I release a new book, subscribe to my newsletter at http://cjarcher.com/contact-cj/newsletter/. You will only be contacted when I have a new book out.

ALSO BY C.J. ARCHER

SERIES WITH 2 OR MORE BOOKS

The Uncensored Memoirs of a Book Hunter

The Glass Library

Cleopatra Fox Mysteries

After The Rift

Glass and Steele

The Ministry of Curiosities Series

The Emily Chambers Spirit Medium Trilogy

The 1st Freak House Trilogy

The 2nd Freak House Trilogy

The 3rd Freak House Trilogy

The Assassins Guild Series

Lord Hawkesbury's Players Series

Witch Born

SINGLE TITLES NOT IN A SERIES

The Warrior Priest

Courting His Countess

Surrender

Redemption

The Mercenary's Price

ABOUT THE AUTHOR

C.J. Archer has loved history and books for as long as she can remember and feels fortunate that she found a way to combine the two. She spent her early childhood in the dramatic beauty of outback Queensland, Australia, but now lives in suburban Melbourne with her husband, two children and a mischievous black & white cat named Coco.

Subscribe to C.J.'s newsletter through her website to be notified when she releases a new book, as well as get access to exclusive content and subscriber-only giveaways. Her website also contains up to date details on all her books: http://cjarcher.com She loves to hear from readers. You can contact her through email cj@cjarcher.com or follow her on social media to get the latest updates on her books:

facebook.com/CJArcherAuthorPage

instagram.com/authorcjarcher